KU-092-376

THE
MURDER
ROOM

LISA STONE

HarperCollins *Publishers*

HarperCollins*Publishers* Ltd
1 London Bridge Street,
London SE1 9GF

www.harpercollins.co.uk

HarperCollins*Publishers*
Macken House, 39/40 Mayor Street Upper,
Dublin 1, D01 C9W8, Ireland

First published by HarperCollins*Publishers* Ltd 2024
1

A catalogue record for this book is available from the British Library

ISBN: 978-0-00-867154-9

Set in Sabon LT Std by HarperCollins*Publishers* India

Printed and bound in the UK by CPI Group (UK) Ltd,
Croydon CR0 4YY

This book is produced from independently certified FSC paper to ensure
responsible forest management.

For more information visit: www.harpercollins.co.uk/green

ONE

Alfie sat at his desk in the attic room and searched the internet. He was alone; his wife was at work and his sons were at school. He was looking for something specific. Something to spice up his sex life, give it a shake-up. No, not a toy. They'd tried that a while ago and the novelty had worn off very quickly. He was looking for something brand new. The answer to his dreams, something that would return them to the heady days of fifteen years ago, before he and his wife had their sons.

It wasn't long before he found something. He browsed the internet some more. God, they were small. You could fit them anywhere, even inside the end of your pen. He looked some more. There were so many to choose from. He scanned the pages, scrolling down one and then the next. Then he began checking the details and found it. This security spy camera was inside a bedside clock, which would be perfect. Just what he wanted, and only £50!

He read the instructions and signed in to his account, then clicked and pressed buy. The parcel would arrive the next day. He checked his email and, sure enough, there was the notification in his inbox. The instructions had said it was easy to fit. He hoped it was. He wasn't an expert at fixing things, not like some men he knew.

He couldn't sleep that night. He was like a child, looking forward to a treat. He wouldn't tell his wife, not yet, if at all. She wouldn't understand. He wanted to test it first and make sure all was well. And anyway, the secrecy added to the drama.

TWO

At 11.30 the following morning the post arrived and Alfie shot to answer the door. His wife and the boys – Mike, fifteen, and Gregory, thirteen – were at work and school again. There was something naughty and mysterious in having this secret. He felt a frisson of expectation run through him.

The delivery guy wanted to take a photo for their records, so Alfie thanked him and stood holding the parcel while the photograph was taken, then he took the package up to his study in the attic. He closed the door, then sat and carefully unwrapped the parcel, examining the box before removing the clock. You'd think it was like any other bedside clock, unless you knew its secret – that it was really a home-security spy camera for looking into a room.

He read the words on the box. Wireless, of course. It was a 1080p camera clock designed to capture and record high-definition video. It had night vison, so would photograph even in the dark. That was a bonus. He hadn't realized it would film when all the lights were out – the infrared allowing you to see detail clearly. 'Whether it's day or night, you will know who comes into your house or office,' he read.

He paused and thought about that before continuing. The camera could synchronize with your iPhone, Android, tablet or PC. Perfect, he thought. It also had a wide-angle lens, designed to capture as much of the room as possible.

He sat back and looked at the box. It didn't need any complicated assembly, the instructions said. It fitted easily wherever you wanted it, allowing you to set up video surveillance in your office, classroom or hotel room. The only question he could think of was what he would tell his wife if she found out.

Alfie wasn't one to rush things. He liked to take things slowly, in his stride. So he put the camera back into its box, out of reach on his desk, and got on with some work. Pre-pandemic, he'd gone into the office in town five days a week, but that had stopped. He was a surveyor by trade, a fully paid-up member of the Royal Institution of Chartered Surveyors. The office had been closed during the pandemic and they'd all worked from home, with the obligatory Zoom calls. Now they only went in for a meeting every so often. His boss hadn't renewed the lease on the premises in town and so instead they went to an office that was a large extension built onto the side of his house.

Alfie worked on some two-dimensional drawings while thinking of the camera and the delights it would shortly present. He worked for nearly an hour, then closed the screen and pulled the box over. He took out the instructions. It seemed straightforward, but best to test it in here first before taking it into the guest room.

He read the instructions again – *These cameras are good at identifying burglars and uncovering partner infidelity*, it said. That wouldn't be a problem here, he thought. Not with Jenny. She would never do anything like that. *You can connect your CCTV security camera directly to your smartphone with the use of a mobile app.* The app, that was the first thing to do. He picked up his phone and downloaded the app.

After a bit of fiddling, the room suddenly came into view on his phone screen. He turned the clock camera around and was surprised by his expression. He looked gruffer and older than he usually did. He gave a little wave, then, tucking his phone into his pocket, he picked up the clock and carefully carried it down one flight of stairs to the guest bedroom on the first floor.

His wife ran their Roomy-Space.com. He hadn't got involved until now. She had been assigned a host from the company to help out at the start. When Jenny had first suggested the idea a year ago, he'd been against it, and so had his sons, vehemently. 'I'm not having strangers in my house,' he'd said, and the boys had said, 'No way!' But when he'd discovered they could charge £90 a night for bed and breakfast that rather changed things. He'd agreed to try it, and so had his sons with the promise of getting more pocket money. Jenny did it all, though. She left the guests breakfast and all they had to do was boil the kettle for coffee or tea. He kept an eye on them, however, and now he'd be able to do so even more. This camera would strengthen his house security, as it said on the box, as well as spicing up his sex life.

Most of the guests had only stayed one or two nights, and had left by 10.30 the following morning. One couple had stayed five nights, and they were the ones who had given him this idea. The attic room was his study, and his and his wife's bedroom was on the first floor next to the Roomy-Space. They'd heard the couple making love every night, although it was more than that. It had sounded like an orgy! They'd lain awake listening to them banging and groaning until after 2 a.m. So much so that Jenny didn't believe they were married, or at least not to each other, and thought they must be having an affair. He couldn't disagree.

They'd listened, then Jenny had felt like making love and made the first move. It was passionate. Like nothing he'd experienced in a long time. The Roomy-Space had been Gregory's room and he'd had to be coerced into sharing Mike's room. From where they now slept, they couldn't hear all the fuss coming from the Roomy-Space. Alfie had said his study was free if one of them wanted to sit in there to do their homework. So far neither of them had.

He left the door open as he went into the guest room. No one was due back yet, and as far as he knew the couple renting the room wouldn't be arriving until this evening, after Jenny was home. The room looked like many of the ones that appeared on Roomy-Space.com, with a double bed, a wardrobe, two bedside cabinets and a chair. Alfie and Jenny had to share their bathroom, which was definitely a drawback. The bed linen was supposed to be washed after every visit, but sometimes they missed a night if they had a lot of couples arriving and leaving after one night. No one had complained yet.

Alfie went over to the existing clock and removed it from where it sat on the bedside cabinet. He looked at it and then positioned the new one exactly where the old one had been. Perfect. Even if you looked at it very closely, there wasn't much difference; all you could see was a small additional embedded circle, just to the left of the clock face where the camera was, no bigger than half a centimetre. It blended in very well, he thought.

He picked up his phone and tested the spy camera, then adjusted it so it was in line with the bed. His heart was racing as he switched it to standby. He then got onto the bed and practised moving around, all the time watching on his phone. He lay still and the camera stopped running. He then made a tiny movement and it began again. He turned over on the bed and there it was. It seemed to be working fine.

Leaving the room, he closed the door and went up to his study, where he spent the rest of the afternoon, every so often checking his new spy camera. He felt a small pang of guilt. It wasn't exactly the done thing to invite people into your home as paying guests and then film them.

Alfie googled so see if what he was doing was legal and a quarter of an hour later decided it wasn't – people had been prosecuted in the past, and it went against Roomy-Space.com guidelines. He spent a few moments with his stomach churning and his heart racing. Perhaps he should have bought just a camera and fitted it properly in a light or something so that he definitely wouldn't get caught. But then again, if he was honest, that was probably beyond his capabilities. He was a surveyor who had very limited DIY expertise.

He put the box away and tried to concentrate on work. The piece he was working on was already late. He focused, but then spent time flicking between the computer and his phone. The guest room was still just as he'd left it. All was well. Then minutes later he heard his sons return home from school. Tucking his phone into his trouser pocket, he went downstairs to greet them.

THREE

'Everything OK with you guys?' Alfie asked as he did most afternoons.

His sons were talking about football – a subject he didn't take much interest in or know much about.

They replied with soporific yeses, poured themselves a glass of water each, and then went to their bedroom as they normally did. Alfie didn't know what they did up there – continued talking about football, he supposed.

Jenny would probably be home soon. She was a teacher – at a different school to the boys – and her home time depended on meetings, and anyone she'd asked to stay behind to see her. It was a Wednesday and Alfie couldn't remember her having meetings on a Wednesday before, so it seemed likely she'd be home on time. She'd returned to work full-time a few years before, to help pay off the debt they'd got themselves into. It had been mainly Alfie's fault. He'd tried to set up a business and go it alone, and had failed, miserably. Jenny had picked up the pieces.

Sure enough, twenty minutes later, Jenny arrived home only a little later than usual. He watched from the kitchen window as she parked on the drive, then got out and let herself into the house.

She was flustered, as she often was when she first returned home from school, and dumped her books, paperwork and laptop on the kitchen worktop. She offered her left cheek for a perfunctory kiss and then talked about school. He made her a cup of tea and listened. He felt he had to listen. It was his duty, since he was the reason she'd had to go back to work full-time.

'And do you know what the little madam said to me?' Jenny asked indignantly. She was talking about a pupil she'd asked to stay behind to see her. 'She told me to take a running jump. She said her mother didn't care what she did, so why should I? I mean, I ask you, where do you go from there? I've filled in a complaint form for the Head, but I don't suppose anything will come of it.'

Alfie shook his head in sympathy and passed her the mug of tea.

'I don't know how you deal with it,' he said dutifully. 'Day after day. I'm sure I couldn't do your job.' This always made Jenny feel important.

'Are the boys in their room?' she asked.

'Yes.'

'Good. I don't want them to start staying out after school and hanging around in a group. That's what leads to trouble.' And she was off again, this time about a lad at school called Sky who'd joined a gang and had disappeared. The police had been called in and were looking for him.

'I'm just going up to say hi to the boys, then we'll get dinner on,' she said and, leaving her empty mug for Alfie to wash up, she left the room.

Alfie stayed where he was and listened as her footsteps went upstairs. He heard her cross to the boys' room, where she knocked on their door, looked in on them and said a few words. Closing their bedroom door, she then went to the guest room to check it was all right. Alfie listened to her go across the laminated flooring – over to the bedside cabinet. It went quiet for a few seconds, then she came out again and came downstairs.

'There's a new clock in the guest bedroom,' she said.

'Yes, that's right. The other one was broken so I bought a new one.'

She looked at him slightly oddly, then said, 'Are you sure it's not just the batteries? Have you still got the old one?'

'No, I threw it out. I checked the batteries first.'

'I just wondered,' she said. 'You know how useless you are about these matters.' And she gave him a fond kiss on the cheek before beginning to prepare their dinner, leaving him to finish off his work.

'Do you know when the guests are due?' Alfie asked as they ate.

'They're going to text me when they leave their

daughter's,' Jenny said. 'Apparently they have family living not far away.'

'Oh, I see,' Alfie said, and continued with his meal.

It was 6.30. The boys gobbled down their dinner and immediately left the table to return to their bedroom. Alfie sighed but didn't comment. They'd had that conversation before. Instead, he cleared the table and washed up as Jenny did her schoolwork. At 7.40 Mrs Maddison and her husband texted to say they were on the bus and would be with them by 8 p.m. They didn't want anything to eat as they'd already had dinner.

'Thank goodness,' Jenny said. 'We'll save the rest for another day.'

'I'll tell the boys they're on their way,' Alfie said, and disappeared up to their bedroom.

'Boys,' he said, knocking on their door before going in. They appeared to have been sharing a joke. 'Our guests will be here at eight. Just to let you know so you can get clear of the bathroom by nine.'

'Thanks, Dad,' Gregory said, hiding a smile. Mike couldn't stop laughing.

'Are you all right, lads?' Alfie asked.

They nodded and tried to maintain straight faces.

Alfie came out and closed their door. There was no telling what they were up to at their age.

His heart was racing now. Whatever did he think he was doing? He supposed he could always return the spy camera and forget about the idea completely. It wasn't too late. Calm down, he told himself, taking a few deep breaths. Then he slowly returned downstairs and went into the living room where his wife was working.

'Everything all right with the boys?' she asked, looking at him.

He nodded. 'Why shouldn't it be?'

'I don't know. You seem a bit anxious tonight.'

'No, I'm fine,' he said, and sat down and turned on the television.

At 8.05 Mr and Mrs Maddison arrived. They pressed the doorbell and then pressed it again in quick succession. Alfie stood.

'No, I'll go,' Jenny said, and went into the hall to answer it.

Alfie waited in the living room. Why did he feel so guilty? He could hear Jenny talking to them as she led them through to say hello.

'Liz and Peter Maddison,' she announced. 'This is my husband, Alfie.'

They all shook hands. Alfie could have kicked himself. How could he have been so stupid? Of course it was unlikely to be a young couple, not mid-week. These two were in their eighties – she was considerably overweight and he had a limp.

'Your room is this way,' Jenny said, not giving them a chance to sit down.

They turned and followed her upstairs.

'We've been visiting our granddaughter,' Liz explained on their way up. 'She lives a short bus ride away, and with the new baby they haven't got room for us to stay

13

any more.'

Jenny eased them into their room. They seemed happy with it.

'As you know you share the bathroom, which is just across the hall. Our two lads will be finished by nine, and my husband and I go in after ten.'

'Fabulous,' Peter said. 'Perfect.'

'He didn't want to come to a Roomy-Space,' Liz explained. 'It's our first visit to one.'

'Well, I hope you'll be fine here,' Jenny said. 'So you have everything you need. There are towels on the bed and I'll leave your breakfast by the door before I go out in the morning. I hope we don't wake you.'

'We'll be up at a reasonable time tomorrow,' Peter said. 'We're going to see our daughter again, and then get the 1.05 train to Doncaster.'

'Very good. I'll leave you to it.'

Jenny smiled, came out, then closed the door and went to the boys' room.

'Our guests are here so keep the noise down, please.'

'Sure, Mum,' Mike said.

'Will do,' Gregory added.

'Good boys,' she said, coming out and closing the door.

Alfie's expectations of anything happening that night were nil, not with a couple in their eighties. It wasn't possible, was it? He waited downstairs, listening, and after a lot of shuffling around in their room he heard them finally settle in bed by 10 p.m. Now he wanted to check the app on his phone, just to make sure it was working.

He gave them half an hour and at 10.30 he went to the bathroom. It was the one place he wouldn't be disturbed. Locking the door, he closed the toilet seat, sat on it and illuminated his phone app. It was dark in the room but the night vision was working and there they were, fast asleep. For a moment he wasn't sure if the sound was working, then he found the volume and adjusted it. He could hear Peter snoring. It was quite loud.

He sat there mesmerized by the sight of other people sleeping. It was a bit like watching the boys when they were younger, only this couple didn't move around the bed as much. Peter was flat on his back and his wife was on her side. He watched them both for a while longer, but nothing happened, so he put the phone aside and got on with his own showering. Once ready, he went downstairs where Jenny was just finishing clearing up. He said goodnight, locked the house, then went to bed. He had one last sneaky peek at his phone. The couple were as he'd left them, same position and fast asleep. He heard Jenny come to bed too, so he switched off the phone. They were both asleep by 11.30.

Jenny got up the second the alarm went off the next morning. Alfie followed. There was no need for him to rise so early – he only had to go upstairs to work. But if he stayed in bed during the week he felt guilty, so rather than wrestle with his conscience, he always got up with Jenny. There followed the usual morning kerfuffle with the boys to get them up and ready for school on time, so that they and Jenny could be out of the house by 8.15.

15

His wife had left croissants and some other pastries on a tray outside their guests' door earlier. It was still there, and no sound was coming from the other side of the door yet.

Alfie went up to his study, opened the app, then sat there at his desk, examining the recording of the night. There were a few blips when Peter coughed and turned over, but nothing of any significance. It was quiet until 2.20 a.m. when Peter woke with a start and got up to use the toilet, switching on his bedside lamp as he went. It disturbed Liz, who mumbled something and turned over away from him. He was gone some time and then returned to bed. There was nothing more until right this second. Now they were getting up. He had no wish to see people in their eighties starkers as they got out of bed, so he closed the app.

He could hear their movements from where he was in the study. They took their breakfast tray in at 8.45 after Liz went to the bathroom. Then he assumed they were eating but didn't like to watch. Once they'd finished, they called up goodbye. Alfie felt he needed to come down to see them off.

'Thanks for everything,' Liz said. 'We'll stay with you again.'

'Good. That's what we like to hear,' Alfie replied.

He was disappointed, but it was only to be expected – a few false starts. He entered the guest room and stripped the bed. It was part of the deal he had with his wife to have it made up ready for tomorrow night's guests. He felt another stab of guilt but shelved it with all the others.

FOUR

It was Thursday afternoon. The boys had just come home from school and they were always high as the end of the week approached.

'You've got exams looming,' Alfie cautioned Mike.

'It's all under control, Dad,' he replied.

In truth, Alfie didn't know what his eldest son did and had long given up trying to find out.

'As long as it is,' he said, and left it at that.

The boys got themselves a drink and went to their bedroom.

Their Roomy-Space was fully booked over the weekend. Couples on Friday and Saturday, and a single man was a possible for Sunday. The good weather helped, of course; people wanted to walk in Coleshaw Woods – a natural beauty spot not so far away. Alfie was optimistic that his spy camera would be useful at some point over the weekend; the couple coming tonight had only made the booking that morning. He'd tried to get a look at the list of bookings on his wife's phone – she had put herself in charge and rarely let him see.

'It's a couple,' was all she said she could remember.

'How old are they?' Alfie asked.

She looked at him. 'I don't know. It's on their booking form,' she replied unhelpfully, and disappeared out the door.

All the booking forms were on his wife's phone, so he still had no idea.

Alfie's anticipation grew during Friday so that by the time the boys were home and ensconced in their room he was in a bit of a state. He'd kept wandering into the guest room and looking at the clock, then going back to his study. His wife didn't get in until after 5 p.m. on a Friday because she had a staff meeting, and then the couple arrived at 7. They were off their heads on something and didn't have any luggage. Jenny took one look at them, refused to let them in, and told them they'd get a refund while Alfie had stood quietly by, contemplating what he'd missed.

So it was Saturday before he got another chance. Alfie was feeling a little frazzled when the doorbell rang shortly before 7.30 p.m. Jenny was in the bathroom, so he shot to the door and answered it. They were early.

'Hello,' he said, smiling.

'Hi, I'm Carl. And this is my partner, Emma.'

Alfie shook their hands and welcomed them in. He was in his late teens and she was about sixteen. They looked exhausted.

'Will you be going out tonight?' Alfie asked, showing them to their room. 'If so, I'll let you have a key.'

'No, we'll be staying in,' Carl replied a little curtly.

'No problem,' Alfie said.

Checking they had everything they needed, he came out and closed their door.

Jenny and Alfie spent the evening in the sitting room. She was marking schoolwork; he sat and flicked through the local newspaper for some minutes. Then, unable to contain himself any longer, he made an excuse and went to his study. It was now 8 p.m. He tapped into the app on the way upstairs, and by the time he arrived he was watching the couple in their bedroom. She was sitting on the bed, clearly not very happy. There was an argument rumbling on and Alfie struggled for a few minutes to work out what it was about. They were both very agitated and she kept shushing him to keep his voice down. She sat on the edge of the bed with her back to the spy camera and he kept moving around. Then Alfie got the gist of it. She wasn't supposed to be seeing him and her parents didn't know. She'd told them she was staying with a friend for the night and now regretted it and wanted to go home.

The argument had reached a plateau and seemed to be going nowhere. Alfie learnt they had been seeing each other for six months, and that the reason she couldn't tell her parents of their relationship was because Carl had been in trouble with the police. Alfie felt quite protective towards her parents.

The argument continued. Alfie began to feel slightly uncomfortable watching it. It was a teenage problem and they needed to sort it out or end their relationship. He deadened the sound, then put the phone on his desk, flicking through a computer magazine, as they continued to speak dumbly. It was quite funny, really. Every so often he glanced at the screen. Then he knew he would be missed. He and his wife spent Friday night together, so he put away his phone and went downstairs where he kept the television on mute until Jenny had finished her marking.

It was after 10 p.m. when they both decided they were knackered and would go to bed. They made love. Alfie briefly wondered if their guests were doing the same thing. He hoped so. He couldn't look at his phone now, though, and he and Jenny fell asleep very quickly.

He was woken briefly in the night by a strange sound, but there were often strange sounds he couldn't place when there were strangers in the house, so he thought nothing more of it and went back to sleep.

The following morning when he woke he went to cross the hall to go to the bathroom. He could see that the guest-bedroom door was slightly open. Strange, he thought. It didn't sound as though anyone was in there, so he looked. Sure enough, the couple had both left already. That must have been what he'd heard during the night.

He had some work to do that morning, ready for a site visit on Monday. The boys always stayed in bed until around 10 a.m. at the weekend, sometimes later. In his dressing gown, he left Jenny in bed and went to his study, closed the door and turned on his phone. Perhaps they'd had a big making-up session before they'd left, he thought. He found the place in the recording where he'd stopped watching last night, and pressed play. There they were, still arguing, and so it continued. He waited for it to subside. It was all becoming too much.

It didn't subside. It grew, with a few breaks. She kept telling him to keep his voice down so they wouldn't wake the owners. It went on for half an hour and Alfie fast-forwarded. He wanted to get to the bit where they were friends again and had sex.

Alfie pressed play again, then watched and waited, becoming increasingly concerned. There was something not right here. Carl was struggling to keep his voice down. He had a temper, that was for sure. It was fast escalating into something dreadful. Alfie could feel it; he could hear it in Carl's tone of voice. It wasn't good. He kept putting his hand on Emma's shoulder, and she kept shaking it off.

By 11.30 it was still going on. It was a wonder they had the stamina to continue. 'Just let her go,' Alfie said out loud. He felt very sad indeed that this was the end of their relationship and it was taking place in his home. If he and Jenny argued it was over and done with in fifteen minutes. He always knew she was right, and he said so.

But what was happening now? He turned up the volume on his phone. Carl had thrown Emma onto the bed and was putting the pillow over her face. 'All right.

Enough. Get off her now,' Alfie said frantically, standing. 'This has gone far enough.'

He waited. 'Now,' he yelled. 'Get off her!'

Carl appeared to suddenly come to and removed the pillow from Emma's face. She didn't move. He shook her, then, after a pause, began giving her mouth-to-mouth resuscitation. Nothing happened. Alfie stared at the screen and was about to go into the bedroom when he remembered it was a recording. 'It can't be,' he said out loud, staring at his phone.

He watched as Carl continued to try to resuscitate her, pumping her chest repeatedly, but despite his best efforts, nothing happened. Emma was dead. Then, instead of shouting for help as he should have done, he sat on the bed, his head in his hands, for some time. Alfie's breath caught in his throat. He stared at the screen and waited. A while later Carl stood, picked Emma up as if she were drunk and threw her over his shoulder. She flopped like a rag doll. He steadied himself and then carried her downstairs and out of the house. The time on Alfie's phone showed 11.46 p.m.

Alfie's heart was racing. He felt hot and cold, and sick to the core. He didn't know what to do. Phone the police? That seemed the right thing to do. He picked up his phone and was about to dial, but then realized he'd have to admit he'd been viewing something he shouldn't have been. He sat down again. What should he do? Jenny would know.

He began heading towards his study door and stopped. Jenny didn't know about the spy camera. What was he going to tell her? He sat down again and tried to calm himself and think rationally about what to do.

Alfie sat there in his pyjamas, his thoughts going all over the place. Gradually, after some time, his mind began to clear. He wasn't going to do anything at all. That was the best solution. He would carry on as normal, because there was nothing else he could do. If he went to the police, they'd question him about the recording. When they found her body he'd rethink.

He could hear Gregory and Mike getting up and going downstairs for breakfast. Jenny was in the kitchen too. He would say nothing. After all, how far could Carl have got carrying a dead body? He assumed that, if anyone had spotted him, he would have said she was very drunk, because that was how she'd looked, flung over his shoulder. Did Carl have a car outside? That would have made it a whole lot easier to dispose of the body.

Alfie was calmer now. He knew what to do. It wouldn't be long before someone raised the alarm and Carl was stopped and caught. Alfie didn't have to *do* anything. He checked his phone again to see if Carl had returned during the night, then remembered they hadn't been given a key. Of that he was certain. Should he delete the recording? He decided against it, just in case. Putting on a brave face and summoning all his strength, he went to the guest room and gingerly peered in. The bed was very ruffled and for reasons he couldn't say, he straightened it and made it look nice again. He then went to the bathroom to get showered and dressed, all the while hoping he was doing the right thing.

The water fell, constant and easy, and he stood under it for far longer than normal, soaking up its soporific effects. Once he was done, he stepped out and checked his face in the mirror for any sign of what had transpired. He couldn't see anything and went to join his family for breakfast. Jenny was at the stove, cooking. They only had a cooked breakfast at the weekend.

'Good morning,' Alfie said, his voice unsteady, and he joined Gregory and Mike at the table.

They were still – as usual – in their pyjamas. Jenny was in her dressing gown. He looked at them as though they were a different family. They *were* different to him now, not tainted by the brush of deceit. He knew something they didn't, and he would keep it that way. He looked at his wife and sons and wondered what they'd make of it – if he were to confess that he'd set up a camera to spy on their guests and had caught a murderer by chance. They'd think he was crazy.

'Are you all right, Dad?' Mike asked after a few moments.

'Yes. Thank you,' he replied, his voice rather loud.

'Do you want your usual fry-up?' Jenny called over.

He thought about it and honestly couldn't face it.

'No, thank you. I'm not feeling great today.' He patted his stomach. 'I'll just get coffee.'

The boys watched him cross to the coffee machine.

'They've gone then?' he said. 'The guests.'

'Yes, I didn't hear them go,' Jenny replied. 'But then we rarely do on a Sunday if they're early.'

24

Alfie didn't know what to say, so he stayed quiet. Jenny brought the boys' plates to the table with their eggs, bacon and baked beans.

'I guess they left very early?' he suggested.

'Must have done,' she said. 'I've checked the room and it's fine. We'll use the bedding for next time. It doesn't look like it's been slept in.'

Alfie's stomach contracted and he thought he was going to be sick. No, Jenny, not that. Not the pillow that was used to smother Emma. They couldn't use that again. He took a deep breath and tried a sip of his coffee.

'Do you know if they had a car?' he asked after a few moments.

'I've no idea. Why?' Jenny replied.

'I just wondered,' Alfie said.

The boys were looking at him oddly. Was he talking normally? He was finding it very difficult to know. That was the problem when you had a secret like this. You didn't know if others were reading your thoughts or not.

'I think I'll go upstairs for a lie down,' he said, and abruptly stood.

'Do you want anything?' Jenny asked.

'No, I'll be fine soon.'

All eyes were on him as he left the room. Alfie hadn't been ill for a long time, but then he'd never witnessed anything so terrible in his own home – a murder! He went upstairs to his study and sat with his head in his hands. Whatever was he doing? Should he go back down and tell Jenny the truth? No, he couldn't. Supposing he tipped off the police anonymously? But what could he say that would help? He stood and paced the room, thinking about last night, then he reached for his phone. He still found it difficult to believe that someone could commit murder in their house. But as he looked again, he saw the proof right in front of his eyes. It had definitely happened.

FIVE

Alfie spent the rest of the day trying to look and behave normally, which wasn't easy. In fact, it was a big effort. Gregory and Mike got dressed and went to play football. He would normally have accompanied them to cheer them on, but using his illness as an excuse, he didn't go today.

'Hope you're feeling better soon,' Mike called as they left.

'Yes, thanks,' he replied as they closed the door.

Jenny was busy with some lesson planning. Teaching full-time was a much bigger commitment than it used to be, and Alfie felt responsible for the amount of work she had to do. They'd been doing fine with her working part-time and now, because of Alfie's bad management, she'd had to go back to working all hours. There was nothing he could do about it, so he left her with her laptop in the living room.

The single man who'd enquired for that evening emailed to say he didn't need the room after all, so they didn't have anyone staying that night.

The hours of Sunday passed slowly. The boys returned from football in good spirits, having won their match 6–1. Alfie congratulated them and kept checking the news on his phone. There was nothing yet. It was too soon. He guessed there wouldn't be anything for a while. It was too early for any report from Emma's parents to be taken seriously by the police, he thought. They would allow at least twenty-four hours before they put out a bulletin and began searching for her.

All in all, it was a wretched day. Alfie felt guilty, and then he began to feel ill again.

Having had no breakfast, he'd refused lunch too, and as dinnertime drew near he was ready to throw up. Then he forced himself to eat something and began to feel a bit better. He went to bed early and watched some television on his laptop, as well as continuing to check the news. When he heard Jenny come up he feigned sleep, and kept pretending to be asleep for most of the night. In actual fact, he lay there working his way through the various scenarios of what might be happening. The girl's parents would have reported her missing by now, surely.

He tried to think of instances where that might not be the case – if she was in care or living on the streets was all he could come up with. Was Emma old enough to be living on the streets? he wondered. Then he caught himself – she'd said she couldn't see Carl again because her parents didn't approve of his criminal record, so she must be living with her parents. How much of her activities were they aware of? And so his thoughts went around and around.

Sometime after 2.30 he must have fallen asleep, because when he awoke it was 7 a.m. on Monday, and the house was on the move. Thank goodness the night was over, he thought, slowly getting up. Jenny had already gone to make breakfast and wake the boys. He felt groggy from only having had a few hours' sleep but pulled on his dressing gown. He went to his study to check his phone – it was safer in there – and that was when he saw it.

The police are looking for Emma Arnold, 15, runaway, who was last seen on Saturday afternoon. If anyone has any information, please call Coleshaw CID. Her parents are distraught.

There followed the number of Coleshaw CID.

Fifteen, was that all she was? It was all he could think about for some time. She was the same age as Mike, and a minor. He suddenly came over faint.

So Emma's parents had reported her missing and the police, believing she would return, had put this out. Only, Alfie knew that she wasn't missing; she was dead. It was a small piece in the local news – there was nothing about Carl. Where was he? How old was he? He guessed a few years older than Emma but couldn't be sure. Clearly, Emma's parents didn't know she had booked their room or the police would have come by now. He'd heard her say she'd told them she was staying with a friend. He wondered whose name the room had been booked under, but the only way he could find out was through Jenny's phone.

Alfie looked again at the piece and his stomach churned. You wouldn't find it unless you were looking for it. It was under local news. Jenny and the boys wouldn't see it, would they? Jenny only read the main headlines on her phone and the boys didn't read anything at all, as far as he knew.

He sat for a moment pondering, then went downstairs.

'Are you feeling better today?' Jenny asked him.

'Yes, I think so,' he replied.

'Just as well you don't have to *go* to work,' she said, and busied herself getting ready.

He ignored the slight and got himself a coffee and a slice of toast. The boys were late up again. They always were on a Monday. Jenny kissed his cheek and left. He called up to the boys to get a move on, then sat at the table with his coffee and toast and thought about what he should do.

If no one knew where Carl and Emma had stayed that night, they were safe. Her parents believed Emma had run away. Perhaps she'd done this type of thing before. Perhaps her body might never be found. In which case there was nothing – as far as he knew – to connect her to here. Did Emma's parents know she was still seeing Carl? he wondered, and decided probably not. It crossed his mind that it would have been so much easier to have gone to the police as soon as he'd seen the recording, but the crime was twenty-four hours old now and he would have to explain why he hadn't come forward before, other than that he'd panicked. Better to say nothing now, surely?

'Bye!' he managed to call to his sons as they left, and poured himself another coffee.

Then he remembered with a jolt that he was due on site at 10 a.m. He grabbed his coffee and took it up to his bedroom where he found a suit in the wardrobe. Once ready, he returned to his study for his laptop, at the same time checking his phone. There was nothing new on Emma or Carl.

He tried to put on his work face as he got into the car, but he was no longer sure what that was. Concentrate on the specifics, he told himself, and he keyed the postcode into the sat nav. It showed twenty minutes to his destination. He knew roughly where the house was.

As he drove, he kept the news on and listened for any mention of the missing girl. There was nothing. He wondered how common it was for teenagers to go missing, and then pressed the car's audio system to ask: 'How many teenagers go missing each year in the UK?' he asked.

'Seventy-five thousand children were recorded missing in the UK last year,' it replied.

That was a lot, he thought. How many of them ever returned? He wondered.

Suddenly he was outside the house. He stopped and parked. It was a three-bedroom semi, which shouldn't take too long to check over. The couple were buying without a mortgage but still wanted the homebuyers' survey. He went up the short path and pressed the bell. The female owner let him in, offered him a tea, which he refused, then she thankfully left him alone. He walked around the inside, checking the ceilings, walls, bathrooms and so forth, then went outside to check the guttering, main walls, windows and doors. He also stole a glimpse at his phone; there was still nothing. He finished by checking the boundary walls and fences, then returned indoors, thanked the lady for her time and said he'd have the report written up and sent by the end of the week. She thanked him and he left.

On the way home a police car pulled in behind him and stayed there for longer than felt OK, then it dramatically pulled out and drove ahead of him, disappearing down the road. He breathed a sigh of relief.

He arrived home frazzled and checked the news on all the channels. There was still nothing further. It was now a day and a half since the murder. Surely something should have been found by now? What the hell were the police doing?

SIX

DC Beth Mayes and DC Matt Davis sat in the office above Coleshaw Police Station, closing their computer files. It was Monday, midday. They'd been assigned the task of going to talk to Emma Arnold's parents to see if they could gather any more information. It was the start of a more thorough investigation into Emma's disappearance, and as the week progressed, if she didn't turn up, their questions would become more searching.

DS Bert Scrivener had given them the details of where the Arnolds lived, together with his assurance that he was 99 per cent certain the girl would reappear over the next few days. But protocol said they had to follow it up now, despite the fact that he was sure she was safe. Hundreds of thousands of people went missing every year and eventually most of them arrived home. 'Every ninety seconds someone is reported missing in the UK,' was one of Bert's favourite statistics.

'Also, phone the school, and find out what you can

about Emma,' Bert said. 'No need to go there just yet.'

'Will do,' Matt replied, picking up his laptop from his desk.

Matt and Beth went down the back stairs of the police station to the yard, where they got into their unmarked police car. They had worked together since they'd joined the force some years ago and took it in turns to drive. Matt now took the wheel while Beth made contact with the school.

'DC Beth Mayes here,' she said to the receptionist. 'Can I talk to the Head, please? It's about Emma Arnold.'

'I'll see if she's in her office,' the receptionist said.

Beth waited and was then put through.

'Yes, hello. Has she been found yet?' the Head asked.

Beth paused, trying to work out what the Head knew.

'Emma's parents phoned in first thing this morning, very worried,' the Head clarified. 'They wondered if we'd heard anything, which we haven't.'

'She hasn't been found, I'm afraid,' Beth said. 'I'm actually phoning for a few more details about her. I was wondering if you could help.'

'Well, what do you want to know? This is confidential, between you and me?' she added.

'Yes,' Beth said. People in positions of authority usually checked to make sure what they said wouldn't be passed on. 'General things. What is she like to teach?'

'She's about average for her class,' the Head said. 'They've got exams looming this summer and she's predicted to get mostly Cs. I'd have to speak to her class teacher for more specifics. If she did more work, she'd be a bit brighter. She spends too much time out with boys. She's gone missing before, you know?'

'Yes, I do,' Beth said. 'Does the name Carl ring a bell? The parents mentioned him when we spoke.'

'Not really. I guess her classmates will know more than I do. Shall I ask them?'

'No, not yet,' Beth said. It would only get them all gossiping.

'All I can tell you is that Emma is a personable girl who could do more at school if she put in the effort. It's an important year, as I keep telling them.'

'Thank you. Anything else?' Beth asked.

'Not really. You'd get more by asking her friends. There are three of them that are close. Are you sure you don't want me to mention anything?'

'No, thank you. We'll speak to her class later this week, if she hasn't appeared by then. Thank you for your time.'

Turning to Matt, Beth said: 'The usual – nice girl, could do better.'

Matt nodded and continued to drive to the Arnolds' home, where he parked outside. Mrs Arnold met them at the door.

'Have you found her?' she asked, genuine anguish in her gaze.

'No, not yet,' Beth said. 'We're still looking.'

'But how hard?' Mr Arnold asked.

As hard as their allowance permitted, Beth thought, but said nothing.

Beth glanced around their neat front room, then back at Mrs Arnold.

'Is Emma your only child?' she asked, sitting down.

'Yes.'

'We've been sent to try to find out some more details about her,' Beth said gently.

'Like what? We've told you what we know,' Mr Arnold replied. 'You just need to get looking for her.'

'Can we go back to the last time she went missing?' Beth asked. 'I believe it was after an argument. Can you remember what it was about and where you found her?'

Mr Arnold looked at his wife. 'I really don't know. It was a silly argument. About clothes, I think. What she was wearing. She came back a day later – wouldn't even tell us where she'd been. That was eight months ago.'

'And she was back a day after the argument?' Matt checked.

'Yes, I think so, but this is different.'

'Can you explain how it's different?' Beth asked.

Mrs Arnold sighed. 'We think she's with that Carl Smith. We told the other officer all about him.'

'What makes you believe she's with Carl?' Beth asked.

Mr Arnold told them that Carl had a criminal record and was no good, as he'd told the other officers.

'Have you actually met him?' Beth asked.

There was a long silence before Mrs Arnold replied. 'No,' she said, before having a go at them about not doing more to find Emma.

It was Monday; Emma was last seen on Saturday, and

36

they simply didn't have the police resources to do more for a fifteen-year-old who'd gone missing before and had turned up safely.

'We gave you Carl's address, which we found in our daughter's room,' Mr Arnold put in. 'I'll go there myself if necessary.'

'I'm afraid you won't find him at the address you gave us. He's never lived there. We checked.'

'Oh, I see,' Mr Arnold said while his wife's mouth dropped.

'So that's proof of what we're saying. He's no good. I mean, why would he lie about where he lived?'

Beth and Matt exchanged the briefest of glances. Mr and Mrs Arnold had high hopes for their daughter and Carl was busy smashing them.

'We're following up all leads,' Matt said. 'I'm sure we'll have some news before long.'

'There's something we remembered,' Mr Arnold said. 'We phoned your duty sergeant first thing this morning. Carl has got tattoos all down his left arm and might have them in other places as well.'

'But you said you've never met him,' Matt checked.

They were silent before Mrs Arnold replied: 'No, we haven't – Emma told us about the tattoos. She wouldn't let us meet him. We haven't met many of her boyfriends.'

Beth and Matt came out with a clearer picture of Emma. She was a victim of judgemental parents and couldn't do anything right, and was a little rebellious as a result. It was a pity, because they clearly loved their daughter, despite some of her behaviour. On the way back to the police station they put Carl Smith's name into the Police National Computer and came up with three Carls living within a ten-mile radius, one of whom had a criminal record.

'We'll see if Scrivener wants us to check him out tomorrow. For now, he wants us back in the office. It's the continuing saga of the Bates family – I wonder what they've done now ...' Matt said.

Beth nodded and thought about Emma and how she herself would have coped with such overprotective parents. She wouldn't have coped at all. She was a free spirit and wouldn't have it any other way. Maybe Emma was the same.

SEVEN

By Monday afternoon, Alfie had come to the conclusion that he needed to take a look at his wife's phone. This was to find out the address and telephone number of whoever had made the booking for Saturday. He would do it as soon as Jenny arrived home. When she first came in she had a habit of dumping everything she was carrying on the centre island in the kitchen, and leaving it there while she went to wash and change her clothes. The boys wouldn't be around then; they'd have gone straight to their bedroom to chill. And luckily, Alfie knew Jenny's passcode.

For now, he went to his study and began filling in the homebuyers' survey for the house he'd seen that morning. His concentration kept fading and he found himself gazing out through the study window. He was high up here and it was early October, but there was little sign of autumn yet. His thoughts kept going to some unspecified grassy ditch some way from here, where Emma's body would eventually be found. What was he going to say then? He trembled at the prospect and tried to bring his thoughts back to his work.

Sometime later he heard Gregory and Mike come back from school. He went downstairs to talk to them, but they weren't interested in what he had to say. They poured themselves a drink each and said they were going to their bedroom.

'What do you do up there for so long?' he asked them.

'Usual stuff,' Mike said dismissively, and left.

Gregory followed him, with a look of feigned seriousness.

One day, when the matter of Carl was all over and done with, I'll ask to see their schoolbooks, Alfie thought, see what's really going on. But for now, he had other things on his mind, and he needed to put dinner in the oven. It was his turn to cook and he thought they'd have meat tonight, as they hadn't for a few days. He got some chops out of the freezer, put them in the microwave to defrost, then peeled the potatoes. He put them together with some glazed parsnips in the oven to cook.

Jenny came in at her usual time of 5 p.m. She kissed him on the cheek, then dumped all her belongings on the island – books, her shoulder bag and, most importantly, her phone – and went upstairs. As soon as she'd gone, Alfie picked up the phone, entered her passcode and found the Roomy-Space.com file. He quickly went to the most recent page. They didn't have anyone coming tonight. Good. Mondays were often clear. He scrolled back and found the page for Saturday night. The booking had been made by Carl Smith. He quickly wrote down the telephone number and address he'd given, then put the phone back just where he'd found it.

Alfie was just stuffing the piece of paper with Carl's details into his trouser pocket when Jenny returned. He made her a cup of tea and she asked how his day had been. Then she talked about school as she usually did. Only this time it was about the Deputy Head and how much time she'd had off already. They were only three weeks into the new school year and it wasn't acceptable, Jenny said. Alfie nodded and thought about what he was going to do later, after dinner, now he had Carl's address and telephone number.

At 6 p.m. he called the boys for dinner and they came down, sharing a joke. He supposed he should be grateful they got on so well. If they'd been continually fighting and quarrelling, he'd have a bigger problem on his hands. They all sat down at the table and he served dinner.

The boys gobbled down their food and Jenny asked them if they had any homework to do. She knew the value of education.

'Yes, Mum,' Mike dutifully replied, then he stood, took his plate to the dishwasher and went upstairs.

Gregory followed his older brother.

'We haven't got anyone staying tonight,' Jenny said, retrieving her phone from the island. They had a rule that mobile phones and other electronic devices should be kept away from the table.

'No?' Alfie replied. 'Oh well. I'm going to the petrol station now. Is there anything you want? I'll wash the pans when I get back.'

'No, nothing,' Jenny replied.

Maintaining his composure, Alfie stood and left the table with his plate, glass and cutlery, which he put into the dishwasher.

'Bye,' he called from the hall as he left, but no one answered.

Outside, he got into the car, where he entered Carl's address into the sat nav. Some hesitation, then it came up. It showed it was ten minutes away. He started the car and drove. As he did, he dialled the number of Carl's phone; it rang and rang. He hung up, tried again. Nothing. He continued to drive to the address.

He parked outside and looked at the house, then double-checked the address on the paper. It was correct. He'd imagined Carl living in a flat somewhere, not a house. It wasn't dissimilar to the one Alfie lived in himself. Perhaps Carl was still living with his parents. What would they say about what he'd done? When Alfie had run through what might happen tonight in his head he'd pictured Carl living with friends in a small flat or even sofa surfing. He'd just have to play it by ear.

He got out of his car and made his way up the path to the front door. It was still light outside. He hesitated, then, summoning his willpower, he pressed the bell. Time to see what Carl had to say for himself! Assuming he was in, of course.

42

A guy about Alfie's age answered the front door.

'Yes, can I help you?' he asked.

'Is Carl in?'

'Carl? I'm sorry, you must have the wrong address.'

Alfie looked at him carefully. 'No, I don't think so,' he said, and repeated the postcode.

'That's this postcode, but I can assure you that there's no one by that name living here, as I've told the police. There's just me, my wife and my two girls. You could try other houses in the road, but not either side. We know them and there's no one there by the name of Carl.'

It took Alfie a moment to realize the man was probably telling him the truth. Unsure of what to do next, he said a polite goodbye and left. The door closed behind him. He was angry with himself for being such a fool, and with Carl for putting him in this situation.

He didn't go to the houses immediately next door but went to one two doors down instead. He knocked and told them he was looking for Carl and received the same reply. 'No, sorry, he doesn't live here.'

It was fifteen minutes later that Alfie came to the conclusion that Carl had lied when he gave his address and didn't live on this street at all. So it was possible to put fake details into the booking form on Roomy-space. com. He wondered if the phone number was fake too.

Angry and upset, he returned to his car and tried the phone number again. It was answered immediately. 'Hello?'

'I don't suppose you're Carl Smith?' he asked.

'No, sorry, mate. Wrong number.'

And with an aching heart for all that was wrong with the world, he thanked the man and ended the call. He was no nearer to catching Carl Smith than the police were, and it hurt. Was now the time to go to them? But what could he say? He sat in his car outside the house, thinking. He eventually decided that he had less incentive to go to the police now than he'd had at the beginning of all this, so he started the car and drove home.

EIGHT

Alfie didn't sleep well again that night. There'd been a murder in his house and he still didn't know what to do. He lay in bed tossing and turning until after 1 a.m. At one point Jenny prodded him in the back and told him she had to be up in the morning and to go to sleep. But Alfie's thoughts wouldn't stay still.

He now knew that it was possible to use a fake telephone number and address when filling in the form for Roomy-Space.com, which left the email address. He hadn't thought to note that when he'd looked at Jenny's phone. It was now lying on her bedside cabinet, recharging.

He lay there until he was certain she was asleep again; he didn't want to wait until the following evening. Then he silently slid from the bed and crept round to Jenny's side. She was still sleeping soundly. Watching her carefully, he took her phone and logged in to the Roomy-Space account. He found the email address: Carl123456@gmail.com. Mmm, he thought; he could remember that.

He returned to his side of the bed. He lay on his side beneath the sheets and added the email address to the contact list on his own phone, wondering how you managed to trace an email address. He lay there thinking for some time, then, with Jenny still sleeping peacefully beside him, he composed an email to Carl.

Carl

I am the man whose house you stayed in on Saturday night. We both know what you did was very wrong. You need to hand yourself in to the police. Now!

Alfie

He read it, thought about it some more, then pressed send before his confidence disappeared. It vanished into the ether. He waited for a reply but none came. He knew that some people kept their phones on all night, but maybe Carl didn't. He listened out for his phone to vibrate and then finally dropped off to sleep after 2.30.

When he woke, Jenny was getting up. He immediately reached for his phone. He had an email from Carl. He waited until Jenny had left the bedroom before reading it.

Why don't you piss off? Remember, I know where you live.

It was a threat. It was impossible to view it any other way. He was being threatened by a murderer who knew where he lived. He frantically replied: *Don't threaten me!*

Back came the response. *Why not?*

Alfie didn't know what to say. What had he done? He

46

decided not to say anything in reply. After all, what could he say?

Agitated, he got up, washed and dressed, all the while thinking of Carl's threat. He had made a huge mistake in emailing Carl. His family were now in danger, and it was all his fault. There were plenty of times when he wasn't in the house. His sons were big for their age, but not that skilled when it came to fending for themselves. And Jenny could easily be got at – at home or at school.

Very worried and unsure of what to do, he went downstairs and slowly made himself breakfast. He ate it steadily and thoughtfully, thinking about his family. Jenny kissed his cheek, then left for work. His sons yelled, 'Bye, Dad!' and then left too. He took his second cup of coffee up to his study and googled: *How to trace an email.*

After an hour of following instructions, he discovered that you couldn't trace an actual email, not successfully anyway. You could trace its IP address, but that wouldn't help him much in the long run. So it was impossible for him to know where Carl had sent the email from. He guessed the police would have more tools at their disposal. Again, he wondered if it would be wise to contact them, but again dismissed it – too much time had now passed.

Alfie checked his phone for any news on Emma and saw an online piece had been updated.

Police are appealing for witnesses to the disappearance of missing schoolgirl Emma Arnold, 15. She was last seen leaving her home on Saturday afternoon. Anyone with information please contact Coleshaw CID. Her parents are very worried.

Alfie read it and didn't know what he was supposed to do. He sat there and did nothing, aware that he had been contacted by her killer. If only he hadn't set up that bloody spy camera in the first place, he wouldn't be in this position. Jenny might have made the connection eventually between Emma Arnold and their guest, but that would have been a while from now, when it all became headline news.

He went to his desk and tried to work, but it was impossible to do anything productive. He kept shuffling papers around, standing and going to his window. Then at lunchtime Jenny messaged to say they had a booking for that night.

'OK, thanks,' he messaged back, and regretted his decision to install the camera even more.

He'd lost any incentive to use it. Supposing he saw something else he shouldn't? He'd already witnessed a murder and now he was being threatened by the perpetrator. It didn't get any worse than that. It served him right for buying the stupid thing in the first place. It was only ever supposed to be a bit of fun.

He went downstairs for some lunch, cut the grass, and by the end of the day when the boys arrived home he'd done virtually no work at all. He watched them mooch around the kitchen. Then it occurred to him that, being kids of the same age, they might have heard something about Emma at school. Schools buzzed with knowledge and gossip. He didn't know which school Emma went to, but it couldn't be that far away.

'Have you seen the news report about Emma Arnold?' he asked them.

They both stopped what they were doing to look at him.

'Yes, why?' Mike asked.

'I was just wondering if you knew her.'

'She's in my class at school,' Mike replied.

'So you know she's missing?' Alfie asked, shocked. When he was a teenager, he'd have told his parents if someone in his class was missing.

'Yes. What of it?' Mike asked.

Alfie stared at him. He really didn't like his attitude sometimes. Emma was in Mike's class at school. It wasn't what he'd been expecting, not at all. He realized he couldn't think what to say next.

'I saw the news report and just wondered,' he said.

'She's gone missing before,' Mike said nonchalantly.

'But this is different,' Alfie said, then stopped. He couldn't tell them how different this was.

The boys looked at him. 'Why?' Gregory asked.

'Well, it hasn't ever been reported before, has it?'

'I really don't know,' Mike said. 'You'd have to check online.'

And they went to their room to chill.

Alfie quickly took out his phone and searched to see if it had been reported before that Emma Arnold had gone missing, but he couldn't find anything. So now he knew which school she went to and that she was in Mike's class. How far did that get him? After some thought he decided no further at all.

'Emma Arnold goes to the boys' school,' was the first thing he said to Jenny when she arrived home.

She looked at him nonplussed as she dumped the books on the centre island.

'Who's Emma Arnold?' she asked.

He stopped himself from saying that she was the girl who'd stayed there on Saturday night, for it now occurred to him that she might not be aware of her name. Carl had made the booking and it was in his name alone. Had he introduced her? Alfie thought back; he might have – well, as Emma at least – but he couldn't be sure.

'She's missing,' was all he said.

Jenny worked at a school in a different borough so she wouldn't necessarily have heard the news.

'Oh, right. Well, let's hope she turns up soon,' she said. 'We've got a woman staying tonight,' she continued. 'She'll be here at seven. She's got a funeral to go to tomorrow.'

Jenny went to wash, and to check the guest room. Alfie could have kicked himself. He needed to be more careful in future. He'd nearly given himself away by mentioning that Emma had stayed on Saturday. Now that he thought about it, Jenny had been in the bathroom when Carl had introduced Emma. Could she know the girl's name was Emma another way? He wasn't sure.

He checked his phone and his heart nearly stopped.

There was another message from Carl.

You'd better not go to the police if you value your life, it read.

Alfie trembled and put his head in his hands and stayed like that for some time trying to think what to do.

That evening – Alfie quieter than usual – was given over to Mrs Saunders, who'd arrived half an hour early when they'd just finished eating. Jenny answered the door and then showed her up to her room, but she wouldn't stay there, and kept coming down with requests and questions. Could Alfie open her bedroom window, please? It seemed to be stuck. Could he close it again? She couldn't do it. Could she possibly borrow some soap? She'd forgotten hers. She talked far too much, Alfie decided. She was in her early eighties and had left her husband alone for the night. He wasn't used to being alone. She hoped he was all right. Then she told them her life story of how she'd met him. They'd been married for fifty-five years!

Finally, around 9 p.m. she came downstairs and asked for help to book a cab for tomorrow. Alfie thought it was evenings like this when he really hated the Roomy-Space – the constant drain on his time, especially when he had other things to think about. The woman was clearly worried about going to the funeral. It was an old family friend of hers who'd died, and she was anxious about being so far from home and being late for the service. She'd come on the train from Wellingborough and Alfie said he'd book the cab to get her to the cemetery in plenty of time. She was very grateful indeed. Jenny didn't have the heart to simply put her into her room after that and close the door. She offered her a cup of tea, although she already had tea and coffee in her room. They were there until nearly 9.45 when she thanked them all again and went to bed. They heard her moving around and then, soon enough, the noise stopped and she was fast asleep.

'Make sure she's up and off tomorrow,' Jenny reminded Alfie as they, too, headed up to bed.

Almost as soon as her head touched the pillow, Jenny was sound asleep. Tomorrow was another day, Alfie thought, as he lay there worrying about Carl. But it wouldn't get any better unless he went to the police and confessed. Could he really do that? he wondered. He spent the next hour thinking about it and what would be involved. Then he put it to the back of his mind, snuggled into Jenny and went to sleep.

NINE

DC Beth Mayes and DC Matt Davis were at their desks by 8.30 the following morning. It was going to be another long day. It was Wednesday and they'd had their morning briefing already. The missing person investigation had dominated and was being taken more seriously now because of the time that had passed. Beth and Matt had been assigned to go to the school that Emma attended to talk to the whole class. They'd phoned the Head and agreed to go at 10.30 when she promised they'd all be together for class time.

The checks they'd run through the National Police Computer for Carl Smiths living within a fifty-mile radius of the police station had drawn a blank. One guy was in his seventies and had a single previous motoring offence, another in his sixties had a conviction for shoplifting, and another in his forties had a breaking and entering conviction and was still in prison. There was no Carl Smith matching their description.

'Mr and Mrs Arnold were convinced our Carl Smith has a criminal record,' Beth said.

'I suppose he could live over fifty miles away,' Matt said. 'I'll check it out later when we return to the station.'

They parked outside the school. The Head was waiting for them and greeted them at the door. Shaking their hands firmly, she showed them down the corridor to the classroom they were using, talking all the time about the weather and Emma. They went into a classroom full of fifteen-year-olds, who fell silent as they entered. The Head addressed them first.

'These police officers have come to talk to you about our missing Emma Arnold. Please cooperate,' she said, and stepped back.

Beth went forward as Matt stood to one side. She spent a little while talking about Emma and how she had last been seen on Saturday afternoon. She said she was aware that Emma had gone missing before, but somehow this seemed different. She then asked if anyone had seen her. A number of hands shot up.

'Yes?' Beth pointed.

'Leaving school on Friday afternoon,' the girl said. 'That was the last time I saw her.'

'Me too,' someone else called out.

'And me.'

'So she was seen on Friday afternoon. Did anyone see her later than that?'

There was silence. Beth threw a look at Matt.

'Does anyone know who she was seeing?' Beth asked.

'Carl,' a few called out.

'She's been seeing him for ages,' someone said.

'He doesn't live that close by. But they're in love, Miss.'

There were some sniggers.

'Does anyone know exactly where Carl lives?' Beth asked.

They shook their heads.

'How did Emma meet him?' Beth asked.

'Don't know, Miss. But I think it was about nine months ago they started seeing each other.'

'No, it wasn't. It was more like six months ago.'

'I don't suppose any of you has his phone number?' Beth asked.

They shook their heads. 'Have you tried Emma's phone?' someone asked.

'Yes, we tracked it. It's one of the first things we do. It's been switched off since she left home on Saturday.'

The enormity hit them and the room fell silent. None of them would ever switch off their phones for a long period. Maybe something bad really had happened to Emma.

'Is there anything else any of you can tell us that might help?' Beth asked. 'Emma's parents are very worried indeed.'

'They should have cared for her better,' one girl called out.

'What do you mean by that?' Beth asked her gently.

'Nothing,' the girl said, and put her head down.

'Anything else?' Beth asked, scanning the room.

The class sat in deep and thoughtful silence.

'Thank you,' Beth said. 'If anyone does remember anything, can you please contact the police station?'

'Or me,' the Head put in.

'Yes, or the Head.'

The class was now told to go to their lessons. They were a bit late and told not to make a noise. As they streamed out, Beth watched the girl who'd made the comment about the Arnolds looking after their daughter better and stepped in front of her.

'Could I have a word with you, please?' she said. The Head was waiting too.

Beth drew her away from the other students filing out.

'What did you mean about Emma's parents taking better care of her?' she asked quietly and non-confrontationally.

'Nothing,' she replied sullenly. Then she said, 'They're too strict with her. I wouldn't be surprised if they've got her locked in a bedroom.'

'Strict in what way?' Beth asked.

'They make her study all the time and she has to stay in during the week. She's only allowed out on a Saturday and has to be back by nine o'clock. It's ridiculous.'

'I see,' Beth said. 'How did she meet Carl? Do you know?'

The girl shrugged. 'I don't know. He's a mystery. I mean, he exists, but Emma keeps him all to herself, at a distance, like. Won't let any of us near him.'

'Do you know why?'

'I think she felt that if she takes him out somebody else

might grab him. She's like that. Because of her parents. She sits in her bedroom and dreams of running away. I guess I'm her best friend at school. I don't think she has any others.'

'I see,' Beth said thoughtfully. 'Anything else you can tell us? That's very helpful.'

The girl thought and then shook her head.

'What's your name in case we want to speak to you again?'

'It's Lorie Philips,' she said.

Beth nodded. 'I don't suppose you have any ideas about where Emma could be now?' she asked.

'Not really. I mean, the only place she knows is her parents' house. She didn't say anything on Friday to me. I think she's at home somewhere.'

'Thank you,' Beth said, and moved away.

'I wonder how well they searched the Arnolds' home?' Matt said as they returned to the car.

'Yes, so do I,' Beth agreed, taking out her phone.

She dialled the station and asked to speak to DS Scrivener.

'Sir, how thoroughly did we search the Arnolds' home when they first reported their daughter missing?' Beth asked. She knew that when a person was first reported missing the police visited the premises and took a short statement, then searched the house.

'I've no idea. Why?' he asked.

'A pupil at Emma's school has painted a slightly different picture of the family and said Emma could be shut away at home.'

'Just a minute, I'll check and see what the officer report says.'

Beth stayed on the line. Matt started the car and began driving towards the police station.

DS Scrivener came back on the line. 'You'd better go and take another look if there's any doubt. The filed report is unclear as to where they looked. I'll speak to the officers when I see them, but we're upping the enquiry. She's now officially a missing person and a press statement will go out later.'

'Thank you, sir,' Beth said. 'We'll go to the Arnolds' now.'

'Then come back here straight after,' DS Scrivener added.

'Yes, sir.'

Matt, who'd already heard DS Scrivener on the police radio, turned the car around.

'We'll look like right numbskulls if she's there,' he said to Beth.

Twenty minutes later, Matt parked the car outside the Arnolds' home. Only Mrs Arnold was in. Her husband was at work.

'Any news?' Mrs Arnold asked them, showing them in.

'Nothing yet,' Matt said. 'We'd like to search your house again if you don't mind?'

'No, not if it's going to bring her back,' she said, with a touch of cynicism. 'Shall I show you around?'

'There's no need,' Matt replied.

They began by taking a good look in the two

downstairs rooms, then the kitchen. They opened and closed cupboard doors. Obviously, Emma couldn't be hiding in one of them, but there could be a handbag or something that belonged to her. They found nothing. Mrs Arnold, who'd been following them around, gave up after a while and returned to her seat in the living room. Eventually Beth and Matt went upstairs.

There were three bedrooms up there. It was immediately obvious which one was Emma's, and they spent some time looking through her belongings and found nothing significant. They looked at the back of the wardrobe, between the clothes and in the drawers under the bed where they found a laptop. They put it to one side to take with them. They checked the bathroom, then looked up at the loft hatch embedded in the ceiling.

'Do you have a rod for the loft hatch?' Matt called downstairs to Mrs Arnold.

'Yes, it's in the airing cupboard. We keep the Christmas stuff up there.'

Matt opened the airing cupboard and found the long-handled hook. He engaged it with the lip from the loft hatch and turned. It dropped down.

'There's a light up there somewhere,' Mrs Arnold called up from the foot of the stairs. 'Goodness knows why you want to go up there, though.'

'Thank you,' Matt called down.

He extended the ladder and went up. The stairs squeaked. Beth followed in through the loft hatch. It was a fair-sized room, but without the height to make it into a usable space. They had to stoop as they made their way around. It had been covered in laminate flooring, so they were able to manoeuvre the few boxes that stood up there. There wasn't much to see. Beth looked in the boxes. It was mainly Christmas decorations and some discarded household items the Arnolds clearly hadn't wanted to throw out. There were no hidden alcoves in the loft, and it didn't look as though anyone had been up there since last Christmas. They came down carefully. Matt switched off the light, and they closed the door.

'Did you find anything?' Mrs Arnold asked them as they came down.

'No. Only this laptop in Emma's bedroom. You don't have a garage?' Matt checked.

'No, just the hard standing at the front of the house.'

'Can we look in your shed, please?' he asked. It was a large shed, situated at the end of the garden.

'Sure, but you'd be better off trying to find Carl. He's to blame for all of this.'

'The force is looking for him,' Beth said. 'There's a newsfeed going out tonight.'

'Here's the key to the shed,' she said, handing it to Matt.

He and Beth went out through the back door. The garden was about forty feet square, mainly lawn. As they walked down the centre path to the bottom of the garden where the shed was, they looked in the flowerbeds for any sign they had been recently dug up. There was nothing.

The shed door took some unlocking. It was full of junk

as well as gardening equipment.

'Emma?' Beth called, peering around a lawnmower.

There was no reply. They listened. Not a sound.

She and Matt moved some of the junk and peered around it, but it soon became clear there was no one there. They came out, locked the door and returned to the house. Mrs Arnold was waiting for them in the kitchen.

'Well? She's not hiding in there, is she?' she asked, her voice tight.

'A girl in Emma's class at school said she thought she could be at home,' Beth said, and handed back the key.

'I don't know who that would be. Emma goes to school to study, not socialize,' Mrs Arnold snapped.

'But surely you allow some socializing. I mean, she's fifteen now,' Beth said.

'Not until she's finished her exams, next June. That's what my husband and I have decided and we'll keep to it. She can socialize all she wants then.'

Beth gave a small, perfunctory nod. It had been felt that the Arnolds didn't merit a family liaison officer yet. Emma had gone missing before and Mr Arnold had gone to work, so she wasn't too worried.

Beth picked up the laptop she'd left in the kitchen.

'We couldn't find the new one her father bought her, when the other officers came,' Mrs Arnold said.

'Is there anything else missing?' Beth asked.

'I don't think so. That's what I told them.'

'Obviously call us if Emma or Carl get in touch,' Matt said as they prepared to leave.

'Yes, I will.' Then her hard exterior dropped. 'Where do you think she is?' she asked, her bottom lip trembling.

'We honestly don't know, but we'll keep looking for her,' Beth replied.

Mrs Arnold came to the door and watched them go, then returned to her living room. Of course Emma would come home soon; she had before.

TEN

Alfie sat at his desk that Wednesday morning, having seen Mrs Saunders off to her friend's funeral. He'd tried to work, but it was impossible with so much going on. He'd got himself into a bit of a state, if he was honest with himself. With each day that passed he knew he should do something, possibly go to the police station and give himself up. He feared it was all his fault, that his actions had spearheaded what had happened. He'd set up the spy camera, after all. But what could he have done differently? He hadn't watched it in real time. He'd been asleep. If he'd been awake and seen it, he would have gone straight in there and stopped Carl from murdering his girlfriend.

He looked again at the recording and cringed when Carl put the pillow over Emma's face. It was driving him mad to watch it. Yet he had to. On and on. He'd have to do something soon or it would unhinge him. But what? Go to the police and explain? But why had it taken him so long to report the crime? they would surely ask. And

63

how seriously would they take the fact that he had been illegally recording his guests? Alfie didn't know, so he sat there getting more and more distraught.

Half an hour later he had a thought. Would it work? He thought it might. If he could copy the part of the recording that was of use to the police – the bit that showed the murder – he could send it to them in the post. They'd know she was dead, so it would become a murder investigation, not a missing person one, which would help a bit. He shouldn't get caught. It could work. He thought about it for a bit longer, then began rummaging in his desk drawer for a spare USB stick.

He found one and plugged it into his laptop to check it was clear. It was. He now had to work out how to copy footage from his phone to the stick, and he spent some time doing this. He ended up copying across far more than he wanted to, so he deleted what he didn't need. The less time the police spent viewing the bedroom in his house the less chance there was of them identifying him or where he lived. The footage now showed some of the argument, up to where Carl put the pillow over Emma's face. He played it through twice and, satisfied, put the USB stick into an envelope and sealed it.

He sat there for a few moments looking at the envelope. Was he doing the right thing? He ummed and ahhed and eventually decided he was. Taking a pen, he wrote Coleshaw Police Station, then looked up the address online. There was nothing on the envelope to identify him, but as soon as they played it they would know what it was about.

Alfie now put on his jacket and went to his car. He drove into town and parked at the far end of the high street. He had to walk past the police station to get to the post office, but he wouldn't have been so daft as to push the letter through their door. There was CCTV all over the place outside the police station, whereas outside the post office there was just one camera. He surreptitiously posted the envelope and thought, with some satisfaction, that his letter looked much the same as the hundreds of others in the post box. Greatly relieved, he bought himself a coffee and then returned to his car.

On arriving home, Alfie thought he'd better change the bedding in the guest room. He didn't know if the room was being used that night. He hated going into that room now and shuddered at the thought. It bore all the traits of a crime scene, for which he felt responsible. Averting his eyes from the bed, he pulled off the duvet and bottom sheet, hoping he wasn't destroying evidence. Surely the recording would be enough for the police, though? Then something small dropped to the floor. He looked down and saw it was a tiny gold earring. He picked it up and examined it. It didn't belong to Mrs Saunders, that was for sure. It contained half a word, which read 'off'. He checked under the bed and in the corners of the room for the matching earring but couldn't find it. He dropped it into his trouser pocket and continued making up the bed.

Alfie didn't like being in the room for longer than he had to be, so as soon as he'd changed the sheets, he left. He went downstairs, pushed the washing into the machine, set it and pressed go. Then he went up to his study, taking out the earring as he went. Could it be Emma's? His heart missed a beat as he looked at it in his hand. He had a way of finding out – a copy of the video footage on his laptop. He sat at his desk and played it, skipping through much of the argument. He slowed it at the point where the argument developed and then zoomed in closer to her head. He watched and waited. There were two earrings and then there was just one. It pinged off onto the floor. So it did belong to Emma. Dear lord. He couldn't just throw it away. But neither could he keep it. Oh shit, he thought. What am I going to do?

Having her earring was personal. It was like a talisman. He studied it in the palm of his hand. It was no use sending it to the police – they wouldn't know whose it was – so he decided to bury it in the garden. Alfie went outside and found a small trowel that Jenny kept for planting bulbs. He dug a hole about eight inches deep and buried it, then put the trowel back where he'd got it from and returned indoors. He felt lighter now. It had been a shock, finding the earring, but now he'd dealt with it.

He managed to do a bit of work before the boys returned home from school. He went downstairs as he usually did. They both stopped talking as he came into the kitchen.

'Good day?' he asked them.

'Fine. Are you all right, Dad?' Mike asked.

'Yes. Why shouldn't I be?'

'You look worried,' Gregory added.

'Do I?' he asked.

'The police came to our school today,' Mike said. 'Not to see us,' he added quickly.

'I'm pleased to hear it. What did they come about?'

'It was about Emma Arnold, the missing girl.'

They were both staring at him now.

'Oh, I see,' he said as nonchalantly as he could. 'I've got to go out to see a client. Can you keep an eye on dinner, please?'

'Sure, Dad.'

Alfie did have to go to see a client, but nonetheless it was a shock that the police had gone to his sons' school. He sat for a while in his car parked out the front and thought. After a while he decided there was no point in waiting any longer and he started the car and drove off to see his client. By the time he was back, Jenny was home and the dinner was spoilt.

'I told the boys to watch it,' he said, annoyed.

Jenny tutted, scraped off the burnt meat, made the rest up with vegetables, then called the boys down for dinner. They sat at the table and looked at the small pieces of meat on their plates.

'It's your own fault,' Jenny told them. 'You'll watch it better next time when you're asked.'

Alfie looked at them through half-closed eyes and felt like offering them his meat. If they were in trouble with Jenny, he often felt he was too. It was an unenviable position to be in. Thankfully, he was still in a good frame of mind from his day's work. He'd sent a copy of the tape to the police and had buried the earring in the garden.

After dinner, as they were clearing away, his phone beeped with a news alert. He had set up his phone to alert him when there was an update on Emma. He moved to one side to read it.

Police have widened their search for missing teenager Emma Arnold. If anyone knows her whereabouts or has any information that could lead to her discovery, please contact Coleshaw Police Station. We are all very worried about her.

Of course the police wouldn't have the recording yet, not until tomorrow, perhaps even Friday. He'd posted it first class but was aware of how problematic the postal service was. He tucked away his phone and began washing the pans. He'd feel better once they'd received it.

After washing the pans, Alfie went to the utility room. The washing would be dry by now. The utility room was a small space on the outer edge of their house. It was just big enough to contain the washing machine and dryer, under the shelf where the boiler was. He reached for the basket and opened the dryer door. Yes, it was bone dry. As he bent to pull it out, he caught sight of something glittering at the back of the work surface. He stopped and picked it up and stared in disbelief. It was the gold earring with the word 'off' entwined into the filigree, exactly the same as the one he'd buried earlier. What the hell? He felt his pulse begin to rise. It hadn't been there earlier when he'd put the washing in. What the hell was going on?

Alfie's chest grew tighter by the second. It was impossible. It couldn't be the same earring. He turned it over in his hand and examined it. It looked like the same one, but there wasn't any dirt or mud on it. He turned it over again and looked at it from all sides, then decided it couldn't have been buried and dug up, that it must be similar to one Jenny owned. The 'off' must refer to something other than 'fuck', although he couldn't imagine what. Still unsure, he put the earring into his trouser pocket and finished pulling the sheets from the dryer.

He spent some time folding them and laid them one at a time neatly into the basket, deep in thought. It had to be Jenny's. There was no other explanation.

Once all the washing was out of the dryer, he picked up the basket and went into the house. He set the basket at the foot of the stairs, ready to take up later, and went into the living room to see Jenny, where she was working.

'Your earring, I believe?' he said, and put it on the arm of her chair.

She stopped what she was doing to glance at it.

'No, not mine,' she said, and continued to work.

'Are you sure?' Alfie said, picking it up.

'Yes, I'm sure. Where did you find it?'

'In the utility room, on the work surface above the dryer,' he said.

'I expect it's come out of the laundry from one of our guests,' she replied.

'No. It was on top of the work surface,' he emphasized.

She glanced up at him. 'I really don't know then,' she said. 'Perhaps it's one of the boys'?' She continued with her work.

Alfie picked up the earring and went into the hall. He took the washing up to the airing cupboard and left the basket outside the door. He went to the boys' room and knocked on the door. After more time than Alfie thought he should have been kept waiting, Mike called, 'Come in.'

Both boys appeared to be studying.

'Does this earring belong to either of you two?' he asked, holding it up for them to see. 'I mean, do either of you recognize it?'

'No,' Mike said, giving it a cursory glance.

'What about you, Gregory?' Alfie asked.

Gregory came over and took it from his hand, looked at it, then said, 'No, I don't recognize it. What do you think the "off" means?'

Alfie wasn't sure if he was taking the piss or not. It was difficult to tell with Gregory.

'I assume the other earring has "fuck" on it?' he said calmly. They probably wanted to hear him say the word.

Both boys gasped in mock horror and then collapsed into laughter.

'Come on, be serious,' Alfie said. 'Do either of you know where it's come from?'

'No, Dad,' Mike said.

Gregory handed it back. 'I haven't got a clue.'

Alfie left their bedroom, closed the door and stood on

the landing looking at the earring for some time. He knew what he had to do, sooner or later. He'd go straight into the garden and dig up the earring. That would prove it was another one. It would still be there.

ELEVEN

Alfie had decided he couldn't go into the garden that evening with his family at home, so he'd have to wait until the following morning. He did go to his study and watch the video footage of Emma again, though. It really did seem to be the same earring. Identical in every way. But then he looked online and saw that similar earrings could be bought from a few different retailers. He decided the most logical explanation was that it had belonged to another guest and been hidden in the sheets. Tomorrow, once he'd dug up the original earring, he'd be satisfied. This earring was from another client.

Alfie was getting used to four hours sleep a night, but he knew it wasn't doing him any good. He lay in bed as his wife slept peacefully beside him. This whole bloody saga of the earring was tormenting him, and it was after 2 a.m. before he finally fell asleep. Then he was awake again when Jenny got out of bed at 6.45.

Alfie didn't get up straight away. He hung back. He

was tired and he'd woken up thinking about that bloody earring again. Added to which, it was pouring with rain outside. He could hear it on the windowpane. He lay in bed and checked his phone for the weather forecast. The rain was supposed to be on and off all day. He slowly got out of bed, showered and dressed, and went downstairs just in time to kiss his wife goodbye on the cheek.

'You're up late today,' she said.

'I didn't sleep well,' he replied.

But she was already out the door, with her head full of schoolwork.

He called up to Mike and Gregory to get a move on. They'd had breakfast, at least; there were remnants of cornflakes in two bowls by the sink. He made himself a coffee as they came downstairs and then left about 8.15, calling, 'Bye,' as they went.

He needed to get this done straight away. When he looked out of the window he saw that the rain had stopped, for the time being at least, although it still looked very murky. He gulped down the last of his coffee, quickly pulled on his jacket and shoes, and went out the back door. The rain began again as soon as he stepped outside. He hesitated. Should he try again later? No, he couldn't do any work until he'd seen the earring buried there.

He put the hood up on his jacket and found Jenny's trowel. He began digging in the same spot as yesterday and expected to find the earring quite quickly. He hadn't buried it very deep. He dug and dug, deeper still, then left and right. No earring appeared. He continued digging. It was raining heavily now, and he was sopping wet. He kept digging, then he stood back and looked at the large hole he'd made. The rain ran down his face. He could have wept. The earring wasn't there. A fox or a dog maybe? But then foxes and dogs didn't fill in the hole again afterwards. He squatted down and dug a bit more, although he knew it was futile. Not understanding what had happened, he stood there looking at it and then dug a bit more. He stared at the hole. He'd buried the earring there yesterday in that exact spot and it had reappeared indoors. It was impossible. Was he losing his mind?

The rain seeped through his coat and he realized he was soaked through. It was raining harder now than it had been before. He began to fill in the hole, gradually, a trowel of earth at a time, sifting through the soil and looking for any sign of the earring. It wasn't there. Once the hole was covered in, he put the trowel back. He looked at where the hole had been, trying to make sense of what had just happened.

Indoors, he took off his sopping-wet coat and shoes, then removed the earring from his pocket and stared at it. Perhaps he'd thought he'd buried it and hadn't really? But then what had he been doing out there in the garden for the soil to have been freshly disturbed? His brain searched for a rational explanation. There simply wasn't one. He wandered into the living room and sat in a chair, thinking. Half an hour later a WhatsApp message arrived on his phone.

You looking for something?

He nearly dropped his phone. It had to be from Carl.

But Carl didn't have his phone number, just his email address. He was sure of it. He stared across the room as if Carl himself might suddenly appear, then looked through the living-room window into the garden. There was no one there. But how did Carl know what he was doing? He pressed the number and called it. The phone rang and rang and eventually rang out. He tried again with the same result, willing it to connect. He then waited a quarter of an hour, pacing the room, and tried again. It rang out.

Alfie went up to his desk and sat down. Should he message Carl? He needed to know how he'd got his phone number and how he knew he'd been in the garden looking for the earring. He tried to get on with some work but couldn't. He was getting behind with all the worry. One of his clients was threatening to take her work elsewhere. Then, as 1 p.m. approached, he picked up his phone and called Carl's number one more time. There was no reply, so he set about composing a WhatsApp message.

What do you want? Was his final offering, and he pressed send.

He sat with the phone in his hand for some time, then put it on his desk where he could keep an eye on it. Nothing happened for about half an hour, then it buzzed with a message. He picked it up and couldn't believe what he was seeing.

£5,000

'You what?' Alfie exclaimed out loud. 'But I haven't done anything. You're the one who killed her.' He texted a reply, then deleted it. He was being blackmailed by a murderer. If only he'd gone straight to the police, it could have saved him a whole lot of trouble.

At Coleshaw Police Station Beth was taking a call from Mrs Arnold.

'You know you said to call if I found that anything else of Emma's was missing?'

'Yes?'

'Well, I think one of her jumpers has gone.'

'What does it look like?' Beth asked, reaching for a pen and paper.

'I can't be certain, but I think it's a new jumper with light-blue bobbles on it.'

'Anything else?' Beth asked, making a note.

'No. Not that I've found so far.'

'Please phone us if you find anything. Thank you.'

'You are doing all you can to find her?' Mrs Arnold asked. 'I mean, I know she's gone missing before, but it was never like this.'

'Yes, of course we are. Everything. We'll be in touch just a soon as we have any updates.'

They said goodbye, then half an hour later Mrs Arnold called again to say she'd found the missing jumper at the back of the wardrobe. Beth thanked her for letting them know, made a note on the file and wondered if it was time to get a family liaison officer involved. Mrs Arnold sounded as if she might need one before long.

Alfie still hadn't replied to the message asking for £5,000. He didn't know what to say, so he did what he normally did in such circumstances: nothing. He couldn't forget it, though. He worried about it for the rest of the day. Five thousand pounds was a lot of money. He was starting to think that maybe he should pay it. That would put a stop to Carl. Then he thought some more and started second-guessing himself. If he made this payment, what was to stop Carl asking for more?

By the time Mike and Gregory came home from school Alfie didn't know if he was coming or going, so he decided to ask for their opinion. He opened his mouth to speak and then realized he couldn't ask them anything without disclosing the whole sorry story.

'It doesn't matter,' he said, and left them to it.

He went to his study, where he sat at his desk and tried again to do some work. It was impossible and some of his client files were now well behind. He phoned the client whose work was badly delayed and explained he'd had some personal issues to deal with. She tutted under her breath but allowed him more time. He'd just put the phone down when another message arrived from Carl.

Leave the money at the old war memorial at midnight tomorrow.

Alfie jumped and stared at his phone in disbelief. He knew where the old war memorial was in Coleshaw – on the edge of the village. It was decorated with poppy wreaths on 11 November, Armistice Day, when the villages held a small remembrance ceremony. He'd been to the service once. But why there?

It was on the tip of his tongue to ask why the hell Carl had chosen that spot. Then he decided that would rather be missing the point, as he was being blackmailed by a murderer. His second thought was to ask what Carl knew about the earring turning up. But how would that advance anything? He wished he could confide in Jenny. That's what he usually did.

He took the earring from his pocket, placed it on his desk and stared at it. Turning up like it had was significant, but how had it got there? He couldn't work it out. Then another message arrived.

Or else.

Carl was threatening him again! He picked up the phone to call him, but as before it rang and rang and then rang out. It was clear that Carl wasn't going to speak to him but just communicate through messages. Alfie gritted his teeth in anger.

The easiest and simplest thing to do was to pay up. He could afford £5,000, but he'd have to go into the bank tomorrow to get it out. He wasn't allowed that much in one go from the cash machine. He sat there considering his next move and thought it wise to message Carl.

Can you guarantee there won't be any more payments?

he asked, and pressed send.

Back came a reply, almost instantly.

Yes.

I'll leave the money there, Alfie wrote.

You'd better.

Now all he had to do was work out how to get to the war memorial at midnight tomorrow without arousing Jenny's suspicion. And who knew, maybe the police would even have arrested Carl by then.

TWELVE

Tomorrow would be Friday, so Alfie could arrange to meet a friend for a drink in the village pub in Coleshaw without Jenny thinking anything of it. It was a way of getting out of the house, going out for a drink on a Friday. The pub stayed open until midnight. But who could he ask? Alfie wondered. He'd lost contact with most of his mates since he'd been working from home for four years. He hardly ever went out now. He thought of Adrian, but he had a young baby. Jack? He was about the same age as Alfie, two kids, and divorced. He phoned him.

'Hiya, mate. You OK?' Alfie asked him.

'Yes, I'm fine. Long time no see.'

'Too right. Do you fancy meeting for a drink tomorrow night?'

'Yes. Sure. Glad to get out. What time and where?'

'Eight o'clock at the Anchor Inn?'

'I can get there earlier if you like.'

'Eight o'clock is fine with me. See you there.'

Having confirmed the plans for the following night, Alfie was able to concentrate slightly better on work. He had another site visit scheduled for that afternoon, a couple who were meticulous about every detail. He made the booking early so he arrived home at the same time as the rest of his family. They talked and ate together, and everything seemed fine, then as he and Jenny were sitting at the table after their meal talking, an almighty fight broke out in the boys' room above. Alfie shot from his seat and flew upstairs. He didn't knock but went straight in.

'Stop it now!' he cried. 'What the hell is going on?' It wasn't like them to fight.

They separated, then stood there fuming, glaring at each other but not saying a word.

'What is it? What's going on?' Alfie asked. Jenny had also come upstairs.

'What's the matter?' she asked them.

'Nothing,' Mike said angrily, sitting on his bed.

'It doesn't matter,' Gregory mumbled.

'It matters to me and your mother,' Alfie said, concerned.

He and Jenny stood there waiting for an explanation, but none came, so eventually they had to let it go. To keep probing would be more trouble than it was worth.

'No more fighting,' Alfie told them.

'Have you done your homework?' Jenny asked.

'We're about to,' Gregory said.

'Get on with it then.'

Alfie and Jenny waited for them to settle, then came out and returned downstairs to the living room.

'Boys.' Jenny sighed as she sat down.

Alfie nodded, thoughtfully.

That night Alfie was so tired after a week of sleepless nights that he fell into a deep sleep almost as soon as his head touched the pillow. He slept through to the morning and woke when Jenny did. He was feeling much better now. The copy of his recording would have arrived at the police station and he very much hoped that meant he was going to get rid of Carl once and for all. He tried to imagine the police viewing the video clip. Would they instantly realize what they were looking at? He hoped so.

It was with these thoughts to keep him occupied that he waited for the bathroom to be free, then showered and dressed. Once he was alone in the house, he went downstairs for coffee. The sun was shining on what was going to be another unseasonably mild day. Alfie wandered around, then at 9.30 he drove into town and parked in a side road from where he walked the ten minutes to Coleshaw High Street. His heart was starting to beat faster. This next step was the beginning of the end. Was it illegal to pay a blackmailer? He thought about it and honestly didn't know.

The queue going into the bank was surprisingly short, given how slowly it was moving. Then he realized there was only one cashier serving. He needed counter service – the amount was too large to draw from the cashpoint

– so he waited. Eventually it was his turn and he stepped up to the counter.

'Good morning, sir.' The assistant smiled.

'Good morning. I'd like to withdraw five thousand pounds, please.'

'Yes, of course. What's it for?' she asked, looking at him. Alfie felt himself grow hot.

'A motorbike,' he lied.

'Can I have your debit card, please?'

With fumbling fingers, he took his card from his wallet and pushed it under the grid. He waited; he was becoming hotter and more worried as she checked his account on a screen he couldn't see. He knew the money was in there, at least; he'd just received a payment from a client.

'Sign here, please,' the assistant said at last, and pushed a form and pen under the grid.

As he picked up the pen, he noticed his hands were trembling. Calm down, he told himself. He carefully signed the form, hoping she wouldn't notice, and pushed it back.

'Thank you,' he said in a small voice, and with a weak smile.

A few more clicks on her computer and she was asking him how he would like it. For a moment Alfie didn't have a clue what she meant, then he realized.

'Oh, I don't know,' he said, flustered. 'I didn't think to ask.'

'An assortment?' she suggested, wanting to move on to the next customer.

'Yes, please. That will be fine.'

'Envelope?'

He nodded.

She tucked the money into an envelope and handed it to him, then thanked him for his custom. He quickly put the envelope into his inside jacket pocket as he stepped away from the counter and left the bank. He took some gulps of fresh air as he walked back to his car. That was just withdrawing the money. He still had to take it to the pub and then leave it at the old war memorial. As he walked he had his hand on his jacket pocket, and kept looking over his shoulder, left and right, to make sure no one was following him. He didn't want to be mugged. Once safely in the car he sat for a moment, taking deep breaths, calming himself, before starting the engine and driving home.

When he arrived home, he took out the money and counted it. It was all there, so he put it safely in his desk, then he managed to do a spot of work. The police had the recording and he had the money for Carl. He hadn't received any more directions and assumed the plan remained the same.

Half an hour later a WhatsApp message arrived from Carl.

Well done. Keep it safe. More instructions to follow.

Alfie stared at the words, then reread them. They implied that Carl knew he'd got the money, but how? He couldn't work it out. The more he read it, the more certain he was that Carl somehow knew. Twenty minutes later he messaged him.

Did you follow me? he asked.

Back came an immediate reply. *Of course.*

Alfie stared at the screen. How did Carl know what time Alfie would be going to the bank? He didn't know where Alfie's bank was. It was a long time since Alfie had last visited it; it wasn't like he went every Friday, after all. He sat there and tried to puzzle it out, then he decided to message Carl again.

How did you know what time I'd be there? How did you know where my bank was?

He waited patiently for the reply. *I followed you.*

Alfie sat there, stunned into silence. He tried to think of his next question, but couldn't come up with anything apart from: *From where?* Which he sent.

Back came an almost instant reply. It was an emoji of a laughing face.

Furious, Alfie pressed to call him. It rang and rang, and eventually rang out.

'Bastard!' he cried, and threw down his phone.

He ran from his study, down two flights of stairs and out the front door. He searched the street, looked up and down it, began this way and that. Then he forced himself to calm down. He told himself it wouldn't be long before the police found Carl, now they had the recording. He began to walk past houses, looking through windows, trying to spot someone behaving oddly. There were new people at Number 23, that was five doors down from him. They had a clear view of his house. He didn't know them at all. Could Carl live there? He stood on the pavement staring into their front room. A woman crossed in front of the window, saw him standing there and moved behind the curtain to continue to watch him. He stayed for a while, looking, and then walked past, crossed the road and walked back again, but he couldn't see anyone now. Some houses had net curtains, which made it more difficult to see in.

He walked back to stand outside Number 23. The woman inside was watching him again, so he went up to the front door and pressed the bell. She took some time to answer, so he pressed it again. She was a woman about the same age as himself, with short blonde hair.

'Hello, I'm Alfie. I live with my wife, Jenny, further up the road. Do you have anyone living here by the name of Carl?'

'No, there's just my husband and daughter here,' she replied stiffly.

He was looking past her, down the hall, trying to see inside for longer than was polite.

'We've had a large parcel dropped off for Carl,' he said.

'No, I'm sorry. It's not for us,' she said, and began to close the door. 'Was that everything?'

'Yes, thank you,' he said.

The door closed, but Alfie didn't immediately move away. He stood there for some moments, listening. As he did, he peered in the downstairs front-room window again, but no one was there, and there was nothing to be seen. Just a neat front room.

He continued along the street. He was puzzled. He

couldn't see anything strange in any of the other front rooms he passed. Did Carl live at Number 23? But why would he use Roomy-Space.com if that was the case? It didn't make sense. Unless it was for show. Pure and simple. Alfie knew that Carl didn't live at the address he'd given on the booking form, so it was possible he lived on the road. If so, it was a hell of a coincidence. He pondered, walked up and down the road on both sides once more, then returned indoors and texted Carl.

Do you live on my road? he asked.

Back came a reply. *No.*

Would he tell the truth if he did? Alfie wondered.

He couldn't think of any more questions to ask, and it was well past lunchtime. He hadn't done any more work and he wasn't hungry. He hadn't eaten breakfast either, he'd just had a coffee. His stomach was churning. It felt tight. If he thought about it for too long, he felt sick.

He made another coffee and took it to the living-room window. As he sipped it he stared out at the patch of soil he'd dug up yesterday. He had time. In fact, he had all afternoon. He gulped down the rest of his coffee and went outside. It was still a mild day. He began to dig in the same spot he had done yesterday. Wider, deeper than before, but no matter how deep or wide he dug he couldn't find the other earring. He'd just begun filling it in when Jenny suddenly appeared.

'What are you doing?' she asked, amazed.

'What are you doing here?' he said, looking up from the shallow grave.

'We've got an inset day, I told you. The staff were in this morning, but not this afternoon.'

She was still staring at him, waiting for a reply. Her expression was a mixture of shock and incredulity.

'I lost something,' he said. 'I thought it might be here.'

For a second it crossed his mind to come clean and tell Jenny everything, but how would he even begin? She was still staring at him, then she shook her head in dismay and returned indoors. Alfie quickly filled in the hole and patted down the soil. It definitely wasn't there, not now or ever. The earring was still in his pocket, and he'd found it on the counter in the utility room.

THIRTEEN

'What the hell?' Beth exclaimed under her breath as she and her colleagues watched the video. 'So Emma *is* dead.'

The video recording showed a young man they now assumed to be Carl Smith, arguing with and then killing Emma Arnold in a bedroom somewhere. They watched in horror as he bundled her over his shoulder and disappeared out the door. The time on the recording showed it was 11.46 p.m. Then there was nothing more and the video ended. They watched it a second time before DS Scrivener switched off the tape and stood up to address them in a sombre mood. Five colleagues drafted in for what was now a murder enquiry. The room fell eerily quiet.

'So there we have it,' he said, his voice flat. 'The package containing the tape arrived by Royal Mail first thing this morning. Forensics are checking it now. Thankfully the wrapping is still intact. I think we can assume it's definitely Carl in the video – Emma calls him by his name – and he could be anywhere.'

'And we don't know where the room is?' Beth asked.

DS Scrivener shook his head.

'It looks like a Roomy-Space to me,' Matt said. 'They have that roominess about them.' No one laughed and Beth shot him a warning look.

'Yes, I wondered about Roomy-Space too. It's a very impersonal room, with just what you'd need to spend a night or two,' DS Scrivener said.

'Do we have any way of figuring out where it might be?'

'I'm pretty certain the video footage has been taken through a small spy camera lens,' DS Scrivener said. 'We'll know more from forensics later. My guess is that it was planted by someone on a bedside cabinet or something like that. Then, for whatever reason, the owner sat on the recording for most of the week before sending it to us. Either that or they've just discovered it. Either way, I can see why they didn't bring it in themselves.'

'I suppose the house could have been empty,' Matt said. 'I mean, no one came to help Emma. Or they were just asleep and didn't hear them.'

'Yes,' DS Scrivener said. 'Which is why I want someone to check all registered Roomy-Spaces in this area. Start local and then work your way out. Harper, can you take the lead on this, please?'

'Yes, sir,' the young man replied.

'If we manage to get a trace on the parcel, plus the Roomy-Space, we'll hopefully be well on the way to finding out who Carl is. Matt and Beth, I want you two to go to see Mr and Mrs Arnold and break the news about their daughter gently. We'll need a family liaison officer now. Give Chloe McNeal a ring – I believe she's free.'

'Yes, sir,' Beth said.

'The rest of you, try to find Carl by any means you know how. Any questions?'

No one replied.

'Thank you for your time,' he said, and moved away.

'Jesus,' Beth said to Matt. 'So she's really dead?'

'It would appear so.'

'And that pun was well out of order – "the rooms have that roominess about them".' She glared at him.

'I'm sorry. I realized the minute I said it.'

Beth phoned Chloe McNeal before they left the office. She said she'd meet them at the Arnolds' house in an hour. She had heard about the investigation, and her daughter attended the same school as Emma. Matt and Beth left the police station in quiet and sombre moods. They were both aware that until now they'd treated the Arnolds with some distance, believing that Emma would return, as she had before. Now they were going to inform them that their only child was dead. They'd been so convinced that she would be found alive and now this.

'I suppose there was always the chance this could be the outcome,' Matt said as they made their way to the police car.

'Yes, I know. I was convinced she'd be found alive, though.'

'Me too.'

They got into the car and Beth drove.

'But I'm puzzled as to what Carl did with Emma's body,' Matt said thoughtfully.

'It was nearly midnight – there wouldn't have been many people around,' Beth replied.

'But where did he go with her? What did he do with her body? I mean, she was murdered last Saturday and it's Friday today. DS Scrivener thinks whoever found the recording kept it for most of the week and then sent it to us. I'm not so sure.'

'What do you think happened?' Beth asked, glancing at him.

'I think the owner and Carl could be one and the same person,' Matt said. 'That would explain why no one heard or saw anything. He killed her and kept her body in a basement or garage and then disposed of her. Or maybe she's still there.'

'I suppose so,' Beth said, giving it some thought. 'But then why would he send us a recording?'

They continued to discuss possible alternatives during the ten-minute journey to the Arnolds' home. They drew up and parked. Neither of them was in any hurry to leave the car, but Mrs Arnold had heard the engine and came to the window to look out.

'Come on, best get it over with,' Beth said.

Reluctantly, they opened their car doors and got out. Mrs Arnold was at the door by the time they reached it.

'You've got news?' she asked, her face creasing with

apprehension.

'Can we come in?' Beth asked.

Mrs Arnold stood aside. Mr Arnold appeared further down the hall behind her.

'He's having today off,' Mrs Arnold said, leading the way into their front room, as she had done before. 'What is it? What have you got to tell us?'

Beth gently directed them both to the sofa and they sat down. Everything was neat and tidy in the room, like the last time they were there. She looked at them with compassion in her eyes. There was no easy way to say this – the worst news a parent could ever receive.

'I'm sorry to have to tell you this, but we have received firm evidence that Emma is dead,' she said, and paused.

Mrs Arnold stared at them, not understanding what she'd been told, then she burst into tears. Mr Arnold sat on the sofa holding his head in his hands, in silent distress.

Beth and Matt were trained in breaking bad news and had had to do it about six months before, after a fatal road traffic accident. But this was different. It was a murder enquiry. The Arnolds' daughter had been taken in the prime of her life. A girl they all believed would walk through the door.

Matt and Beth waited for some moments as Mrs Arnold wept and Mr Arnold just sat there holding his head in his hands. There was nothing they could say or do to help them through this time.

'I'm so sorry,' Beth said eventually.

Matt always felt uncomfortable in these situations and

often said nothing, as he did now.

Beth waited some more and then asked, 'Is there someone we can call to be with you?' She touched Mrs Arnold's shoulder.

Mrs Arnold shook her head and continued to cry, then looked up. Beth passed her a box of tissues she found on the side; Mrs Arnold took one and wiped her eyes.

'When and where?' she asked quietly.

Mr Arnold looked up too but didn't say anything.

'A package was posted to Coleshaw Police Station. It contained a video recording,' Beth said. She may as well tell them the truth now as there would be a short piece with a picture of Carl on the news tonight. 'It showed the murder of Emma by a man we believe to be Carl.'

'I knew it,' Mrs Arnold snapped, and she began to cry again.

'The bastard,' Mr Arnold spat under his breath.

Beth waited for them to recover.

'When?' Mrs Arnold eventually asked again.

'Late last Saturday night.'

'That's nearly a week ago!' Mr Arnold exclaimed.

'That's correct,' Beth said. 'We don't know where Emma's body is yet. But we expect to have more news quite quickly.'

'But why?' Mrs Arnold asked through her tears. 'Why did he kill her? Emma never did wrong to anybody.'

'We don't know the motivation for the attack,' Beth said. 'It wasn't clear on the recording, but it seems like it might have been an argument that got out of hand.'

Mrs Arnold shook her head in despair.

'And now my Emma is dead.'

'How did she die?' Mr Arnold wanted to know.

'She was suffocated with a pillow,' Beth said.

'Oh no.' Mrs Arnold gave a small wail and began to cry again.

'I'm so sorry,' Beth said. 'Are you sure there's no one we can call for you?'

'No.' Mrs Arnold shook her head.

Beth waited for Mrs Arnold to calm herself again and then said, 'Chloe, your family liaison officer, should be here soon.'

'We don't need one of those,' Mr Arnold said.

'It's up to you. She's on her way now and will have a chat with you. To see if there is anything we can do. Then you can decide.'

'So Emma just went off to sleep?' Mrs Arnold was asking.

Not exactly, Beth thought. She was last seen with her feet thrashing and her head stuffed under a pillow, fighting for her life. But Beth gave a small nod.

'Do you have any more questions?' she asked them.

Neither did. They just sat there looking like their very existence had been ripped out of them, which in a way it had. Beth knew they would never fully recover. Not from the death of their only daughter.

Beth made a cup of tea for the Arnolds and she and Matt stayed with them until they saw a car pull up outside and Chloe get out. Beth went to greet her.

'How are they?' Chloe asked.

'Not great.'

'Any news on the murder hunt?'

'Not as far as I know. I'll keep you posted.'

She nodded and they went into the house, where Beth introduced her to Mr and Mrs Arnold.

'Your family liaison officer,' Beth said.

Chloe immediately fell into her role, drawing up a chair and sitting beside the Arnolds, dealing with them in a compassionate and caring manner. It took a special person to be a family liaison officer, Beth thought. As well as answering the Arnolds' questions, she would pass any further information they might share about Emma back to the police. When there wasn't a family to support, she did normal police work.

Beth and Matt waited until Chloe was settled with the Arnolds, then they said goodbye and went towards the front door. Mr Arnold jumped up and rushed after them, grabbing Matt's arm.

'You will get that bastard Carl, won't you?' he said, seething.

'Yes,' Matt said.

'We will, I promise you,' Beth added.

Mr Arnold looked as though he was going to say something else but thought better of it and let it go.

FOURTEEN

Alfie played the video on his phone one last time and then decided to delete it. He'd been thinking about doing it all afternoon and had finally come to the conclusion that it was the right thing to do. The police had a copy – that was enough to catch Carl – and Alfie wanted nothing more to do with it. He'd gone into his study after Jenny had caught him in the act of filling in the hole in the garden, and was now pretending to work, but of course he couldn't do a thing. Five more hours, he thought, until he met Jack.

He checked his phone to make sure the footage had completely gone. It had. Then he took the earring from his pocket and looked at it. Should he send it to the police as well? he wondered. He would need to send a note with it, explaining what it was and how if fitted in, because unlike the video footage, it wasn't self-explanatory. He decided against it. It was too much trouble, and he couldn't think what to write. He put the earring safely into a drawer in his desk. It was the only connection he had with Emma.

His mind flickered to the many murderers who'd kept souvenirs of their victims – Ed Gein, Ted Bundy, Jeffrey Dahmer and many more. He wondered why they did that. Then he stopped. Alfie wasn't a serial killer, just an unfortunate victim of chance. If he hadn't installed the spy camera, he'd have been none the wiser.

He heard the boys come home from school at around 4 p.m. He stayed in his study; it was safer up there for now. He sat there fiddling with items on his desk and thought about what he was going to talk to Jack about until midnight. Jenny always said he wasn't much good at making small talk. At 5.30 she called up that dinner was ready.

He stood slowly. He didn't feel much like eating but supposed he'd better have something. He'd be drinking tonight and didn't want to get tipsy early on half a lager. He needed his wits about him. If he did this right, by this time tomorrow everything would be back to normal.

He went downstairs, sat in his place at the table and waited as Jenny served dinner. It was braising steak from the slow cooker, which had been on all day.

'I wondered what was in there,' Alfie said, and began to eat.

It tasted good – Jenny's food usually did, better than his. As they ate she mentioned they were having guests arrive later that night. A married couple who shouldn't give them any trouble. He nodded, continued eating and looked at his sons. He tried to make conversation with them like he did most evenings.

'Another week has passed then,' he said.

Neither of them replied. He looked at them as though they were strangers. They'd grown so big and tall recently he hardly recognized them. Could they ever do anything like Carl had? His first reaction was no, but then again, in the heat of the moment, maybe they were capable of it. He had to admit he hardly knew them now. He supposed that Carl had a mother somewhere, and presumably she never thought her son could be a murderer either ... Unless he was in care, maybe?

'Everything all right at school?' he tried again.

'Yes,' Mike said.

Gregory nodded.

Jenny and the boys left the room as soon as the meal was over, but Alfie stayed behind to wash the dishes. Jenny always had a lot of work to do on a Friday evening and went straight to the living room to do it. The boys were soon ensconced in their bedroom, which suited Alfie. Tomorrow, he'd take them out somewhere nice like he used to on Saturdays. But tonight, he needed to concentrate and get ready.

'I'm going for a drink with Jack in a bit,' he reminded his wife.

'Yes, you said. Give him my best wishes.'

'Will do.'

As Alfie went upstairs a message arrived. He took his phone from his pocket and saw it was from Carl.

Leave the money under the vase at the old war memorial at midnight.

Alfie texted back, *OK*.

Another message followed: *Then get into your car and go home.*

That seemed an odd thing to say, he thought, but texted back, *Yes, I will.*

All this texting was starting to assume an air of normality that left Alfie feeling very uncomfortable. He continued to his bedroom and as he did Mike came out of his room and said their television was broken. Alfie went in. The air was stale so he opened a window. The place was in a mess now the two boys shared it. He had to move some of their stuff to get to the television. Both boys watched him as he tried the on/off button first.

'We've tried that. It didn't work,' Mike said.

They were right. Alfie had a checklist of things to cover when it came to fixing electronics, and second on the list was the fuse in the plug. He spent some time getting to and removing the old one, then went downstairs for a new one. He came back, fitted it and the television worked fine. Satisfied, he came out of their room.

'Thanks, Dad,' Gregory called after him.

'Yes, thanks,' Mike added.

'You're welcome.' At last, he had done something right!

It was now nearly 7 p.m. and a news update arrived on his phone. The article showed a photo of Carl, and the wording beneath said that following some new evidence the case was now a murder enquiry and if anyone had any information to contact this number. Alfie breathed more easily. The police had looked at the video tape and at last things were moving.

On the way to the Anchor Inn that evening Alfie went via the old war memorial to check he knew where to leave the package of money, which was firmly secreted inside his jacket pocket. He drove slowly around it. No one else was there. It was pitch black at this time in October, no lighting at all. On the second trip around he spotted the vase. It had a few old flowers in it. He assumed the money wouldn't be there long. Carl would be watching him, and as soon as Alfie returned to his car he would collect it. Satisfied that he had done everything he could to make sure the handover went smoothly, he continued to the Anchor Inn.

It was packed on a Friday evening; there was little else to do in Coleshaw. There was live music on from 8 till 10 p.m., which Alfie hadn't realized. Fortunately, Jack had grabbed a two-seater table in one corner. He saw Alfie and waved. Alfie made his way over.

'Hi, Jack, you OK?'

Jack stood and they greeted each other with slaps on the back.

'Do you want another drink?' Alfie asked him. Jack's glass was half empty.

'Yes, why not? It's a pint of their Special, please.'

Alfie went to the bar to wait his turn. He looked around to see if there was anyone else he recognized, but there wasn't. He had to wait some time to be served. He just had a half of lager, as he was driving, then made his way across the crowded pub to Jack, who'd now drained his previous drink.

'So how are you?' Alfie asked, sitting down.

'Not so good, if I'm honest,' Jack said.

That makes two of us, Alfie thought.

'No? What's the matter?' he asked.

Jack took a long drink from his beer before he started to speak. In a nutshell, he regretted his decision to leave his wife, nearly two years ago. The last time Alfie had met him was a year ago and everything had seemed fine then, but clearly Jack had discovered that the grass isn't greener on the other side. Far from it. He missed his kids dreadfully and had now broken up with the woman he'd left his wife for.

'I'm dating again,' he said miserably, and took another long drink.

'That must be fun,' Alfie said, wishing he could swap confidences and tell Jack of his own problems.

But Jack was shaking his head. 'You find someone online, spend ages messaging them and think you've got a lot in common. So you arrange to meet and discover you haven't. It's happened too often now and it's pissing me off.'

Alfie could see how miserable Jack was and he'd already finished his second drink, so he offered to buy him another one.

'Please, mate,' he said, and pushed his glass across the table towards Alfie.

He went to the bar – another half of lager for him, he'd

still be fine driving on that – and a pint of Special for Jack. It wasn't cheap. He returned to the table.

'I met someone last week,' Jack continued. 'Everything was fine until she said she actually lived in St Ives and she was just up here for the weekend. I mean, I can't start going down to St Ives. It turns out all she wanted was a shag.'

Alfie wondered if Jack had given her what she wanted, but he didn't like to ask. He nodded and tried to divert him to other topics, but Jack kept coming back to the matter of his ex-wife.

'Why don't you just admit you made a mistake and go back to her?' Alfie eventually asked, exasperated, unable to remember her name. Another hour had passed.

'I can't,' Jack said. 'She's got someone new. I'm not allowed to go near the house. There's a court order in place.'

Jack then spent the next half an hour talking about the non-molestation order his ex-wife had taken out against him after he turned up there drunk a couple of times and hit her new partner.

'Jesus, I didn't know you were the violent type,' Alfie said.

'I never used to be,' Jack lamented.

Jack finished his drink and went to the loo. When he came back, Alfie waited for him to offer to buy the next round of drinks. Their glasses had been empty for some time, and Alfie had ended up buying two more rounds – lemonade for him, Special for Jack.

'Do you want another one?' Alfie eventually asked, the awkwardness getting the better of him.

'Cheers, mate,' Jack said. 'I'd offer to buy this round, but I don't have any money. I'm a bit short at present.'

So Alfie stood, got more drinks, and returned to his seat, bitterly regretting ever having asked Jack out for a drink. Jack was now too pissed to notice that people were slowly leaving. The live music had stopped over an hour ago.

At 11.30, Alfie realized with a jolt that they were the last people left in the pub.

'How are you getting home?' he asked, standing.

'I thought you could drop me off,' Jack slurred.

Oh shit, Alfie thought.

'I can't, mate. Sorry.'

'Oh, OK, no problem,' he said, with the drunk's attitude to life that everything would get fixed in the end.

'Can't you get a cab?' Alfie asked, helping his friend to his feet.

'I haven't got any money. I'd assumed you'd take me home.'

Alfie looked at him. What should he do? The landlord called, 'Time, please.' Alfie took a few steps towards the door. Jack wasn't his problem.

'You taking your friend with you?' the landlord called after him.

Alfie hesitated, then went back and, with one arm under Jack, steered him out of the now-empty pub and into his car.

Not pleased, but consoling himself that Jack would probably fall asleep during the drive to the war memorial, Alfie buckled him into the front passenger seat, then got into his own side. He began the drive, keeping an eye on Jack, who was asking a few silly questions like 'Where are we?' and 'Where's my sister?' Two minutes later his head rolled to one side, his mouth fell open and he began to snore.

Alfie now felt the adrenalin kick in. Not long now until this whole sorry business was behind him.

During the short drive to the war memorial, he vaguely wondered where Jack was living now. Not the same address as he'd lived in with his wife, he thought. It must be local. He'd either walked to the pub or caught the bus there. Alfie would need to ask him after he'd delivered the money. He continued towards the war memorial with Jack snoring beside him. He put his hand on the package in his jacket pocket and gave it a reassuring squeeze. In no time at all they were approaching their destination so Alfie slowed down and looked around. There were no people or cars here, but as he got closer to the memorial he saw the vase was empty now. So Carl had emptied it at some point in the evening.

He parked as close as he could get and checked the time. Two minutes to midnight. He looked at Jack, who was still fast asleep and hadn't noticed the car had stopped. He was now drooling from one corner of his mouth. Alfie felt sorry for him. He wasn't a bad sort, really.

At exactly midnight, Alfie took the package from his jacket pocket, quietly opened his car door and got out. He closed it again equally quietly and then walked the dozen or so steps to the war memorial. He lifted up the vase – it was surprisingly clean – placed the package under it, then looked around. Everything was still and quiet. If Carl was there, he was well hidden.

He waited a moment to see if anyone would appear, and then went back to his car. He waited a little longer in the car, then slowly drove away. As he did, he looked in the rear-view mirror and to his astonishment saw a bloke on a bike riding out of the bushes. He dismounted briefly to grab the package and then rode off again.

Alfie braked hard and stopped the car. Jack flopped forwards with a small groan. On the spur of the moment, Alfie turned the car around and headed in the direction the cyclist had gone. He could catch a guy on a bike, but even though he was sure he'd driven in the right direction, there was no sign of him. He turned the car around and drove towards home, wondering what on earth Carl was playing at.

Jack stirred and semi-woke. 'Where am I?' he blurted, rubbing the spittle from his chin.

'You've been asleep, but I can take you home. Where am I taking you?'

'My sister's house,' he replied.

'Where does she live?' Alfie asked with patience.

'Fifty-three St Leonard's Close.' He slowly recited the postcode.

Alfie slowed the car and put it into the sat nav. It was seventeen miles away!

'I'm staying with my sister. She dropped me off,' Jack muttered, and then fell asleep again.

Alfie drove to Jack's sister's house and rang the bell. Her husband answered and Alfie eased Jack in.

'He's all yours. Good luck.'

It was after 1 a.m. when Alfie finally arrived home, exhausted but relieved that the evening was over. He climbed the stairs to his bedroom and just before he opened the door he thought he heard a noise coming from his sons' room. He went up to the door and listened, but the noise had stopped. He listened for a while longer, then continued on to his own room and climbed silently into bed with his wife.

FIFTEEN

The team were working late on Friday night at Coleshaw CID. Since the additional newsfeed had gone out earlier that evening they had been inundated with phone calls. They all knew it would die off as quickly as it had started so they'd agreed to work late.

Forensics had returned their initial findings on the packaging containing the copy of the video clip. It showed a clear set of fingerprints, but they didn't match anyone on their database. The saliva on the stamp and the envelope flap would very likely contain DNA – if the person hadn't thought about wearing gloves, they likely hadn't considered DNA evidence either, but those results wouldn't be available for a few days.

The street's CCTV had come in too, and that was what Beth was working on now. The camera covered the main post office in Coleshaw High Street, which was where the parcel had been posted, according to the franking stamp. But the parcel could have been dropped off at any time that day.

Beth was now scouring the footage, looking for someone depositing a package of the right size and shape. She was marking the tape at every possible point, highlighting suspects. There were lots of markers now. Then she found something of particular interest and zoomed in. The picture was quite good, and the man posting the envelope seemed to be behaving oddly. He looked up at the camera before surreptitiously pushing the package – the right size and shape – into the post box. Beth stopped the footage and went back to the point where the man appeared. She then went slowly forward, advancing the clip a frame at a time. When she came to the frame of him looking up at the camera she stopped and zoomed in. It was a good image and Beth was pleased. She gave it another marker and moved on.

Meanwhile, Beth's colleague Harper had been given the task of checking the Roomy-Spaces within a ten-mile radius of Coleshaw. They'd quickly eliminated the ones that were empty on the night of the murder, and he was making significant progress on the others. He now had a shortlist of just three that needed to be visited. He'd started off with twenty-four.

'It's not too late to visit tonight?' he checked with his boss, DS Scrivener.

'No, lad, it's a murder enquiry. You can go if they're close.'

'Very good, sir. Then I'll go home after.'

Harper drove to the first address and eliminated the

room quite quickly. While it was of a similar size, the wallpaper certainly wasn't the same and neither was the furniture. He thanked the owner for her time, got back into his car and drove to the second, five miles away. He went up the path and rang the bell. It was answered by a middle-aged woman. He explained why he was there and asked if he could see the room she rented out.

'Can you come back tomorrow?' she asked. 'The couple I have staying have been travelling all day and are asleep now. They have an early flight in the morning so will be gone by seven.'

'Are you sure we can't wake them just for two minutes?' he asked. 'I'll be in and out as quickly as I can.'

'I'd rather you didn't. They'll give me a bad review.'

He asked again, but when the woman insisted he left. He tried the third address, another two miles away, and again eliminated it straight away. It was part of a bigger room that could accommodate a family of four. When he'd seen the photographs of it online he'd assumed he'd been looking at two rooms. He thanked the homeowner and said goodnight.

Harper returned to his car and phoned DS Scrivener. It was now 9 p.m. He explained the progress he'd made, or rather hadn't made.

'You'll have to leave it for tonight,' DS Scrivener said. 'Go back first thing in the morning to the one you haven't checked. Never mind that it's a Saturday. As soon as you're done, I want you to come back to the station and continue searching for other possible Roomy-Spaces. We'll shift the boundaries out another ten miles.'

'Very good, sir.'

Harper went home exhausted, having worked a thirteen-hour shift, but at 8.30 the following morning he was standing on the doorstep of the property he hadn't seen inside the night before. He pressed the bell once, twice, and waited. It took a long time before Mrs Watson, the owner, answered, still in her dressing gown.

'Good morning, ma'am.'

'Oh, it's you,' she said. 'You're early.'

He smiled bravely. 'Can I have a look at your room now, please?' he asked.

'Yes. Come in.'

He followed her up the staircase to the Roomy-Space and went in. His heart nearly stopped. Unless he was very much mistaken, this was the same room as the one on the video clip. The bed was unmade, but apart from that it was identical. He took out his phone to check the still photo. It matched. He looked at the woman, who was by the door watching him, expecting him to be in and out so she could go back to bed.

'Have you touched anything?' he asked, and immediately knew it was a daft question. It was a Roomy-Space, after all. They'd probably had lots of guests since Emma and Carl had stayed here.

'Touched anything?' she repeated.

'Did you have a young couple stay here last Saturday?'

She thought for a moment. 'Yes, Carl Smith and his partner.'

'When did they leave?'

'I'm not sure. They were gone by the time I'd got up in the morning. Why?'

'Do you live here alone?' he asked.

'No. I have a husband and two boys. What's all this about?'

'Just a minute,' he said, and phoned Coleshaw CID. DS Scrivener was already there.

'I have a match,' Harper said. 'I'm at the property now.'

'You're sure?'

'Perfectly.'

'Good. What's the address? I'll send the team.'

'What's going on?' Mrs Watson asked as he finished up on the phone to his boss.

'Can you ask your husband to get up, please?' Harper asked.

'No. He was in very late last night and he's still asleep. What is it?' she asked again, clearly very anxious.

'We have reason to believe that the young lady who stayed here with Carl Smith last Saturday was Emma Arnold, the missing teenager.'

She stared at him, bewildered.

'I do need to see your husband, and your sons. How old are they?'

'Fifteen and thirteen.'

He nodded. 'We believe Emma spent her last night in this room.'

'I'll fetch my husband,' she said, and disappeared out

of the door.

Harper stayed where he was and looked around the room. There weren't that many places you could hide a spy camera, but this was definitely the room they'd been looking for. DS Scrivener had been right with his hunch about the place being local. Harper's gaze travelled around the walls and ceiling and then to the pictures. He was by the door now and didn't like to go into the room until the scenes of crime officers had arrived. His gaze went to the bedside clock just as Mr Watson arrived in his dressing gown. He looked shocked and disorientated.

'What's the matter?' he asked.

'Could you come downstairs, please, sir, and bring your sons as well?'

'I can, but what's all this about?'

'I would rather wait until my boss is here,' Harper said. 'Which rooms are your sons in?'

'I'll get them,' Mr Watson said, and he left to fetch the boys.

'You need to get up,' Alfie said, looking around his sons' bedroom door. 'Put on your dressing gowns and go downstairs. The police are here.'

'What?' Gregory said. 'The police?'

Mike merely turned over in bed, clearly trying to shut out the noise.

There was some groaning and moaning while Alfie waited with the detective outside their bedroom. Eventually both boys were up.

113

'Downstairs, please,' he said as they emerged.

'What's all this about?' Mike asked. 'I need to use the bathroom.'

'Go to the bathroom,' Jenny said, who had just come to join them. 'Then come down. This is serious.'

They left Mike and Gregory to use the bathroom, and DC Harper followed Alfie and Jenny down the flight of stairs, and into the living room.

'What's all this about?' Jenny asked. 'You said it had to do with that missing girl, Emma Arnold.'

'That's correct,' Harper said. 'I'll answer any more questions when my boss is here.'

Alfie remained quiet. It was slowly dawning on him that the police must be there because of the tape he'd sent. Jenny looked completely confused as to what was going on and sat down nervously on the sofa. Alfie sat down too.

'What's all this about. Do you know?' Jenny asked him.

He shook his head.

Soon Mike and Gregory came down the stairs and sat down in the living room too.

A police car that was patrolling the local area arrived first. It contained two officers who knocked on the door. Harper went to talk to them while Alfie and the rest of the family, in their dressing gowns, stayed in the living room. A man who introduced himself as DS Scrivener arrived next, followed, fifteen minutes later, by the scenes of crime officers and forensics, who came in and went straight up to the bedroom. It wasn't their home any more, Alfie thought.

DS Scrivener started asking them about a recording that had been made in the guest room, the one they used for Roomy-Space.

'A recording?' Jenny repeated as footsteps sounded across the ceiling.

Alfie said nothing and slowly looked up. He had never imagined in his wildest dreams that the police would be able to trace the room. He took a moment, then said: 'It was me. My wife doesn't know anything about it. Neither do my sons.'

The boys exchanged worried glances.

'What?' Jenny said. 'What are you talking about?'

'I planted the spy camera,' Alfie continued. 'I made the recording and posted it to the police.'

'What are you talking about?' Jenny snapped again, with a mixture of anger and uncertainty.

'It was me,' Alfie said to the police. 'No one else is involved.'

'Is there just the one room you use for Roomy-Space or do you have more?' DS Scrivener asked.

'Just the one,' Alfie said miserably.

'Would you like to get dressed, sir, so you can come to the police station to answer some questions. I'll have your mobile phone, please.'

Alfie handed over his phone as Jenny looked on, becoming even more upset.

'Will someone please tell me what's happening?' she cried.

'I set up a small spy camera in our Roomy-Space. Inside

the clock on the bedside table. I captured Carl murdering his girlfriend, Emma Arnold. I sent a copy of the recording to the police,' Alfie said, hoping that might be enough.

She opened her mouth as if to speak, then closed it again, obviously struggling to think of what to say.

DS Scrivener waited for Alfie. He stood and, without speaking to or looking at his wife and sons, went upstairs to dress.

'Why did Alfie set up a spy camera in the guest room?' Jenny asked her sons, perplexed.

There was silence, then Mike said, embarrassed, 'I guess it was to film people staying in the room without their clothes on.'

She stared at him. 'But why would he want to do that?' she asked, looking at her sons. They said nothing. Gradually the penny dropped. 'Oh my,' she said. 'But that's illegal.' And she buried her head in her hands and wept. The police continued to thoroughly search the Watsons' guest room, photographing it as they went. They even took up some of the carpet.

Alfie dressed and left for the police station, calling goodbye as he went. No one replied. Jenny was in tears and was still trying to get her head around what Alfie had been doing. Then DS Scrivener wanted to search the rest of the house.

'Alfie spends most of his time in his study,' Jenny told them.

'We'll start there then,' DS Scrivener said.

'It's in the attic,' Jenny replied. 'Top floor.'

DS Scrivener called to another officer to join him, and Jenny followed them up. The boys had gone to their room to get dressed. Jenny was still in her dressing gown. She thought how long it had been since she'd last set foot in the study. It was considered Alfie's domain. There wasn't much to see, really, but it was his bolt-hole, when he wanted to escape the rest of the family.

She was still struggling to come to terms with what he'd been accused of. Her husband, a secret photographer. Did she know him at all? When this got out she'd be struck off the register for Roomy-Space.com for sure. She waited as DS Scrivener and the other police officer looked around. There was a desk, a chair, and bookshelves on one of the walls. Two computers stood on his desk, and she knew he had a tablet too. The second officer began to open and close desk drawers. Some he just looked in, others he went through more carefully.

'Are we taking these computers?' the police officer asked his boss.

'Yes,' he replied. Then to Jenny, 'We'll give you receipts.'

'You're taking them?' Jenny asked. 'But they've got all of Alfie's work on them. You're treating him like a criminal.'

And as she said it, realization dawned; that was exactly what he was – a criminal.

SIXTEEN

At the police station Alfie was checked in at the desk, then taken to a cell where he sat and waited with a cup of water. They'd wanted to know if he needed a duty solicitor present and he said he did. That took time to arrange. It was nearly midday when Mr Brunson arrived and Alfie was shown to Interview Room 2. Mr Brunson was very young. He shook Alfie's hand and said rather glibly that he'd rather be on the golf course on a nice morning like this.

'I'm sorry,' Alfie said grumpily. 'I've been stuck in a cell.'

Two detectives appeared, introduced themselves, and then DC Beth Mayes gave the date, time and the names of those present, before beginning the interview.

'Mr Watson, can we first establish that it was you who sent the recording of Emma's last moments to us?'

'It was me,' Alfie said. He could hardly deny it.

'Good. Because we have a very clear photograph from

118

the CCTV camera at the main post office in Coleshaw of you posting it.'

'It was me,' he said more loudly. Then, before DC Mayes could go any further, Alfie, who was frustrated at having to wait so long in the cell, blurted out, 'I didn't even see anything. It was a complete waste of time.'

'What do you mean, you didn't see anything?' DC Mayes asked.

'I didn't ever see anyone take off their clothes. I only set up the spy camera last Wednesday, but that night a couple in their eighties arrived, so I didn't watch them. Then there was no booking for Thursday. And my wife Jenny turned a couple away on the Friday.'

'Why?' DC Davis asked. 'Why turn a couple away?'

'Because they were unsuitable. They were off their heads on something and didn't have any luggage. Jenny took one look at them and told them they'd get a refund.'

DC Mayes nodded. 'Then what?'

'The spy camera was running during the whole of Saturday night when the murder happened. I haven't used it since. The app is on my phone.'

'Your phone is still being checked,' DC Mayes said.

Alfie wondered what else they'd find on his phone and tried to think. They'd had it during the hours he'd been waiting for his solicitor to arrive.

'I understand you deleted all the recordings from your phone,' DC Mayes said. 'Why was that?'

Alfie sighed as Mr Brunson typed. He hadn't yet said a single word.

'There was just the one recording of that night. I thought it might help me move on if I removed it. I was sick of the whole thing and wanted to put an end to it. I regretted even doing it in the first place. It was just supposed to be something to spice up my sex life. But I didn't ever see anything – apart from the murder.'

'And you thought that by deleting the video you could just pretend none of it happened?' DC Davis asked.

Alfie shook his head. 'Maybe, but that's not what happened,' he admitted gloomily. 'I thought you'd catch Carl using the recording and that would be an end to it. I never dreamt you'd all come to my house. The only trace of Emma there now is the earring, anyway.'

Alfie immediately realized what he'd done.

'What earring?' DC Mayes asked.

Shit. He rubbed his forehead with his hand. How much should he tell them? He'd have to talk about the earring now, but maybe he could avoid telling them about his dealings with Carl. Somehow, he thought if he admitted to that, it could make his situation a whole lot worse. Although now that he thought about it, the police already had his phone, which contained all the messages between him and Carl. He would just have to play it by ear.

'The earring?' DC Mayes prompted.

'Yes, all right. Emma was wearing earrings, one of which came off in the struggle that night. It had the word "off" on it. I found it in the bedroom when I was cleaning. I assumed the matching earring had "fuck" on it. I didn't like to just throw it away, so I buried it in the garden.'

Alfie paused and looked at them for a reaction. They were both expressionless. 'Then miraculously it reappeared in our utility room,' he continued. 'I checked the garden and it's definitely not there any more.'

'Do you still have the earring?' DC Mayes asked.

'No – well, yes. It's in the desk drawer in the study.'

'Is there anything else from Emma in your house?'

'No, nothing, as far as I know.'

Standing and looking at Mr Brunson, DC Mayes said, 'I need to make a phone call. Does your client want a break? Ten minutes?'

Mr Brunson nodded.

DC Davis switched off the recording equipment, then stood and followed DC Mayes out.

'I hope the rest of the team are still at the property,' Beth said, taking out her mobile phone.

DS Scrivener answered his phone. He was still there.

'It's Beth, sir. Have you found anything? We're interviewing Mr Watson now.'

'Nothing of significance,' he replied. 'We're taking samples of the carpet in the bedroom for forensics to have a look at.'

'Can you check the drawer of the desk in the study, please? There could be a small earring in there that belongs to Emma. It's got "off" written on it. Mr Watson has just told us.'

'I'll go up there now,' he said. 'We've got his computers and iPad already.'

Beth waited while DS Scrivener went upstairs, then she

121

could hear him rummaging in the drawer.

'Got it,' he said. 'Is that everything?'

'Yes, sir.'

'We'll be leaving soon. See you at the station.'

Beth and Matt returned to the interview room and sat down. Beth switched on the tape and reminded Alfie he was still under police caution.

'Did you find the earring?' he checked.

Beth nodded. 'When you said the earring reappeared, what did you mean?' she asked. 'It couldn't have dug itself up. Surely the most likely explanation is that someone you know, possibly a member of your family, watched you do it, and then dug it up later?'

'No,' Alfie said adamantly. 'I asked them all and they didn't know anything about an earring. They were all out at the time anyway. Jenny was at work and the boys were at school. It was just me at home.'

'Let's move on to your phone,' Beth said. 'We're assuming the person you have listed under the name Carl is the same Carl we are looking for?'

'Yes,' Alfie acknowledged. 'It is.'

'What can you tell us about him?'

'Nothing. I don't know him.'

'But you met him last night at midnight?' Beth said.

'I just dropped off the money,' Alfie said, looking very downcast. 'I didn't actually meet him.'

'But you know him a little?' Beth asked.

'No. Not at all. I thought if I gave him the money, he would stop harassing me. He killed Emma. I didn't know what he would do if I didn't pay up. I don't know him. Honestly.' Alfie found he was getting more distressed the more they questioned him.

Beth ignored his plea of honesty and concentrated on the phone. 'I note that your phone is set up to receive updates about Emma Arnold. When did you set that up?'

'Just recently.'

'After she'd gone missing?' Beth asked.

'Yes. I think it was Wednesday or Thursday.'

'Why?'

'Because I was worried, and I wanted to know what was happening. If you'd caught Carl.'

Beth held his gaze just long enough to let him know she doubted his version of events.

'You had some email contact with Carl,' she continued.

'Yes, I did. That's how we started speaking. Then it changed to the messages.'

'Why?'

'I don't know,' Alfie said, rubbing his head.

The interrogation continued for another half an hour, with Alfie continuing to tell them what little he knew about Carl. It was all he could do, and he found himself repeating what he'd already said. He didn't know him and he never would.

DC Mayes wound up the interview, and he was taken back to a cell. His solicitor had said nothing throughout, as many did.

Alfie waited for another half-hour. He didn't even have his phone to distract him. Then an officer came in and said he was free to go and they'd be in touch.

Thank goodness for that. 'Can I have my phone?' he asked them on the way to the desk.

'Not yet,' the officer said. 'Tomorrow or the day after. Phone the station to check.'

'But why?' he persisted. 'I haven't got another one.'

'Sorry, sir, it's protocol. We have your computers and iPad here too. We'll contact you when you can collect them. Would you like me to call someone to come and pick you up?'

'My wife,' he said. He wondered how pleased Jenny would be to see him.

The officer on duty phoned Jenny's mobile and told her that Alfie was ready to go and she could collect him. She replied and then the officer hung up.

'You can go and sit in reception until she's here,' he said.

Alfie sat down. There was another person in reception who was busy on his phone. Alfie felt lower than he'd ever done in his life before. What a total mess. He vaguely wondered if Carl had contacted him in the interim – he had no way of knowing until they returned his phone. Then he wondered again what Jenny was going to say.

SEVENTEEN

Fifteen minutes or so later, Jenny arrived. Alfie saw her through the outer glass door of the police station. She entered, came over and just stood there looking at him. He could tell she was angry and upset. He stood, picked up his jacket and followed her out, down the steps, and then to their car, which was parked a little way up the street. He didn't like to ask if he could drive as he usually did, instead slipping silently into the passenger seat.

Jenny hadn't said a word, but he could see she was seething with anger. He could sense her wrath. After about five minutes she blurted, 'Are you going to tell me what the hell has been going on, Alfie?'

He told her – about buying and setting up the camera, about the murder on Saturday night, about the subsequent correspondence from Carl, the blackmail threat and handing over the money to Carl last night.

'You gave away £5,000!' she exclaimed. It was the only part of the story she'd latched onto.

'I know. I'm sorry. I hoped that would put an end to it. But it seems it was just the beginning.'

She was silent for a moment, then said, 'I'll have to close my Roomy-Space business when this all gets out.' A girl had been murdered, Alfie thought. In their home, no less. Why was she so concerned about Roomy-Space right now?

'Will it get out?' he asked in a small, quiet voice.

'Will it get out!' she said, her voice rising. 'Of course it will get out. If it hasn't already. People are supposed to feel safe when they stay in a Roomy-Space property, not spied upon. How could anyone ever feel safe in there again? I'll be struck off.'

Alfie didn't know what to say. It was all his fault. He looked out of his side window. It was another fine autumn day. He remembered that he'd thought about taking Mike and Gregory out somewhere nice today. He didn't suppose anyone would be in the mood for something like that for a long time. He certainly wouldn't.

'Then there's the matter of my job,' Jenny continued, crunching the gears. 'A teacher with a voyeur for a husband! What will the board of governors say? I wouldn't be surprised if they ask me to resign. How will I ever be able to hold my head up in the staffroom again?'

He had no idea if they could make her resign or not. He was still processing what had happened. He didn't always understand women. He glanced at Jenny and could see tears forming at the corners of her eyes. He put his hand gently on her arm and she pushed it away.

'It's all right for you,' she snapped. 'You can do your job wherever you like, but I'm police checked. What am I supposed to do, Alfie? What are we supposed to do for money?'

There was silence again, then she turned to him and asked, 'How long has it been going on?' As if he was having an affair.

'Only a week. I promise you that's all.'

She tutted and continued to drive, then said, 'The police were all over your study once they'd found the earring. Whatever possessed you to put it in your desk drawer?'

He shrugged. He really had no answer. He'd assumed he was safe.

'I take it there are no more spy cameras hidden around the house?'

He shook his head. It was as if she was going through everything that had happened step by step.

'The police took the clock and they searched the rest of the house.'

'What were they looking for?' he asked.

'Evidence. More spy cameras, I suppose. Have they charged you with anything?'

'No, not yet,' he said dejectedly. 'But I'm pretty sure they will.'

'Yes, so am I,' she said, her voice catching.

She continued in silence until they arrived home, where she parked on the drive. She turned off the engine and sat there staring around her. Alfie sat there too, staring out of his side window.

127

'Do the neighbours know?' he asked.

'I've no idea. They all had a good look at the police, though. They were here all morning. What are we going to do, Alfie?'

'Perhaps we should move,' he suggested.

'And what about the boys?' she said. 'They're settled at school. What do we tell them?'

'What have you told them so far?' he asked.

'Nothing more than they already know.'

She sighed and got out of the car and went into the house. He followed her.

Inside, the boys were holed up in their bedroom as usual.

'We have to say something to them,' Jenny said.

Just at that moment they heard the boys' bedroom door open. Their voices immediately hushed. 'What are we going to say?' Jenny hissed. Then, 'Come down, boys.'

They stood at the foot of the stairs and waited for Mike and Gregory to appear.

'Let's go and have a seat in the living room,' Jenny said. 'Your father and I have to talk to you both.'

Mike wanted to get a glass of water first and Gregory went after him.

'Delaying tactics,' Jenny said, and they went into the living room.

Alfie wandered over to the living-room window and looked out at the patch of soil he'd dug up. He still couldn't work out how the earring had rematerialized, and the police hadn't seemed particularly interested either. He thought about it, then turned away from the window, sat down and looked at Jenny. She seemed more in control than he was; perhaps she was starting to work through what had happened. The boys appeared, looking dispirited. They sat down and it was a few minutes before anyone spoke.

'So, it seems your father has made some mistakes,' Jenny said slowly. She glanced at Alfie. All three of them were looking at him now, straight-faced and disappointed in him. He threw the boys an embarrassed smile, then looked away.

'The police have talked to your father about the recording he made of Carl and Emma. We don't know yet how much trouble he's in. We're going to wait to see what happens before we make any decisions on what to do. It might be that we decide to move away or we might decide to just sit it out. It's too early to say at the moment.'

The boys were still looking at him, waiting for a proper explanation. They weren't kids any more. They were young men.

'I made a big error of judgement,' Alfie offered. 'I did something that I shouldn't have done and it could have repercussions for the whole family.'

Neither of the boys spoke. Alfie waited for them to ask some of the questions he would have done. But they remained silent. Perhaps it was too big for them to deal with.

'Is there anything you want to ask me?' Alfie said at last.

'No,' Mike said, while Gregory shook his head.

'I love you both,' Alfie said.

Mike sighed. 'Have you finished?' he asked.

'Well, yes,' Alfie said.

Mike stood and headed for the door. Gregory stayed where he was.

'Are you OK,' Alfie asked him, 'with what I've told you?'

Gregory nodded, stood and went out of the room.

Alfie breathed a long, deep sigh of relief. 'I got out of that quite lightly,' he said.

'I wouldn't be so sure. The boys have a way of processing information and then they come back to you. They'll be discussing what we've said now among themselves.'

Alfie knew from previous experience that this was likely to be the case.

He and Jenny sat there for a few moments longer, then Jenny asked him, 'What are you going to do about your work?'

'Everything is on my phone or the computers,' he said dejectedly.

'Perhaps the police won't keep them for long,' she said. 'There's nothing more to be found on them, is there?'

'No, of course not.'

Jenny went to make them a coffee, so Alfie headed upstairs. He looked in the guest room on his way. The clock had gone, of course, and the room had obviously been searched. He closed the door and continued up to his study. That had been searched too and left in a mess. He was annoyed. He crossed to his desk and checked the drawer. The earring had gone too, as he knew. He looked at the big space on his desk where his computers had been. The police wouldn't find anything on them, nothing at all. He was sure of that, at least. One of them was just for work, and the other was mainly for back-up and photos. He ambled around and then went downstairs to the living room where his coffee was ready. He and Jenny were mainly silent as they drank it. He didn't know what to do without his phone to distract him or his wife to comfort him.

He offered to help make lunch. He and Jenny shared the cooking at weekends. It was a homemade cheese and onion quiche with mash. He was good at mash, but they worked in an uncomfortable silence. The atmosphere was unpleasant, and Alfie didn't know what to say. He couldn't keep going to his study because there was nothing for him to do up there now.

The atmosphere persisted over lunch.

'I think I'll go for a walk,' he said as soon as they'd finished. 'Does anyone want to join me?'

No one replied so he went alone. He just walked and walked, trying to walk off all that was wrong with his life. He was gone for over an hour. On the way back he passed Number 23, where the new people lived. He looked in and they appeared to be arguing. He shook his head and continued home. People should be nice to each other, he thought.

Late that afternoon, the CID were still working at Coleshaw Police Station. Beth had filed her report from the interview with Mr Watson and was now studying the video tape again. They'd put out a photograph of Carl, but so far there'd been very little response. Nothing much to work on. She stared at the CCTV footage taken at the post office, looking for inspiration. It showed Mr Watson dropping off the parcel, which they now had confirmation was definitely his. His fingerprints were all over the package, and besides, he'd admitted it during the interview. She checked the spy camera tape again and saw the earring spring off during the struggle that night. It landed out of sight. Then there was nothing else of significance.

Beth rewound the tape and went through it again, this time studying Carl Smith on the footage. A young man, thought to be in his late teens or early twenties, five foot ten inches, with black hair and regular features. They were double-checking everything to make sure they hadn't missed anything. Where on earth could he be? All the addresses they'd tried so far had turned up nothing. And Emma's body? It was a week now since she'd been murdered. Bodies usually appeared quite quickly. In fact, they were usually the first clue that a murder had even taken place. It was very unusual to have a murder investigation without either a body or the suspect.

At 8 p.m., Beth switched off her computer and went home. It had been another long day.

EIGHTEEN

Sunday passed as Sundays do, with Alfie staying in bed much later than was usual for him. When he eventually got up, he slouched downstairs in his dressing gown, which got him a telling-off.

'How do you expect the boys to behave when they see you dressed like that?' Jenny said. 'You should set a good example. It's noon.'

Alfie had had a sleepless night and was in no mood to be snapped at, so he had a go at her.

'They can come down in their pyjamas if they want to!' he said. 'It's Sunday, for goodness' sake!'

'Typical!' she snapped back.

'Typical of what?' He rounded on her. They fell silent but glared at each other across the kitchen.

The silence continued as Alfie made himself a coffee, then the boys appeared, both fully dressed and ready to go out.

'Where are you two going?' Jenny asked them, amazed.

'Away from this dysfunctional family,' Mike said.

'Don't be cheeky,' Jenny snapped. 'I asked you where you were going.'

'To the shopping centre,' Mike said, heading for the door. Gregory followed him.

'How long will you be gone?' Jenny called after them.

'A couple of hours,' Mike said, and the front door slammed shut.

'I don't know how you can be so calm,' she said after a moment. 'Five thousand pounds!'

'I thought that would come up again,' he said, aggrieved.

'Well, this whole thing started because you set up that bloody spy camera in the room. You should never have done that!'

'Do you think I don't know that?'

They argued on and off for most of the day, until the boys returned, four hours later.

'Where have you two been?' Jenny asked, turning on them. 'You said you'd only be gone a couple of hours.' She'd been worried, Alfie could tell.

'Shopping,' Mike said nonchalantly.

Alfie looked at their array of bags and nearly asked where they'd got the money from, but then he remembered that they had birthday and Christmas money, as well as a weekly allowance that they rarely spent – along with the extra pocket money they'd got when they'd begun sharing a bedroom.

'What have you bought?' Jenny asked.

'An Xbox with some games,' Mike said.

She nodded. They went to their bedroom, where they spent the rest of the day and all evening playing games, only coming down to drink and eat.

The following morning, as the boys were getting breakfast, Jenny felt it prudent to give them a short lecture.

'You may hear things at school about your father in relation to Emma Arnold. Just ignore them.'

'What sort of things?' Mike asked.

Jenny wasn't sure if he was joking or not.

'Things that don't put him in the best light. Don't reply, is what I'm saying. Just ignore them.'

Mike nodded and went upstairs to get ready for school.

Alfie was up and dressed that morning too. He thought it wise after the bollocking he'd received the day before. It had created a bad atmosphere. He had been downstairs when Jenny had spoken to the boys about ignoring any rumours at school, and took a moment to thank her for saying what she had.

'Well, they're bound to hear something,' she said. 'It's better they know how to handle it.'

'Yes, indeed,' Alfie said. 'I was going to phone the police station this morning to see if they've finished with my devices.'

Jenny nodded and, grabbing her bag, she left the house without kissing him goodbye. He supposed it was asking a bit much after everything that had happened, but even so, he would have liked a kiss on the cheek as she usually gave him. He hoped the affection between them would

135

return in time.

He saw the boys off to school, then went to his study and waited until 9.15, when he used the seldom-used landline to phone the police station.

'Good morning, my name is Alfie Watson and I would like to know when my electrical devices will be returned to me,' he said.

He was left on hold for some time, only to be told that the officer taking care of his case was on a later shift and that he needed to phone back after twelve.

'Fine,' he said, irritated, and put down the phone.

Three hours to wait. He decided to put the time to good use and tidy his study, since he couldn't do any work. Jenny had decided it would be advisable to suspend the Roomy-Space for the moment and she had notified the management, so there was nothing for him to do there.

The time passed slowly and at 11 a.m. Alfie made himself another coffee, which he took to his study and drank as he finished sorting and tidying. At 12 he used the landline again to phone the station and asked to speak to DC Beth Mayes.

'Can I have my phone and computers back now, please? It's Alfie Watson.'

'You can have your phone back – we've finished with that – but we're holding on to your two computers and the iPad for now.'

'Why? I need the computers for work,' he said, annoyed.

'Something has shown up on one of them. We're still

having the other one checked.'

'What sort of something?' he asked, his heartrate beginning to rise. 'Which computer?'

'I am not at liberty to discuss that, Mr Watson. We still have further checks to make. But you're welcome to come and collect your phone.'

Alfie sat there, the landline pressed to his ear, perplexed.

'And you can't tell me what it is you've found?'

'Not at this time, no.'

He ended the call and thought about what they could have found on his computer. He mainly used them for work. They were both full of CAD drawings and things like that. They hadn't even told him which computer was affected. Alfie wondered if it might be just a misunderstanding. Perhaps they'd mistaken some of his drawings. But for what? He'd ask them again when he got to the police station.

He put on his jacket and shoes and prepared to leave the house. The mail popped through the letterbox and he picked it up and put it on the hall table to read later. He got into his car and drove to the police station, all the time thinking about what they could have found on the computer. It was very worrying and something didn't add up. When he arrived at the station, he had to park in a side road. It was busy, he supposed because it was a Monday morning, and he was kept waiting at the desk for nearly fifteen minutes.

'I've come about my phone and computers. It's Alfie

Watson,' he told the desk officer.

'When did they come in?' he asked.

'On Saturday morning.'

The officer found them on his computer and told Alfie to take a seat. He joined the other people who were waiting patiently in reception. After about ten minutes, DC Beth Mayes appeared through a door at the back. She came over to him carrying his phone in a plastic bag.

'There's not much on there, is there?' she said, passing it to him.

'I guess not,' he replied. 'I don't really know many people now.'

She handed him a receipt form to sign, clipped to a board. He stood to sign it.

'Can you tell me what you're looking for on my computers?' he asked. 'I might be able to help you.'

'No, I'm sorry. We can't do that.'

'How long will you have them for?' he tried, passing back the board.

'I'm not sure yet.'

'You must have some idea? A couple of days, a week?'

'We can keep your computers and any other electrical devices for as long as is necessary. It could be months.'

'What? But there's nothing on them apart from my work.'

'Then you'll have them back quickly, won't you?'

Alfie was going to say something else but thought better of it. He thanked her and left. He was furious; any satisfaction at getting his phone back was now overridden by not having his computers, or any idea when they would be returned, or even why they'd kept them in the first place. It was preposterous and the law needed changing. The police shouldn't be allowed to take an innocent person's electrical devices and keep them indefinitely. It was outrageous. He switched on his phone to find that the battery was flat. He was in a very bad mood by the time he arrived home.

Going in his front door, he slammed it shut and grabbed the mail from where he'd left it on the hall table. He marched through to the kitchen where he plugged in his phone, then looked at the letters. There were three, all for him, but the top one was handwritten. Unusual. He picked it up and opened it, still not a happy man. He was expecting an invitation to a wedding or something similar. That was the only reason he could think of for the envelope being handwritten. But when he opened it, he couldn't believe his eyes. It was another demand from Carl.

Leave £1,000 by the old war memorial at 9 p.m. on Wednesday.

Carl

'Got you, you bastard,' he said out loud. 'Got you.' He marched over to the landline, phoned Coleshaw CID and asked to speak to Beth Mayes. She wasn't available so he was put through to her colleague, DC Matt Davis.

'I've just received another ransom demand,' he exploded. 'Carl wants a thousand pounds on top of the five thousand he's already had. As if! You'll get him now, won't you? You have to.' He felt excited by the prospect.

'We'll certainly try,' Matt said. 'What does the note say exactly?'

'"Leave £1,000 by the old war memorial at 9 p.m. on Wednesday, Carl." That's the day after tomorrow.'

'Don't touch the envelope or the letter any more than you already have. Forensics will need it. I'll send someone to collect it. Just leave it on the side. Was there anything else in the envelope?'

'No, just this handwritten letter.'

'OK. I'll be in touch.'

Alfie suddenly felt quite important as he carefully placed the letter and envelope into a small plastic bag. He left it on the dresser in the kitchen. It would be safe there. What a cheek, he thought. He wanted to tell Jenny, but she would be teaching. An hour later, a police car drew up outside his house and an officer got out. He knocked on the door and Alfie gave him the plastic bag.

'Do you want a receipt for it?' the officer asked.

'No, I don't think so.'

He thanked him and Alfie returned indoors, feeling they were getting somewhere now. His phone was charged so he unplugged it from the charger and read his messages. It was true, he didn't have a lot on the phone, as Beth had said; perhaps he should get some more apps? He scrolled through his messages and emails. What was strange was that Carl hadn't WhatsApped or sent an email. He'd written a letter, which he'd posted to Alfie's home address. Alfie leant on the counter in the kitchen and thought about this. Why had he sent a handwritten letter? After some time, he decided Carl must have assumed his phone would still be held by the police. It was the only plausible explanation as to why he would write rather than email or text.

He now set about answering the emails on his phone. He answered two queries that had been sent over the weekend, and phoned the senders, making a definite appointment for one. It was awkward for him to type on his phone – he preferred using his computer – but he managed it. He also saw that he had a meeting the following morning in a nearby town – a team briefing session. It showed on the calendar of his phone. It crossed his mind as he worked whether he should mention what was going on to his boss and he couldn't decide. He'd think about it some more. There was plenty of time.

Alfie was relatively happy, finally being able to do a little work, although he had several lapses in concentration when he sat and thought of Carl, and his anger flared. The cheek of it. Another thousand pounds! He'd only made the last payment on Friday, and now Carl was asking for more when he'd promised he wouldn't. He must be crazy if he thought Alfie would pay more now.

At 1.30 p.m., DC Beth Mayes phoned his mobile. She was in receipt of the letter now.

'I don't know what your view is on this, but ideally we'd like your help to stake out the old memorial on Wednesday,' she said. 'We're no nearer catching him.

Your role would be to do what you did before and let us do the rest. What do you think? You can say no.'

'Yes, absolutely. I'll do anything to help catch Carl. Count me in.'

'Good. I'll need to speak to you in person. Can you come into the police station this afternoon?'

'Yes. When?'

'Just a minute.' She covered the phone and discussed it with someone there.

'At three-thirty today?' she said, coming back on the line.

'I'll be there,' he confirmed.

'Come into the station and ask for me. And obviously don't talk to anyone else about this.'

'Will do. We'll catch him.'

Alfie felt a great sense of relief. He was now part of the police team that would apprehend Carl on Wednesday, and all his troubles would be over. He would play an important part in tracking him down and arresting him. He thought of Jenny, who would love him wholeheartedly again, maybe even more than before, and his sons, who had shown a distinct lack of respect recently, who would admire him again very soon.

He couldn't settle to anything that afternoon, and at 3 p.m., for the second time that day, Alfie drove to the police station. He'd forgotten how much school traffic clogged the roads at this time, and he arrived ten minutes late. He rushed in and gave his name to the desk officer. 'I'm here to see DC Beth Mayes,' he said. 'Alfie Watson.'

'I remember you from this morning,' the desk officer replied. 'Take a seat, please.'

Alfie went over and sat on the same chair he had that morning and looked around him. It was a depressing place, outdated, and badly in need of a refurbishment. Thankfully, he wasn't kept waiting long and presently DC Mayes appeared.

'Good afternoon,' she said brightly, greeting him with a firm handshake. 'Thank you for coming in.'

She led him through a labyrinth of corridors and into a room at the back that had four people in it, whom he assumed to be police officers.

'This is Alfie Watson,' DC Mayes said. 'Do sit down, Mr Watson.'

She introduced them – DS Scrivener, whom he'd already met at home, and others who he hadn't. They were going to be part of the stakeout on Wednesday, the plan for which she now explained. Alfie needed to email Carl to confirm he was going, then drive his car to the exact spot he had done on Friday, park it and wait. At 9 p.m. he would get out and walk to the war memorial, where he would leave the package. It would contain counterfeit bank notes, all marked, of course. He would leave them in the same place, under the vase, then return to his car. Carl would be watching, so it was important he behaved as he did on Friday, i.e. act normally. Then he would drive home, leaving the officers to do their job.

'Got it?' DC Mayes said.

'Yes, sir,' Alfie said. 'I mean, madam.'

'Remember, you're to drive straight home,' DC Mayes emphasized. 'One of us will update you later.'

'It's a good plan,' Alfie said. 'I don't see what can go wrong.'

'Neither do I,' DC Mayes agreed, and looked at the other officers.

When the meeting had finished and they were all in the corridor again, Alfie quietly asked DC Mayes if they'd finished with his computers. She went to check and came back saying, 'No. We need them for a bit longer.'

Despite this, Alfie headed home feeling elated. He was about to apprehend a murderer.

NINETEEN

It was after 5 p.m. when Alfie arrived home and kissed Jenny on the cheek. She'd got in just ahead of him and was busy in the kitchen. She returned his kiss and he suddenly remembered it was his turn to cook so he tried to help her.

'I've been to the police station,' he said, feeling he had to say something to break the silence. 'They asked me to go. They've finished with my phone and handed it back to me.' He took it from his pocket to show her. 'But not the laptops or the iPad,' he added. 'They want to keep those for a bit longer.'

'Why?' Jenny asked, looking at him.

'I don't know, really. It's a mistake, I'm sure of it. Time will tell. But I have to go out on Wednesday evening to see a client. At seven. It's the only time he can do.' He felt he needed to tell her something to explain where he was going on Wednesday, even if he couldn't tell her the whole truth. It was better than saying nothing and then Jenny arranging something for herself. Although it was true that she hardly ever went out mid-week and the boys were old enough to be left home alone for a couple of hours in any case. Alfie did feel bad about lying to Jenny, but the police had been clear that he wasn't to tell anyone about the plan. And he didn't want to risk doing anything that might jeopardize that.

Jenny nodded and continued with what she was doing, making a béchamel sauce for the tray bake. He tried to make himself useful, but it was difficult to know how to do that with her sometimes. He didn't always know what she wanted, even more so since the murder.

When their meal was ready, he called the boys. They came down immediately and were exceptionally quiet. Alfie would have liked to share his day with them – they would be so proud to know he was part of a police operation – but he knew that was impossible right now, so he bit his tongue.

'How's your schoolwork?' he asked. He didn't know what else to say.

'Fine,' Gregory said.

'And yours?' He turned to Mike. Jenny raised her eyes.

'OK,' Mike said, pulling a face, and got on with eating. Alfie knew there was no point pushing the conversation when they were like this, so he left it at that.

After dinner, Alfie washed the dishes and put them away, then he watched television while Jenny worked at the dining table in the corner of the room. He would normally have spent some of his evening in his study, but now he'd finished tidying it, there wasn't much to do. He watched television until the 10 o'clock news, but there was nothing more about Emma or Carl. He then went upstairs, emailed Carl to confirm he would drop off the money, as the police had directed, then had a long shower and got into bed. Jenny followed, having got her lunch ready for school tomorrow. He put his arm around her and she didn't pull away.

'Your name was mentioned at school today,' she said. 'And this house.'

'What?' Alfie asked, astounded. He took his arm away so he could see her better. 'In what way?' A feeling of dread settled in his stomach.

'One of the kids who lives on this road came to me at registration and said they'd seen my house on Twitter. It was when the police were here on Saturday. Someone must have taken a video. I agreed it was my house as there was no point in denying it. I said it was to do with a Roomy-Space guest that stayed with us the week before. It's not like anyone apart from us and Emma's parents and the police knows that Emma was here the night she died. And we want to keep it that way for as long as possible.'

Alfie immediately reached for his phone from the bedside cabinet and scrolled through Twitter, but he couldn't find anything.

'I expect the photo's gone by now,' Jenny said. 'But it was there at morning break. I checked.'

'How quickly these things come and go,' Alfie said, still scrolling through the feed.

He continued checking for another fifteen minutes

but he still couldn't find anything, so he put his phone beside his bed. Jenny fell asleep quickly – nothing ever kept her up, not even a murder in their house. Alfie was unsettled, though, and lay awake trying to work out which neighbour had taken the video and uploaded it. Then he realized it could have been anyone walking past the house who chanced to see it.

Eventually he dropped off to sleep around midnight and was woken the next morning by the alarm. He had to head out today for their monthly team meeting. It was an hour's drive to his boss's house and the meeting was due to start at 9.30. Alfie put on his suit and tie and left at the same time as his family.

He parked outside his boss's house – a massive six-bedroom place built to his boss's specifications, with a double garage and a water fountain in the front garden. He'd been here twice before, but it still impressed.

He walked up the winding path to the front door and rang the bell. An ostentatious chime reverberated down the hall. He was greeted by Mrs Shelby, his boss's second wife, who showed him through to the office, the large extension built onto the side of the house. It was a huge room that looked over a perfectly landscaped garden with another elaborate water feature that had appeared since their last meeting. He sat and chatted to his boss and the dozen surveyors who were already sitting around the table, then accepted a coffee. There was a plate of biscuits too, which he happily tucked into.

Mr Shelby waited until everyone was present before

he stood and began by welcoming a new member of the team – Ms Haywood – then said how great the figures looked, apart from a couple of glitches. Alfie wasn't sure if those glitches were to do with him. He didn't even know if Mr Shelby still worked as a surveyor himself, or simply managed them all. Running his own business was what Alfie had tried to do and failed when Jenny had bailed him out. It was more difficult than it looked.

They took it in turns to speak, standing up to give their figures, taking just five or ten minutes each. Each person received a quick round of applause and sat down again. It was like a used-car salespersons' meeting. When it was Alfie's turn to speak he began by apologizing for the drop-off in work over the last week, and was about to say that he had acquired some new business when his boss interrupted.

'You had the police at your house on Saturday? My wife saw it on Twitter – it said it was the Watsons' house,' he said.

Alfie felt himself colour up; everyone was looking at him. He didn't know what to say. 'It was just in connection with the Roomy-Space we have. Or rather, had,' he said.

'Not good for business, though, is it?' his boss said.

'No,' Alfie agreed. 'It's not.'

He continued with his report, all the while thinking he would have really liked to tell them about his role in catching a murderer this coming Wednesday. That would shut them up once and for all.

The meeting lasted two hours and afterwards, when they'd all finished, Mr Shelby came up to Alfie. 'So, you had a bit of trouble?' he asked.

'Just a bit, but it's been taken care of now.'

'Why were the police at your house?' he asked.

'They wanted to check the room we used for our Roomy-Space. I don't know why, but they haven't bothered us since, so whatever's happened, it's nothing to do with us,' he lied.

His boss seemed to accept this; he nodded and went off to talk to someone else.

Alfie knew how important it was not to let anything slip about the operation on Wednesday, so he slipped away at the first opportunity. He felt aggrieved. It was as though he and his house were common property now and anyone could pass judgement! First at Jenny's school and now here.

On the way home he stopped for a wee and bought himself a sandwich for lunch. He checked his phone for news. There was no reference to him, his home or Emma, which he assumed was a good thing. Mrs Shelby must have seen the Twitter feed at the weekend – news travelled fast on social media and disappeared just as quickly.

He was relieved to get home. He took off his suit and tie and hung them up, then, reinvigorated by the meeting, he went straight to his study to work. Using his phone, he tried to complete a homebuyer's survey of a house he'd visited the week before but it was virtually impossible on such a small screen. It crossed his mind as to whether he should pop out and buy a new laptop, but that would be the whole day wasted. Then he suddenly remembered that his sons had a laptop each, which they needed for school sometimes. What were the chances of one of them being left at home today?

He went to their bedroom, nearly knocked on the door, then remembered they were at school. The room was a mess. Jenny refused to tidy it and said it was their responsibility – they were old enough, after all. There were wires connecting electrical devices running everywhere. Alfie didn't hunt around – he knew the importance of privacy at their age – and concentrated on trying to find what he needed. He found an iPad and then a few minutes later spotted Mike's laptop underneath a pile of dirty washing. Little wonder Jenny refused to clear up in here, he thought. It was disgusting. With a final glance around the room, he carried the laptop to his study, where he opened it. It had 80 per cent battery life – excellent. Mike must have used it recently.

It was password protected but Alfie knew Mike's password and quickly put it in. There were files everywhere – Science, English, Geography – he supposed that meant Mike must be doing some work for school, at least. He ignored his email account – that was of no concern to him – and created a new folder, which he named 'Dad'. He put it on the desktop so he could find it again easily, downloaded a new homebuyers' form and began to work. This was so much better than trying to do it on a phone. An hour had passed before he knew it. He was already over halfway through filling in the boxes about the house and uploading the photos. At this rate he'd be able to complete another study today.

It was now nearly 2.30 p.m. and he saved the file and went downstairs for a tea, which he took to his room to finish the report. The screen saver had come on and when he brought the laptop to life again, he noticed a file on Mike's desktop named 'Mable Crescent'. That was the name of the road they lived in and Alfie assumed it must be a school project. He continued to work for a while longer, then the doorbell rang, so he pressed save and went downstairs to answer it. There was a delivery van parked outside and a brown boxed parcel on the doorstep. It was addressed to Gregory, so Alfie brought it in and placed it on the table in the hall. He went back to his study and continued. He noticed again the file labelled with their address and wondered what it was but continued working. He didn't want to pry.

Alfie completed the form and emailed it to his phone. He was still thinking about the file that Mike had created marked 'Mable Crescent'. It must be schoolwork, and Alfie wondered what Mike had said about them. He sat there staring at the folder and then decided to have a quick look. It was a large file; it probably contained photos of their home. He clicked on it and the folder opened.

For a moment, Alfie didn't understand what he was looking at. There were photos of the house all right, five large, still photos of the rooms, including one of the study with him in it, and one image window blank. Why would

Mike take one still photo of each room and why was the folder so large? He looked at the photo of his study and suddenly his image moved. Jesus! He jumped back. The image did the same. He stared at the screen and then slowly looked around the room. Realization dawned. This wasn't a still photograph, but a live stream. He was being filmed.

What the hell! He tried to breathe, to think calmly. Why was Mike filming their home? A school project? If so, it was a strange one, and shouldn't he and Jenny have been notified? He looked more closely. There was a feed coming from nearly every room, including his and Jenny's bedroom and the bathroom. Nothing from the guest room, though. He sat and paused. This was no school project, so what the hell was going on? He continued to stare at the images. What had Mike been doing? Gregory shared the same bedroom so there was no way he wouldn't have known what Mike was doing. When did all this begin? He thought back to all the evenings and weekends when Mike and Gregory had been in their bedroom – watching them! What the hell?

Alfie pushed back his chair and suddenly stood. He began hunting around his study for the spy camera. It was a wonder the police hadn't found it. They couldn't have done a very good job of searching. He supposed it was too well hidden. He looked along his bookshelf at where the camera could be situated and after a few minutes he found it lodged between some books. He took it down and examined it. It was the size of a button. He switched it off, then crossed to the laptop. There were two blank screens now. The other was for the Roomy-Space. Had the police found their spy camera in the spare room, as well as Alfie's? They'd be in serious trouble if so. His heart sank.

He went to his and Jenny's bedroom, taking the laptop with him so he could see the angle. He found the spy camera lodged into a picture frame. Jesus. Then he went to the bathroom and found the camera in a plant pot. He checked their guest room; there wasn't much in there now. He looked at the smoke detector, the picture frames and a mirror on the wall, but couldn't find anything. He assumed the police had taken it. He now hurried downstairs. He was hot and clammy. What the hell had they been doing? His humiliation and temper flared. How dare they intrude! Were they getting their own back? Teaching him a lesson for what he had done?

Downstairs, he found the spy cameras easily using the angle of each camera lens on the laptop. There was one on the edge of a mirror in the dining room, another just balanced on a picture frame. The last one was tucked inside a table lamp. They had sticky bits of Velcro on them to make them easy to position. He switched them off as he removed them, then checked the laptop. Six blank boxes where the images would have been.

He glanced at his watch. It was nearly time for the boys to return, followed by Jenny. He needed time to think. He went to his study and removed the folder labelled 'Dad' from the laptop, sending the contents to his phone. He then transferred the Mable Crescent folder to his phone too, then returned the laptop to his sons' bedroom. The spy cameras he locked in his desk drawer in the study. Then he sat down and tried to breathe deeply. In and out. What should he do?

If he confronted the boys with what he'd found and asked them what the hell they'd been up to, they'd just turn hostile. If he said nothing and waited, what would happen then? He couldn't imagine.

He thought about everything for some time, then the front door opened and closed as the boys came in, laughing and joking. Were they laughing about him? Jenny wouldn't be long behind them. Should he tell her first? She'd want to confront the boys for sure.

Alfie stayed in his study and gave them time to take off their shoes and go to the kitchen, then he went down.

'Hi, everything OK?' he asked them.

'Sure, Dad,' Mike said. 'You OK?'

It was on the tip of his tongue to start laying into them, but he held back.

'Yes, couldn't be better,' he said.

He watched them saunter off, not a care in the world. I'll show you, you cheeky buggers, he thought.

TWENTY

Alfie went up to his study while the boys went to their bedroom. Little wonder they couldn't wait to get in there when they came home from school, he thought. He waited, expecting noise to erupt, but nothing happened. There were no live feeds now to amuse them. He went onto the landing and heard them whispering from behind their closed door. He hung around and then returned to his study and waited some more.

Jenny came home at her usual time, and he went downstairs to greet her. He'd already decided he wouldn't tell her about the boys' cameras yet. He wanted to find out more first. She was still blaming him for everything that had happened with Emma and Carl. When tomorrow night had been and gone and the police had Carl in custody, then he would tell her everything, and she'd be proud of him.

Jenny was in a reasonably good mood this evening though, and was happy to talk. She asked him how his meeting had gone and he told her, omitting the bit about Mrs Shelby seeing their home on Twitter. He supposed it was ancient history now; there didn't seem to be anything about it on Twitter any more, so why bring it up? Jenny was eager to tell him her own news, that a new piece of legislation was coming into force next year that would affect all schools. It was to do with safety in the toilets.

He listened patiently and made her a cup of tea. She kept talking and he kept listening out for the boys. They'd been up there in their bedroom for over half an hour now. What were they talking about? They must have discovered the live feeds were missing by now, or maybe they hadn't? Mike's laptop had been under a pile of dirty washing, where Alfie had returned it. When did they view the footage of them? Perhaps it was something they only did occasionally in the evening or at weekends? In which case he might have to wait a bit still for them to realize something was wrong.

Jenny continued to chat as they made dinner together. When it was ready he called the boys. They thundered downstairs, always ready for food, and sat at their places at the table. He glanced at them as Jenny served. They seemed normal; perhaps they really hadn't noticed that their recordings had gone. He ate the meal and it turned into a normal family dinner for once, which, despite everything, was nice.

When they'd finished, the boys both stood and returned to their bedroom.

'Homework,' Jenny called after them. 'Before television.'

'Sure, Mum,' Gregory called back.

How much homework they actually did was a matter of contention, Alfie thought.

'Do you think they really do work upstairs?' he asked Jenny as he helped clear away the dinner things.

'Yes, why not?' she said, always protective of her sons. 'They know the importance of schoolwork, and their grades are fine. I've discussed it with them enough times.'

'So you don't think we should check on them from time to time?' Alfie asked tentatively. 'See what exactly they're doing?'

'No, certainly not. You can try if you want to, I suppose. But you have to give them some responsibility at their age.'

She finished tidying the kitchen and went to the table where she took out her laptop. Alfie hovered in the living room, not sure what he should be doing, then went upstairs to his study. As he passed the boys' bedroom door, he could hear that the television was on. He now had an excuse to knock.

Gregory answered the door. 'Hi, Dad.'

'Homework first,' Alfie reminded them, and peered past Gregory into the room. The pile of washing was still there so he assumed Mike's laptop was beneath it. 'Is that dirty washing?' he asked.

Gregory turned to look and nodded.

'We'll bring it down with us later,' he said.

'And turn the television off until you've both done

your homework,' Alfie added. Jenny should be firmer with them, he thought.

Mike had been lounging on his bed watching the television, but he now got up and switched it off.

There was nothing else Alfie could say or do.

'Don't forget your washing,' he said, and came away.

He waited on the landing, but the television didn't go back on so he supposed they'd begun their work. Maybe they did their schoolwork first, before settling down for an evening's entertainment, watching him and Jenny on their recordings? He still couldn't work out why on earth they would want to do that.

Alfie went to his study and whiled away an hour or so, not doing an awful lot. He heard the boys' bedroom door open and one of them go downstairs – presumably for a drink or to raid the fridge. He then heard them come back up again. Tomorrow night would be different, he thought – the sting at the old war memorial. By the time he returned home afterwards they'd still be up. He supposed he'd have to give evidence in court for the part he'd played – recording the murder on his secret camera and then leaving the money at the old war memorial – but that was all in the future.

He wandered around, lost without his laptops, and checked the news on his phone. There was just an old piece appealing for news about Emma, nothing new. At 9.30 Alfie went out and stood on the landing again. The boys' television was back on. He wondered if he should ask if they'd finished their homework but thought better of it.

Jenny came up. She gave a perfunctory knock on the boys' bedroom door and walked in. Alfie had just come out of the bathroom. He heard her ask them if their homework had been done. They must have replied that it had or nodded because she kissed them both goodnight and came out, closing their bedroom door behind her.

'They're good lads,' she said to Alfie, who was still hovering.

He gave a small nod of acceptance. What would she say when she found out the truth? he wondered. The two of them had wired their entire home. It was unforgivable. But he only had himself to blame. He'd set a bad example and now they were following it.

Jenny went downstairs. She had finished her schoolwork now. Alfie joined her, checking the laundry basket on the way. It had the boys' dirty clothes in it. Good, that meant they must have discovered Mike's laptop.

He hadn't received any more messages from Carl about tomorrow night, since he'd sent the email confirming it was on. He wondered if he should email him again to check it was still going ahead. In the end he decided not to. He had an early night but found he couldn't sleep again.

On Wednesday morning, Alfie sprang out of bed. He needed to use the toilet – his insides were in a mess. He was anxious and sat there contemplating the coming evening's events, then he finished, got dressed and went downstairs. Jenny was just leaving and the boys were getting their things together. As soon as they'd left, he went straight to the boys' bedroom. The laptop had gone. He hunted around to see if they'd moved it to a different spot, but he couldn't find it anywhere. He couldn't find Gregory's either and he supposed they'd needed them for school today. What would they say when they found out all their CCTV had gone?

DC Matt Davis phoned mid-morning to check that Alfie knew the arrangements for that evening. He had to go to the police station at 7 p.m., where they'd all be briefed.

'I'm ready,' he said, and he felt it. He was ready to go and do his bit.

He sat at his desk that morning and did a little work using his phone but couldn't really concentrate. He kept standing up and pacing around the room. In the end he got some details wrong and had to phone the owner of the house, very apologetically.

During the afternoon he went for a walk but was back again before the boys or Jenny returned. He was expecting Gregory or Mike to confront him, since by now they must have seen that the CCTV was missing. He waited in the kitchen as they came into the hall. They left their bags by the bottom stair and came through to the kitchen.

'Hi, Dad,' Mike said calmly, and poured himself a drink.

Hadn't they realized what had happened yet?

'Everything OK?' he asked them.

'Yes, thanks, Dad,' Gregory replied, while Mike nodded.

He stood and watched them as they rummaged in the cupboards for a snack. How could they not have checked the laptop either last night or during the day? He waited as they took a snack and disappeared up to their bedroom. Then a horrendous thought occurred to him. Supposing they sometimes watched the feeds at school? His heart clenched. Their friends might have seen him or Jenny naked!

He was halfway up the stairs ready to confront his sons when he stopped. It was 4 p.m. Did he want this confrontation right now? He had enough on his mind, what with the rendezvous tonight. He stood on the stairs, pondering, then came down again and agitatedly waited for Jenny. He suddenly realized she'd mentioned she was going to be late that night so reluctantly he searched the freezer for something to make for dinner. His thoughts were all over the place.

Dinner was ready by the time Jenny came home; she kissed him on the cheek as usual. He'd decided not to say anything tonight about the boys wiring the house; he'd wait until tomorrow. His mind was fully occupied with the sting at the old war memorial.

'I'm meeting a client later, remember,' Alfie reminded Jenny as she ate.

She nodded and got on with her meal.

Alfie had a good reason to eat his meal very quickly. Afterwards, he went upstairs to change and then left the house. He drove to Coleshaw Police Station, his heart pounding with anticipation. He just had to get this out of the way, then he could think about what to say to the boys and Jenny. He walked up the steps to the police station and asked for DC Matt Davis.

'What's it in connection with?' the duty officer asked. Alfie told him.

'Take a seat over there, please,' the officer said, and made a phone call.

Alfie sat down and felt very apprehensive. He rubbed his hands together and kept smoothing his hair. Thankfully, he wasn't kept waiting long before DC Matt Davis appeared.

'You all right?' he asked him, coming over.

'As all right as I'll ever be,' Alfie admitted.

He stood and followed DC Davis through the locked door at the rear of the station and down a corridor that led into a room full of officers – about ten in all.

'Welcome, Mr Watson.' DS Scrivener was at the front, addressing the officers. 'Please sit down.' Was he late? Had they started without him?

He took a seat at the back. Some of the officers turned to look at him and DS Scrivener continued.

'Mr Watson is driving his car tonight to the old war memorial,' he said, by way of an introduction. 'Don't worry. You're not late.' He then went through what was going to happen that evening. Alfie would drive, with an unmarked police car following him, to the old war memorial. He would park in the same place as he had done on Friday. The police car would be out of view. He'd wait until exactly 9 p.m., then deliver the money.

He would return immediately to his car and drive home. 'No hanging around,' DS Scrivener said. Then looking at Alfie, he added, 'We'll contact you tomorrow. Does anyone have any questions?'

Alfie was going to ask if they'd finished with his laptops now, but it didn't seem the right place or time, so he shook his head, as did some of the others. They then spent the next hour getting ready, during which time one of the officers gave him an envelope containing the counterfeit money. At 8 p.m. two unmarked police cars left the police station and at 8.15, Alfie was told to fetch his car and wait for another unmarked police car. One of the officers showed him out via the side entrance. He then got into his car and waited. Presently, a black Ford Focus drew up behind him and flashed its lights. He started his car and pulled away.

Alfie drove steadily, within the speed limit, towards the war memorial. His heart was drumming in his chest. The roads were clear at this time on a Wednesday. He kept glancing in his rear-view mirror at the unmarked police car behind. As far as he could see, there were four officers in it. He supposed the others had left in the other unmarked police cars that had gone earlier.

It was 8.50 when they drew up and parked. He licked his lips and looked around. There was another car where he'd parked before with no one in it. He stopped behind it, hoping he was doing the right thing, and switched off his lights. The police car that had been trailing him overtook. Alfie wondered where it was going. It must have turned around, for he saw it disappear down a country lane, then come back and park down a side road a little way behind him.

He looked around. It was very dark. He couldn't see anyone or any movement. There were some houses with their lights on in the distance. He sat watching the clock as the minutes slowly passed. At exactly 9 p.m., with his palms sweating, he picked up the parcel and left the car. The air was cold; there was definitely an autumnal chill to it now. He went over to the war memorial and looked around. He still couldn't see anyone, so he carefully placed the package beneath the vase, then returned to his car. As instructed, he left immediately, checking the rear-view mirror as he went. Still no sign of anyone. With utter relief, he drove away. He'd done his bit.

TWENTY-ONE

'That was a complete fuck-up!' DS Scrivener said, addressing the three officers in the room. 'No one collected the money and we're no nearer to catching bloody Carl Smith after nearly two weeks!' He paused for effect. No one spoke.

'Forensics have come back this morning, and while they've managed to get DNA from the envelope he licked and sent to Mr Watson, there's no match on the system,' he continued. 'So as far as we're concerned, Carl doesn't have a criminal record. I want you to go back to your desks and check everything you have. Visit Emma's parents again. There must be something we're missing.'

As he finished, a knock sounded on the door. 'Come in,' DS Scrivener yelled gruffly.

A uniformed officer came in.

'Mr Watson is here, sir,' he said. 'He wants to know if he can have his computers back. He says he can't work without them.'

DS Scrivener sighed.

'I'll speak to him,' Beth offered.

'Give him back the one we've finished with,' DS Scrivener said. 'And the iPad.'

'Yes, sir.'

She left the room. It was now Thursday. It would be two weeks on Saturday since the murder and they *were* no nearer to catching Carl, Beth acknowledged, as she went down to the basement to sign out Mr Watson's laptop. Scrivener was right, they must still be missing some vital detail, but what the hell was it? Perhaps it would show itself when they worked through all the files and re-examined everything.

She made her way to the wire cage in the basement that housed people's personal property and signed out the laptop. She went up to the ground floor and through reception. Alfie was sitting in a chair at the front.

'Your laptop and iPad, Mr Watson.' Beth handed them to him. 'We're keeping the other computer for now.'

'Why?' he asked as he signed for it.

'Forensics still have it – they want to look at something,' she replied. 'I'm not sure what it is.'

'So you're no nearer to catching Carl?' Alfie asked. As promised, Beth had phoned him that morning and told him that nothing had resulted from last night, but she didn't have any more details.

She shook her head. 'Has he been in contact with you again?' she asked.

'No. Do you want me to contact him?'

'No point. The email address he's been using doesn't work any more. He's using a VPN, which takes longer to trace.'

'VPN?' Alfie frowned, puzzled.

'Virtual private network,' Beth clarified.

Alfie nodded as though he understood.

'Anyway, I'd better go,' she said. 'We've been told to go back to square one and start again.'

'That doesn't sound hopeful,' Alfie said. 'So you really haven't got any new leads?'

'So it would seem.'

'Let me know if I can be of any help,' Alfie said.

'Will do.'

On the way home, Alfie wondered why they'd kept his other computer but didn't dwell on it for long. He had the most important one back. This was the one he worked on. He supposed he'd get the other one back eventually.

It was 1 p.m. when he arrived home and he went straight to his study where he plugged in the laptop. It sprang into life and he began checking his files. It all looked OK. He got himself a sandwich lunch, which he took up to his desk to eat. He had some files on his phone that he now needed to transfer to the laptop. He continued working for the next two hours. When he heard his sons come home from school, he saved the file he was working on and went downstairs.

'You'll be pleased to know I've got one of my laptops back,' he said proudly.

'Good,' Mike replied, pouring himself a drink. Gregory poured one too.

Alfie had decided to wait until dinnertime to confront them on the matter of their secret cameras, when they'd all be together. If Jenny was there too there'd be some support. With the previous night out of the way, and time passing, he was now feeling more chilled. Yes, the CCTV was cheeky and the boys would be duly punished, but on the scale of things, it could have been a whole lot worse. He had decided that they surely hadn't viewed the recordings at school – they wouldn't do that – and most likely they had just had a bit of fun watching them at home in the evening. He'd tell them off, think of a suitable punishment, and that would be it as far as he was concerned.

Jenny arrived home in a tolerably good mood and had started telling him of a student called Chelsey when he put in about the secret cameras he'd discovered via Mike's laptop. It went down fairly well; Jenny was calm and agreed that Alfie should have a talk with the boys. Then, for the next quarter of an hour, she continued telling him about her day. It seemed Chelsey had been missing school and had been emailing pretending to be a parent, saying she was ill. It was far easier now to fake sick notes, Alfie thought; in his day he'd had to send a handwritten letter with a signature. He nodded, agreed it was terrible, and Jenny got dinner out of the freezer. It was chicken Kiev so not much for him to do tonight. He went up to the study, did a bit of work, and thought about what he was going to say to the boys over dinner.

Jenny called everyone down and as usual the boys arrived first. They came crashing down the stairs, took their plates and sat in their places. They ate ravenously. He wasn't going to create a scene during dinner by raising the topic as they were eating, and the boys knew they had to wait for everyone to finish before they could leave.

Alfie was last to finish his meal; he took his time with the final few mouthfuls and ceremoniously put down his knife and fork. He sat back in his chair. Mike jumped up, ready to go. Gregory was about to follow.

'Can you sit down, please?' Alfie said in his best authoritative voice. 'There's something I want to talk to you about.'

Gregory sat back down while Mike hesitated.

'And you please, Mike.' He looked at them. There was no suggestion that they knew what was coming.

Mike sat on the edge of his chair. Alfie sat more upright and looked from him to Jenny.

Alfie began. 'On Tuesday, I was working from home, which as you know hasn't been easy since losing my laptops. I used my phone for a while, then I remembered that you two had a laptop each. I found yours, Mike, in your bedroom under a pile of washing.' He paused. Still no sign of awareness of the coming revelation. 'I needed to download some files for work and I didn't snoop around. I took your laptop, Mike, into my study and worked for some time. As I did I noticed a file named with this address and eventually I had a look. What do you think I found?'

He stopped and looked at them. The boys were staring at him.

'Dad seems to think I know,' Mike said. 'But I haven't got a clue what he's going on about. What did you find?'

'I found that you, and presumably Gregory too, had wired the whole house with CCTV cameras. I naturally went round each room and gathered together all the cameras.'

'That wasn't us,' Mike said categorically. Jenny was staring at them.

'Of course it was you two,' Alfie snapped. 'Don't be ridiculous. Who else could it be?' His voice had risen slightly at Mike's denial and he was glaring at them now.

'Not me,' Mike replied. 'I'll fetch my laptop, shall I?'

'Not me either,' Gregory added.

Jenny was looking at Alfie in a manner that said he had better be right.

'Go on then,' Alfie said. 'Fetch your laptop.'

Mike gave an indifferent shrug as he left the table and went up to his room. He was quick – he wouldn't have had any time to delete the folder before he came downstairs again, straight into the room. He set up the laptop on the table and opened the lid. It sprang into life. There was no folder marked with their address. Alfie hunted around to see if they'd renamed it.

'You've deleted it,' Alfie accused him. 'Anyway, I still have a copy on my phone.'

He took his phone from his pocket and scrolled through. There was no file marked with their address. With growing agitation, he continued looking for it and then looked up at his family, bemused. Without speaking, he stood and went upstairs to where the five spy cameras were in his desk drawer. He opened the drawer. They'd all gone. He came running downstairs two at a time.

'I locked the cameras in my desk drawer and now they've gone! Where are they?' he demanded of the boys.

'I honestly don't know what you're talking about,' Mike said with an air of nonchalance that upset Alfie even more.

Alfie glared at him. 'You've taken them! It couldn't have been anybody else.'

'I'm sorry, Mum,' Mike said. 'I don't know anything about spy cameras. I thought it was Dad who had the problem with spying.'

'They were here, you silly arse, but I found the others,' Alfie spat.

'Alfie!' Jenny exclaimed. 'Don't talk to your sons like that.'

Alfie was seething. 'You would too if you knew what they'd been up to. Someone must have been in my desk drawer. Which one of you was it?'

He stared at Mike and Gregory. He was very angry now, enraged.

'Well? Which one of you was it?' he asked again when neither of them replied. 'I'll search your bedroom if you don't own up to it.'

Neither boy moved or answered. Mike gave a small shrug. Alfie jumped up and ran upstairs into his sons' bedroom. He began searching it, turning it over for the spy cameras. Mike and Gregory sat with their mother at the table in the room below.

After about ten minutes, Alfie had to concede defeat. The cameras were nowhere to be found.

Alfie spent the whole evening in his study, feeling annoyed. He was very disappointed with his sons and no longer trusted them. When trust was broken it was very difficult to repair. He'd hoped he'd brought them up to be honest and truthful. They should have just admitted their wrongdoing, received the telling-off he'd planned, and then they would have all moved on with their lives. Instead, they'd deleted the folder on Mike's laptop, they'd deleted the files on Alfie's phone – he must have left it lying around – and they'd disposed of the spy cameras. But how had they known where to find them? Alfie wondered. They hardly ever went to his study. It was in the attic. And how did they know the folder had been sent to his phone? He supposed the file left a trace of some sort on Mike's laptop?

At one point he stood and went to his sons' bedroom door, ready to have it out with them. But then he didn't know what else he'd say other than what he'd already said, so, feeling defeated, he returned to his study. The whole house simmered with the unpleasant odour of a family out of step with each other, and it hurt.

Jenny came up at 9.30 and knocked on his door. 'It's me, can I come in?' she asked quietly.

'Of course, come in,' he replied.

She slowly opened the door and then gingerly entered

the room. Alfie was sitting at his desk looking very down and Jenny sat in the spare chair opposite him.

'I know you're upset,' she said. 'But don't take it so harshly. I'm sure the boys didn't mean anything by it.'

'Mean anything,' Alfie repeated.

'I know they look almost like adults, but they're not really. They're still kids and they're worried that you've taken it so badly.'

'Have they confessed?' he asked.

'Not exactly, but I'm sure they will in time.'

She stayed and talked to him for a while longer, offering platitudes, then left to get ready for bed.

TWENTY-TWO

Chloe McNeal, the family liaison officer for the Arnolds, was having a frustrating time of it. Although the police had told Mr and Mrs Arnold about Alfie's recording, there was no more news. It was nearly two weeks since Emma Arnold had disappeared and a week since the police had received the tape from Alfie showing their daughter's death. Mrs Arnold was still beside herself with grief and burst into tears at any mention of her daughter's name. All Chloe could do was put her arm around her and make her a cup of tea. Mr Arnold had gone to work for the morning.

'Supposing we don't ever find our beautiful daughter?' Mrs Arnold cried helplessly.

'I'm sure we will in time,' Chloe said.

In fact, that morning Chloe had been talking to her own daughter, Teddy, who was in the same class as Mike Watson at school. They'd just finished breakfast and Teddy had said that some of the kids in the class thought the Watson lads might know something.

'What did they say?' Chloe had asked.

'I don't know, really,' Teddy said evasively, and finished her glass of juice.

'You must have some idea, love. Can't you tell me, please? Anything. It would help Mrs Arnold.'

'There was a lot of talk yesterday that Mike and Gregory knew more than they were letting on about Emma. That's all I know. I shouldn't have said anything.'

'In what way?' Chloe had asked.

'Just things. Chatter, you know how it is.' She'd picked up her school bag, ready to leave.

'And that's it?'

She'd nodded.

'Do you want a lift to school?' Chloe had asked.

'No, I'll get the bus. I'm meeting someone.'

'OK, see you later.'

They'd kissed goodbye and she'd left.

It was probably nothing, Chloe had thought, as she'd finished getting ready. Of course the boys were acting oddly. It must be pretty dismal for them at home at the moment. A chance word, some overheard chatter – it would all add up to a perfect storm. Chloe pushed the thought from her mind as she left the house, returning a phone call as she went. Now, she was sitting with Mrs Arnold doling out meagre words of sympathy that in the end meant nothing at all. Mrs Arnold just wanted her daughter back.

She waited until Mr Arnold returned at midday before she stood to leave. She had to repeat to him what she'd told Mrs Arnold about the investigation, because Mrs Arnold wasn't in any fit state to take in what she was saying.

Later that day, Chloe arrived at the police station in Coleshaw and went to see DS Scrivener. What Teddy had said was playing on her mind and she wanted to sound him out.

'Sir, how well do you know Mike and Gregory Watson?' she asked him.

'I don't. Not at all. Why?'

'My daughter, Teddy, is in the same class as Mike and said there was a lot of talk going on yesterday that the boys might know something about Emma. She didn't know what, and it could be playground gossip. You know how these schools work.'

'Did she say anything specific?' he asked.

'No, I asked her and she just brushed it off. I have the feeling she knows more than she's letting on, though. It was obviously newsworthy enough for her to bring it up with me, and she knows I'm involved with the case.'

'I see. Do you think it's worth a follow-up visit to the school?' he asked.

'I'm not sure,' Chloe admitted.

'We haven't got any leads at the moment, so it can't hurt. I'll ask Beth to go.'

Chloe nodded. 'But do it subtly,' she suggested.

'Yes.' Subtly wasn't his strong point. 'Leave it with me,' he said.

Beth was sitting at her desk concentrating on her

computer screen. It was 1.30 p.m. She stopped what she was doing to look at DS Scrivener.

'What do you know about the school that Emma Arnold attended?' he asked her. 'You and Matt visited.'

'Not much, sir. It wasn't a long visit and nothing came from it. We spoke to Emma's class, then to a girl, Lorie Philips. She said she wouldn't be surprised if Emma was at home hiding, because her parents were very strict, but we've discounted that.'

'Did Mike Watson make himself known?'

'No. We didn't take a register. And the Watson family weren't on the radar then.'

DS Scrivener looked thoughtful. 'What are you working on right now?'

She told him.

'I want you to go to the school and quietly speak to both Watson boys, separately. Keep it subtle. Use an unmarked police car and park around the corner. Their mother is a teacher at a different school.'

'Yes, sir. What am I looking for?'

'Anything they may know. You'd better get a move on. Schools finish at 3.30. But do make sure to see the boys separately.'

Half an hour later, Beth parked the police car in a side road near the school and got out. She'd phoned ahead and left a message at reception saying she needed to speak to both the Watson boys separately. The Head hadn't been free, and the receptionist said she'd pass on the message. Beth now made her way into reception, where she gave her name to the woman there.

'Just a moment,' the receptionist said, and left her to make a phone call.

Almost immediately the Head came along the corridor.

'I got your message, but you know if you're here to interview the Watson lads you need an appropriate adult present.'

'It's not an interview, more a chat,' Beth said.

The Head paused and looked thoughtful.

'What's it about?' she asked.

'We're still gathering information about Emma Arnold,' Beth said.

The Head nodded and showed Beth up a flight of stairs to her room.

'You can use my room for now. I'll get Mike first, shall I?'

'Thank you,' Beth said.

She sat down and pulled the other chair over so it was opposite hers. Beth gazed around. The room was full of paperwork and books. She'd been here before, some years ago. It was a different Head now. A few minutes later the door opened and Mike Watson came in.

'Shall I stay?' the Head asked.

'No, thank you,' Beth said. Then to Mike, 'Hi. Take a seat.'

'I'm in the room next door if you need me,' the Head said. 'Knock when you've finished.'

Mike sat down. He was a tall, wiry lad whose arms and legs didn't know if they'd finished growing yet. He also looked very anxious – from having to meet CID, Beth assumed.

'It's nothing to worry about,' she said with a smile. 'I just want to ask you a few questions.'

He gave a stiff nod.

'This is a nice school, isn't it?' she began.

Another stiff nod.

'What's your home life been like,' she asked, 'since all this started?'

He shifted uncomfortably, then said, 'It's been OK.'

'You're living in the same house as your father. There must have been a strange atmosphere there with the police ransacking the place and everything.'

'I guess,' he said.

'Tell me about life in the Watson household,' Beth tried again.

'It's normal really,' he said with a shrug.

'I'm not sure what normal is,' Beth said, and paused. There was no response. 'What do you and Gregory like to do in your spare time?' she asked.

'Dunno, really. Watch television, do our homework, I suppose. Sometimes we game,' he said.

'Anything else?'

'Not really.'

'Do you have a laptop, Mike?' she asked.

'Yes. Everyone in school does.'

'Is it with you now?'

'No, it's at home.'

Beth nodded and took a moment. 'It's very sad about

Emma, isn't it?'

'Yes, it is,' he said.

'Is there anything you can tell me that would help us find Carl, or find Emma's body? Even if it's quite small.'

A brief pause before Mike shook his head.

'Nothing? Are you sure?'

'Yes.'

'Does anyone else in your class know anything that might help us? It's very important.'

'No,' he replied.

'Thank you for your time, Mike. Here's my card.'

'Is that it?' he asked, accepting the business card.

'Yes. Why?'

'I thought—' he began, then stopped.

'You thought what, Mike?'

'Nothing,' he said, and stood to go.

Beth gave another cheerful smile and showed him out. He disappeared down the corridor as if Satan was after him. He knew more than he was telling, for sure, Beth thought. The Head heard movement from the room next door and came out.

'Is everything all right?' she asked, coming into her study.

'Yes, thank you. I'll speak to Gregory now,' Beth said.

Presently Gregory came in, a smaller version of his older brother.

'Hi, love. Sit down. How are you?' Beth said.

'OK.'

'I've just spoken to your brother and now I'd like to

hear from you. What can you tell me about life in the Watson household?'

He shrugged. 'I don't know what you mean,' he said defensively.

'Well, is it good?'

'Yes. Generally.'

'What isn't so good?'

'When I get told off,' he said.

'And what do you get told off about?'

'Not keeping our room tidy,' he replied.

She nodded. 'What do you like to do in your spare time?'

'Play in our bedroom.'

'At what?'

'Games, and we watch television after we've done our homework.'

'Do you have a laptop?' she asked.

'Yes.'

'Is it with you?'

'No, it's at home.'

'What do you do on it?'

'Schoolwork,' he said.

'I was talking to your brother about Emma Arnold.' She paused, because Gregory was looking away now, refusing to meet her gaze. 'Have you heard anything about what happened to her?' Beth asked.

He didn't reply.

'Do you know where Carl is?'

'No.'

'Does someone in Mike's class know?' she asked him.

'I don't know,' he said, and shifted in his seat.

'You know we'll find him eventually, and withholding information is a serious offence.'

This lad was holding back on something. She looked at him and waited. For a second it seemed like he might say something, but he clearly decided against it.

'I'll tell you what, you have a good think about what you know and give me a ring,' she said. 'Here's my business card.' She handed it to him. 'OK. You can go.'

Gregory stood and quickly left the room. Beth stood too. She thanked the Head on her way out and returned to her car.

She drove back to Coleshaw Police Station, deep in thought. The boys knew something about Emma's murder, without a doubt. But what was it? She'd give them both time to think and then try again.

When she arrived at the station, she relayed the conversations she'd had with the Watson lads to DS Scrivener.

'I suggest you take a look at their social media accounts. See what that turns up.'

Beth spent the next hour or so on Facebook and TikTok, the only social media accounts the boys held, but other than references to Emma being missing there was nothing of any significance. Beth decided to phone Chloe to ask her if she could try to get some more information from her daughter, Teddy.

'I'll try,' Chloe said. 'But she's not giving much away at the moment.'

'Perhaps the class is running scared, as there's been a murder in their midst,' Beth suggested.

'I'll try her again this evening and give you a ring.'

Later that night, Chloe called Beth's mobile and said there was nothing to report. Teddy had said again that there was some talk yesterday of Mike and Gregory knowing more than they were letting on, but she wouldn't say anything else.

TWENTY-THREE

Alfie sat at home with his head in his hands, unsure of what he should do. He'd spent the day in his study until Jenny had returned home. She was furious when she got in and he felt annoyed too. It seemed DC Beth Mayes had gone to the boys' school that afternoon and interviewed them separately in the Head's room. Jenny had received a message at school informing her of it, so she had come home early from work. The boys had come in and gone straight to their rooms, but that wasn't unusual. Jenny had called them down again almost straight away and they had told them all about DC Mayes's visit.

Jenny went ape and said she was going to phone the CID after she'd spoken to the school. Wasn't it illegal to question minors without an appropriate adult present? Alfie felt even sadder than he already was, and even more unsure of what he should do now. If he called the police and told them about his sons' spy cameras, they could have them both in again for even more questioning.

The boys fled to their rooms and Alfie went upstairs to have a shower as Jenny picked up the phone.

She was put through to Ms Clements and asked her what the hell she was doing.

'I can assure you that the correct rules were followed,' Ms Clements said, when she was able to get a word in. 'I was in the room next door and I could hear every word DC Mayes said. It wasn't an interview, more like an informal chat. It didn't last long.'

'I don't care how long it lasted. My boys are not to be questioned by the CID in your school again. Do I make myself clear?'

'Perfectly. I'm sorry if you felt it wasn't appropriate.' She paused. 'On another matter, the boys have had quite a bit of time off in the last two weeks. I know you've emailed in, but I thought I'd check with you to make sure everything was OK.'

'Which days?' Jenny asked, puzzled.

'Just a minute.' Jenny waited, hearing the Head tapping the keys on her computer. 'Wednesday and Thursday last week and Tuesday this week.'

Jenny thought. She'd left the house before the boys on those days, but Alfie would have said if they'd had time off together. 'That's correct,' she said, wanting to protect them.

'I thought I'd check because they were both off together and they don't usually have time off school.'

'It was a sickness and diarrhoea bug,' Jenny said tightly. 'We all caught it. It came back again.'

'All right, I'll make a note.'

Jenny ended the phone call more subdued than she'd begun it. Three days off in the last two weeks! She called up to Alfie. He didn't hear her so she went up to the bathroom. She knocked and went in. He was out of the shower and dressed.

'Have the boys had any time off school in the last two weeks?' she asked him.

'No, not that I know of. Why?'

'The Head said they'd had three days off in the last two weeks.'

'Must be mistaken,' he replied.

'No, she wasn't. She said it was Wednesday and Thursday last week, and Tuesday this week. I lied for them because I don't want them getting into trouble, but I'll speak to them about it. I knew they'd get in with a bad lot. And on top of everything else!'

Jenny now phoned Coleshaw CID where she asked to speak to DC Mayes. She was put through, but a male voice answered.

'DC Matt Davis,' he said.

'I want to speak to DC Beth Mayes,' Jenny said.

'I'm afraid she's out at the moment. Can I help you?'

'I don't know. It's about the interview she conducted with my sons this afternoon.'

'What about it?' he asked.

'She had no right to do it without an appropriate adult present. And I want to know what was said.'

'My understanding is that they weren't formal

187

interviews,' he said.

'And you were there?'

'Well, no.'

'Ask her to phone me as soon as she gets back,' Jenny said, and ended the call.

Incensed, she hung up, waited for half an hour, then phoned again, only to be told that DC Mayes was still out and likely to be so for the rest of the day.

Frustrated, Jenny called the boys down from their bedroom. 'I've spoken to your Head,' she said. 'I don't believe you should have been questioned without another adult present. Let me know if they try to do anything like that again, please.'

Both boys nodded and were about to continue to their bedroom when Jenny added: 'And what's all this about the time you've both had off school?'

They looked at each other and Gregory said, 'I don't know, Mum.'

'Yes, you do. You were both off school together on Tuesday this week and Wednesday and Thursday last week.'

She waited, hands on her hips.

'Sorry, it won't happen again,' Mike said.

'Whatever made you take three days off?' she asked, astounded. She thought she'd taught them the value of a good education.

They looked at each other and then Mike replied. 'It was silly, really. We got away with it once and so we tried it again. Some of the other kids do it all the time. But we won't do it again, I promise.'

'Where did you go?' she asked.

'To the shopping centre, mainly,' Mike replied.

She continued looking at them, trying to gauge if they were telling the truth. It had been a lot easier to know when they were little. After a few moments she decided to give them the benefit of the doubt.

'And those are the only days you've had off?' she asked them.

'Yes, Mum.'

'Don't do it again or there'll be serious consequences,' she said. 'And can we talk more about why the CID wanted to talk to you both?'

'We told you – to find out what life was like at home. I said it was fine,' Mike said.

'What about you, Gregory?'

'The same,' he said.

'OK, let's leave it there for now, then. Dinner isn't ready yet. Find something to do.'

The boys went up to their bedroom and closed the door.

'Now what?' Gregory asked angrily. 'What are we supposed to do? I think we should tell Mum what we've done. It's not right.'

'No. We'll go on as normal.'

'But how long can we keep this up?'

'For as long as is necessary,' Mike said.

TWENTY-FOUR

The following morning, Mike and Gregory were up and dressed by 9 a.m. They seemed to be talking intensely about something in low voices. Alfie joined them for breakfast and tried to make conversation, with very little success. Jenny was having a lie-in. She was entitled to it on a Saturday, after getting up early the rest of the week. Alfie asked the boys where they were going so early.

'Shopping,' Mike said. 'Beat the crowds. It was very busy when we went last weekend.' He finished the last of his cereal.

'Do you want a lift into town?' Alfie asked, wanting to feel useful.

'No, it's OK,' Mike said.

Alfie waited by the front door to see them off, then made Jenny a cup of tea, which he took up to her. She was on her side, dozing, eyes closed, and moaned a little when he set the cup on the bedside cabinet.

'I've made you a tea, darling,' he said, and left her to drink it.

He then got dressed, wondering what the boys wanted to buy from the shops that was so important.

The boys were both pleased and apprehensive to be out of the house. They walked to the bus stop at the end of their road where they waited for a bus. They stopped talking the moment a woman joined them and then said nothing for another five minutes. When the bus arrived they got on, showing their passes. They didn't say much during the journey in case someone overheard them. Mike made a comment about Liverpool playing Newcastle and Gregory agreed. They were just two young lads out for the day. After a while they put their earpieces in and listened to their music for the rest of the journey. Half an hour later, they got off and changed buses.

The boys gazed out of the window as the second bus left town. It made its way through a much older area of residential housing, twisting through the streets. Then, after about ten minutes, the bus entered what looked like a building site with crumbling houses and a row of old shops – none of which were still in business. They were all boarded up. In fact, most of the houses were boarded up too. The area, about a square mile, was part of a massive regeneration programme. The few who still lived in the houses were waiting to be rehomed. The bus only stopped intermittently when someone wanted to get off. When Mike and Gregory pressed the bell there was only one other woman left on the bus. The driver looked at them with pity as they got off. They guessed he felt sorry for them, having to live in an area like this.

Mike and Gregory took out their earpieces and walked in silence through the semi-derelict streets. No new buildings yet. The council needed to clear the area first before they could start to rebuild. A solitary child could be seen playing at the far end of a mostly abandoned street, bouncing a ball against a wall. Mike and Gregory turned left into Bulwarks Road. It was Number 27 they wanted, halfway along. This house wasn't boarded up like both its neighbours, but even so, something said it wasn't lived in. To a passer-by it was just another Victorian terraced house that had been earmarked for demolition. This was the address they had come to on the three days they'd skipped school.

Mike looked up and down the street – no one was around – then he banged on the door. It was no good pressing the bell – that was broken. Gregory stood close beside him, nervously keeping watch. After a while Mike took out his phone and dialled. 'It's us,' he said, when the other person answered.

Even then it took a few moments for the door to be opened, by none other than Carl Smith, looking agitated and anxious.

'She's still saying she's changed her mind and wants to go home,' he said.

'Well, she can't, not yet,' Mike replied brusquely, going in.

He quickly closed the front door and the three of them

stood in the dim hall.

'What are we going to do?' Carl asked. 'This was your idea. You've got us into this mess so now you need to get us out.'

'Emma was supposed to be fully involved,' Mike said. 'She was up for it.'

'Well, she's not any more,' Carl said.

'We could just let her go,' Gregory suggested.

'And what do you think she's going to tell her parents?' Carl demanded. 'That this was a joke that went horribly wrong?'

The boys remained standing in the hall, glaring at each other. The wallpaper was peeling off and the only sunlight filtered through a pane of pink frosted glass above the main entrance. A musty, shut-up smell pervaded the air as if the place had been abandoned, which it had been for three months, when Carl's gran had moved out. She'd taken what she'd needed and had left the rest for the council to deal with. There was no heating and very little lighting, which they couldn't put on after dark in case someone saw. A faded and damp-stained net curtain covered the front window downstairs. In just three months, the whole place had started to smell of decay.

'We've been caught out at school,' Mike said grimly. 'We can only come here at weekends now.'

'Shit, that's all we need!' Carl said. 'Have you brought her some food? She's starving.'

Mike took a bundle from his pocket and passed it to

Carl. He and Gregory followed Carl upstairs and into the back bedroom. Emma sat in the middle of the room, tied to a chair, a gag over her mouth. Her eyes cried out to them, imploring them for mercy.

'What's with the gag?' Mike asked, going to her.

'She kept shouting that she wanted to go,' Carl said, agitated. 'I was worried someone outside might hear.'

Mike took off the gag.

'You won't cry any more?' he asked her.

She shook her head. 'Please let me go. I won't say anything. I promise. Please.'

He untied her hands, but left her feet tied to the chair.

'Here's your food,' Carl said, and he gave her what Mike had brought from breakfast. She began to eat ravenously.

'Come outside, Mike,' Carl said. 'You can stay with her,' he told Gregory.

They came out and Carl closed the door.

'So what are we going to do about this?' Carl asked. 'We set this up to teach Emma's parents a lesson for being too strict, and your father for spying on your guests, but it's all got seriously out of hand.'

'I have no idea,' Mike said.

Mike ran his hands through his hair and began pacing the small, narrow hall.

'I don't know either. But I've had enough,' Carl said, his voice rising. 'I'm fed up with coming in day after day, sometimes staying the night. I've had a gut full. My gran wonders where I keep going – just as well she has dementia.'

'I'm doing what I can,' Mike snapped. 'It's not easy for us either, you know?'

'I don't care. I've got things to do. You can take over,' Carl said. 'You need to untie her legs so she can go to the toilet. But make sure she's tied up again before you leave. I need a break.'

'When will you be back?' Mike asked, desperation in his voice.

'I don't know. I'm not sure I'll be coming back at all. Bye, Emma!' he shouted and ran downstairs. Mike followed.

'You've got to come back tonight,' Mike cried as Carl opened the door.

'Not sure. I've got stuff to do. This has all gone so bloody wrong.'

And he left, slamming the door behind him.

Mike stood in the hall, stunned. Carl would return tonight, wouldn't he? He stared at the front door, and it crossed his mind to run after Carl, but he let that thought go. He'd never get him to change his mind right now. He had been going out with Emma for a while, but now it seemed like he'd had enough of her. Mike's heart was racing; he felt hot and clammy. Now what? What were they supposed to do? This had all gone horribly wrong.

After a moment, he turned and trod slowly upstairs, feeling very tired. This had gone on for too long, far longer than they had intended, and now it had backfired. He went into the bedroom Emma was using.

'I need to speak to you,' he said to Gregory.

'What's happened?' Emma asked.

'Never you mind.'

Gregory came outside the door.

'Carl's had enough,' Mike said. 'He said he's not coming back.'

'What?' Gregory cried in dismay. 'Oh shit. What are we going to do?'

'I don't know. Perhaps he'll change his mind.'

'Do you think he will?' Gregory asked.

'I said I don't know.'

'Mike, Gregory!' Emma called from inside the room.

They went in.

'I need to use the toilet,' she said.

Mike went over and untied her feet. She stood. She was starting to smell. She hadn't had a bath in hot water for two weeks. There was only cold water in the building. Mike stood back as she went to the bathroom and pushed the door to. The lock had long since broken. He waited outside while she went to the loo and then washed her hands in cold water. A small, pathetic gesture amid so much chaos. When she came out Mike asked her, 'Do you want to walk around first before you sit down again?'

'Yes. I want you to let me go.'

That wasn't an option. Mike watched her as she walked slowly around the upstairs rooms, stretching her legs and arms. In and out of the other single bedroom where Carl's clothes were on the chair. He would come back, he had to. Emma had lost weight, Mike thought.

She was skinnier than she had been. What were they going to do with her?

She stopped walking and turned to him.

'Will you tell my parents I'm alive, please?' she said. 'I wasn't supposed to have been gone this long.'

'I can't,' Mike said helplessly.

'Please. Carl wouldn't tell them. But I've been sitting here thinking, and they need to know I'm still alive.'

'Mike … I think she's right. Maybe we do need to tell Emma's parents she's OK. Even if we do it anonymously, and don't tell them where she is,' Gregory said.

'I'll think about it,' Mike said, deep in thought.

Emma paused at the top of the stairs and looked down.

'Tell them I'm sorry,' she said. 'You don't even have to see them. Just write down that I'm OK on a piece of paper and push it through their letterbox.'

'I said I'll think about it,' Mike said, and told her to go into her bedroom. He and Gregory were still on the landing. She went in.

'What are we going to do?' Gregory asked as soon as he'd closed the door.

'I don't know,' Mike returned. 'Let's hope that Carl comes back tonight, because one thing's for certain, we can't stay here all night.'

'Gregory! Mike!' Emma called from inside the room. She was playing up. 'Can I have a tissue, please? I think I'm getting ill.'

They went into the room and Mike passed her a tissue. She certainly didn't look well, but then wouldn't anyone

197

shut in a place like this for two weeks? No wonder she wanted out.

'Can we get you something from home?' Gregory asked her.

'Yes, please. Do you have any Lemsip?'

'We'll bring you some back,' Mike said.

He looked at the time on his phone. It was only just gone twelve. They could go to a chemist, buy what she needed and then bring the medicine back, rather than going all the way home.

'Do you need anything else?' he asked her. 'We could go to a chemist now.'

'Only for my parents to know,' she said. 'I think they've learnt their lesson.'

Mike nodded. She seemed very different from the girl who never did what her parents asked and had been flaunting herself on social media. He'd seen comments on there about her when she went missing, and some of them weren't very complimentary.

As Gregory watched, Mike tied her feet and then her hands.

'Carl left me untied,' she said as Mike worked.

'Well, Carl's not here now,' Mike said. 'If I leave you untied, you'll be off. You asked for some Lemsip and we're going to get it, along with some more food. You'll be fine for a while until we think what to do.'

He began to tie the gag back on.

'Do you need to do that?' Gregory asked.

Mike hesitated and then left it off. He checked her

bindings and then, together, he and Gregory walked to the door.

'We won't be long!' Gregory called to Emma.

On the way out of the house, Mike tried to phone Carl, but as expected it went through to voicemail. It was a burner phone and he was keeping it switched off to avoid it being detected by the police. He didn't leave a message. When he turned the phone on Carl would see who had phoned and would guess what he was going to say.

'He'll get back on board,' Mike said as he and Gregory left the house and made their way to the deserted bus stop.

'What if he doesn't?' Gregory asked, worried. 'What if he's gone for good?'

'Don't be stupid,' Mike snapped. 'He must just be worried about what to do with Emma, like us. I think we should ask Dad for some more money.' Gregory looked at Mike, astounded. 'I know we didn't get it last time, but the first time went to plan. We got those games we've been wanting.'

'But what about the police?' Gregory said, still shocked.

'They only got involved because Dad told them that Carl had written to him. I've been thinking, and if we tell him not to tell the police I don't think he will. We'll make it clear that our lives will be in danger if he tells, and his will be too. What do you think?' he asked Gregory.

'I don't know. This was never supposed to be about money. We just wanted to teach Emma's parents and Dad a lesson,' he said. After a pause, he asked, 'What's Dad doing now?'

Mike took out his phone and clicked on the icon that allowed them to watch their father. They both peered at the screen. Alfie's phone was standing upright in its holder on the desk and they could see him through the lens.

'He's working, or at least pretending to,' Mike said.

Just at that moment, a bus came into view and they put away the phone. They got on and went right down to the back. They were the only ones on board.

'I think we should ask for some more money.'

'Why?'

'We could offer some to Carl to come back and look after Emma,' Mike said, under his breath. 'A reasonable amount, say seven thousand pounds.'

'Dad hasn't got that much!' Gregory exclaimed.

'Keep your voice down,' Mike hissed. They both looked at the driver, who was fortunately concentrating on the road. 'Yes, he has,' Mike said. 'I've watched him do his online banking. He has over ten thousand pounds in his current account. The alternative is that we just keep helping ourselves a bit at a time.'

'But won't he suspect?'

'He hasn't so far,' Mike said.

TWENTY-FIVE

Mike and Gregory were in town longer than they'd anticipated and it was nearly five o'clock by the time they got off the bus again in Bulwarks Road. They'd bought some Lemsip and food, and had then gone into a gaming shop where the time had slipped by, as they tried out various games. They still had a good chunk of the money their father had inadvertently 'gifted' to them. Then, at just gone 4, they'd got on the bus and it had taken nearly an hour to get there.

There was no one else in Bulwarks Road and they walked quickly to Number 27. It was only when they got to the front door that Mike realized he didn't have a door key.

'Oh shit. Hopefully Carl will be back by now,' Mike said.

He knocked on the door. No one answered. He tried again, with the same result. 'Shit,' he said again. He tried phoning Carl but it went through to his voicemail.

He stepped back and looked up at the front of the building. There was no way they could get in. All the windows were tightly closed.

'Come on, we'll have to go round the back,' he said, and headed up the street.

They went to the end of the row of terraced houses and then around the rear. Most of the houses were vacant. They turned left into a narrow alleyway full of rubbish that people moving out didn't want. As they approached Number 27 they heard Emma screaming.

'We left her gag off,' Gregory said.

They ran to the tall wooden gate at the rear of the yard. It was broken; the latch was off. They heaved it open and then crossed the small yard, which was littered with more rubbish. At the rear of the house there was a metal-framed fan-like window in what had been the kitchen. It was partly open and wouldn't close properly. Mike pulled over some old tin cans that had been used for car engine oil. He stood on one of them and, reaching in, forced the window open. He reached further in and opened the window next to it, then clambered inside. Once in the kitchen, he unlocked the back door for Gregory. The key was still in the lock, so he locked the door after them, putting the key in his pocket.

Emma was still screaming as they ran upstairs and into the rear bedroom.

'What's the matter?' Mike shouted, going to her.

She stopped screaming the moment she saw them. Her face was bright red, and her cheeks stained with tears.

'I thought you'd left me,' she stammered. 'I thought the noise I could hear was someone breaking in and I would be raped.'

'Has Carl been back?' Mike asked.

'No.' She was crying again. This time more quietly, with silent tears running down her cheeks.

Gregory looked at his older brother for help.

'I'm ill,' Emma said. 'Did you get the medication?'

'Yes, here it is. Sorry we're late,' Gregory said.

He took the packet of Lemsip from the bag, then went to the bathroom for some water.

'She'll need her hands untied,' he said on returning.

'You do it. I'm trying to get hold of Carl,' Mike said.

Gregory put down the mug of Lemsip, went round the back of the chair and gently untied Emma's hands.

'Thank you,' she said quietly, and began to drink the fluid.

There were beads of perspiration on her forehead – from all the crying or from illness? Gregory touched her forehead. It was burning hot.

'She's got a temperature,' he said, worried, to Mike.

'I really don't feel well,' she said.

'The Lemsip will help,' Mike said. He was still trying to contact Carl, and now left a message.

'What time are you heading back?' he asked down the speaker. Then added, 'Sorry, mate.' And ended the call.

'Dad's been texting,' he said, still looking at his phone. 'He wants to know what time we'll be back.'

'He's messaged my phone too,' Gregory said.

203

'Don't reply,' Mike said. 'We've got to work out what to do here first.'

They both looked at Emma, who was sipping her drink. Her legs were still tied to the chair.

'Do you have a change of clothes with you?' Mike asked her.

'No,' she said.

'We could have got her something today,' Gregory said.

'Tomorrow,' Mike replied absently, and continued to look nervously at his phone.

Emma finished her drink and Gregory gave her the sandwiches. She ate slowly, just one, and put the other one on the floor.

'Aren't you going to eat that?' Gregory asked.

She shook her head. 'Can I have another drink, please?'

Gregory filled the cup with water and gave it to her. She really did look ill.

'Carl used to bring a flask of tea,' she said.

'We can do that tomorrow,' Gregory replied.

'And he untied my legs as well as my arms.'

'Shall I untie her legs?' Gregory asked Mike.

Mike looked over and nodded, then returned to his phone.

Gregory knelt down and began untying her legs. Just as he finished, she gave him a hefty push and ran out of the door and downstairs. They were after her in seconds and caught up with her as she tried to get out of the front door. Mike had put the latch down. He grabbed her.

'I want to go home. Please, let me go home, please. I won't tell anyone what happened, I promise. Just let me go.'

Mike, the bigger of the two, picked her up and carried her, sobbing, upstairs and into her room, where he sat her on the chair.

'Stay there, please!' he said. 'Or I'll have to tie you up and gag you again.'

Gregory looked on helplessly. 'You mustn't try to run away,' he said.

'What are you going to do?' she asked, fresh tears forming.

'I don't know,' Mike said, looking as helpless as Emma did.

His phone rang. 'It's Dad. I'd better take it. Can you keep her quiet for a bit?' he asked Gregory. 'Hi, Dad … Yes, sure … We've just left the gaming shop. We're on our way back now.'

Emma suddenly cried, 'Help me, Mr Watson!'

Mike hung up as Gregory quickly put his hand over her mouth.

'That's the last time I trust you,' Mike said to her angrily.

He quickly phoned Carl again and left another message. 'Call me back now.' He was panicking and he knew it.

Emma quietened down and the three of them sat in the room as the natural light began to fail. It turned 6.45. Mike switched on the small lamp, hoping it wouldn't be seen from outside. It gave enough of a glow to illuminate the immediate vicinity but no more. The near-night sky peered in through the curtainless window. There'd been nothing from Carl, but their father was calling again. Mike texted, *Back soon.*

They sat waiting for another hour with the vague hope that Carl would return, then Mike began to tie Emma up again. She didn't struggle; the fight had gone out of her.

'Do you want anything before we go?' Gregory asked her. He didn't want to go and leave her, but he couldn't think what else they could do.

She stared back at him, her wide eyes frightened.

'We'll come back tomorrow,' Mike reassured her. 'Just stay where you are and you'll be all right.'

They had to go. With a final glance over their shoulder, they left the house by the front stairs.

It was completely dark outside now. The boys walked in silence to the bus stop in the next road. They passed two other houses that were occupied, with their front-room lights on. The place was even worse at night.

'What are we going to do?' Gregory asked as they waited for the bus. He pulled his jacket closer. It was a chilly but dry night.

Mike shrugged. 'If we don't hear from Carl tonight, we'll come back tomorrow, and have a chat with her. We'll have to think of an excuse to give Mum and Dad.'

'But what happens on Monday?' Gregory asked, dismayed. 'We can't come back then. This has all gone on way too long.' He looked at Mike in desperation.

'Carl will be back by then,' Mike said.

'What if he's not?' Gregory persisted. 'We're already in trouble at school for non-attendance, but we can't leave Emma alone all day.'

Mike was checking his phone again – it had buzzed with a message.

I'm not coming back. You can deal with her, Carl had written. *I've had enough.*

Mike's phone rang again.

'Shit, it's Dad,' he said, and answered it. He'd ignored him for long enough.

'Where are you two?' Alfie asked. 'Your mother's worried sick. She's ready to call the police. Why don't you answer your phone when I call?'

'Sorry, Dad, we're about to get on a bus. Tell Mum not to worry.'

He ended the call before his father could question him further. The bus arrived shortly after that, and they got on. They sat at the very rear. There were two other passengers travelling, and now Gregory's phone started buzzing.

'It's Dad,' he said.

He answered it and listened, then said, 'We'll be back in an hour.' Unlike Mike, he listened to the bollocking Alfie gave him before he hung up.

'I don't know why you listen to him,' Mike said, gazing out of the side window at the passing derelict streets.

As the bus pulled out of the regeneration area and headed towards town, Saturday night began to kick in.

Stop by stop, the bus gradually filled up with happy people going out for the evening. By the time they got to the centre of town the bus was nearly full. A hen party had got on with lots of loud, giggling girls. Mike couldn't help but smile. The boys got off at the next stop to change buses and the girls all called goodbye.

They arrived in their street at 9.15 p.m.

'I hope Emma's all right,' Gregory said, subdued.

'She will be. We'll go back first thing in the morning. For now, you need to concentrate on what to tell Dad. Just say we lost track of time. The gaming shop doesn't close until nine. There was a special display on.'

Gregory nodded and dug his hands deeper into his jacket pockets.

They walked up the short path to their house. Their father was waiting and opened the front door. Now they were in for it, Gregory thought.

'Where the hell have you two been?' he asked, with a mixture of anger and relief.

'Sorry, Dad,' Mike said. 'We lost track of time in the gaming shop. It won't happen again.'

'You haven't been in the gaming shop all this time?' he asked suspiciously.

Mike nodded. 'They had a display on. It was really good. What's for dinner?' he asked, taking off his shoes and coat and leaving them on the hall stand.

'When I phoned,' Alfie said, 'I thought I heard my name being called, someone crying for help.'

So he *had* heard. Gregory glanced at Mike, but he was

looking away.

'Did you?' Mike said, unruffled, heading into the kitchen. 'I've no idea what that was about. Someone in the shop, perhaps. There was definitely no one calling your name, though. You must have misheard.'

Their father glanced at them briefly, then their mother appeared.

'So you've decided to come home at last?' she said. 'In future, please tell your father or me when you'll be back. Your dinner's in the oven.'

'Thanks, Mum,' Gregory said. 'Can we take it upstairs to eat in our room?'

'Yes, your father and I ate quite a while ago.'

They took their plates from the now-cold oven and pinged them in the microwave. Their father was still hovering, watching them closely. He clearly didn't trust them, not one little bit. He knew, as they did, that he had removed the recordings from the laptop, and they hadn't simply disappeared. Neither had the spy cameras simply vanished from his desk.

They filled a glass of water each and carried their plates upstairs to their room. They sat on their beds, relieved to have got off so lightly.

There were no more phone messages from Carl that night.

'I hope Emma's all right,' Gregory said again.

'So do I,' Mike said.

They both lay awake, Mike becoming increasingly annoyed about Carl, and Gregory worrying about Emma, who was now all alone in the semi-darkness of that room. He could picture her tied to the chair with just the dim lamp on, in that practically deserted housing estate. Carl had stayed with her quite often, but now she was all alone.

'I think we should just let her go,' Gregory said. 'We can deny everything if she tells on us.'

'Go to sleep,' Mike said. 'Things will be different in the morning.'

TWENTY-SIX

'What are we going to tell Mum and Dad?' was Gregory's first question on waking. Not that he'd had much sleep. He'd been lying awake most of the night, as had Mike. 'That we're going to football this morning as normal?'

He was looking at his brother, who was checking his phone. There were no messages from Carl.

'We won't tell them anything,' Mike said. 'I doubt they'll be up yet, so we'll just slip out as if we're going to football. I wonder if Carl is going to the house today?'

'He's not going back,' Gregory said, finally losing patience. 'He told us that yesterday – he's had enough.'

Mike texted Carl: *Are you there yet?* He waited. No reply came.

'What the hell does he think he's playing at?' Mike asked, throwing back the covers and getting up. Gregory did likewise.

'We'll buy some food for her on the way?' Gregory asked. 'And some more clothes?'

'Yes, sure,' Mike said. 'The supermarket opens soon.'

'We've got to make her a hot drink as well,' Gregory added. 'She said Carl always took tea in a flask.'

'You'd better go down now and make it then,' Mike said. 'But be quiet, for God's sake.'

Mike quietly got up as Gregory crept downstairs in his dressing gown. He found the flask that his father used for business trips and brewed the tea. He tucked it into the pocket of his dressing gown and took it upstairs together with a glass of juice for each of them.

They heard their father get up to use the toilet, then return to bed. There was no movement from their mother; presumably she was still asleep. As soon as Gregory was dressed and ready, they quietly slipped from the house. Outside, it was another cold, dry day. When they arrived at the bus stop they realized it was only a Sunday service operating, and so they had to wait for nearly half an hour for a bus to take them into town. From there they went straight to the supermarket and bought plenty of food and a change of clothes for Emma, grabbing the first outfit they saw.

'What time are we planning on going home?' Gregory asked as they waited for the next bus that would take them to Bulwarks Road.

'Lunchtime, after football, that's when Mum and Dad will expect us,' Mike replied.

'What are we going to do tomorrow?' Gregory asked, concerned.

'I don't know yet,' Mike said tetchily. 'Perhaps one of

us can go.'

Gregory couldn't imagine how that would work at school, but he decided to say nothing for now.

The bus came and they got on. They didn't talk; there were others on the bus who might overhear. They watched out of the window as the bus made its way from town to the derelict housing estate. It was 10.45 a.m. when they got off and walked towards Bulwarks Road. There was no noise coming from inside. They let themselves in with the key Mike had taken last time. It was still quiet upstairs.

Mike trod solemnly up the threadbare carpet of the stairs – still no noise – and into the back bedroom. It was empty. She'd gone!

'Where the hell is she?' Mike asked frantically, looking around.

He ran into the bathroom, then the other bedroom. Gregory stayed where he was, staring at the rope that had bound Emma's hands and feet. She must have wriggled her hands free and then untied her legs. He heard Mike run downstairs, cursing as he went, then return upstairs.

'She's gone,' he said, his face ashen. 'I don't believe it. After two fucking weeks, we lose her!'

'What are we going to do?' Gregory asked. 'She's going to tell people it was us.'

'I don't know,' Mike said. 'But if she tells, the place will be searched for sure.' He began tidying up, but there were things everywhere from the two weeks she'd stayed here. The chair, all the food wrappers with their fingerprints all

213

over them. It would soon be obvious to the police who'd been here.

'We're done for,' Mike said in a panic. 'We're just going to have to tell the police we don't know what they're talking about and hope for the best.'

Gregory stared at him. 'Shall we tell Mum?' he asked, his voice trembling.

'I don't know. I need time to think. But I do know we need to get out of here now, before the police arrive.' Mike headed downstairs.

'What time do you think she left?' Gregory asked, going after him.

'Come on, quickly,' he said. 'Bring the bag.'

He'd opened the front door and was now checking the street to make sure it was clear. It was completely empty.

They stepped out. Mike shut the door and they hurried along the pavement. They didn't see anyone. The place was thankfully deserted on a Sunday morning, with the few remaining residents still in bed.

'We'll go to the next bus stop along in case the police arrive,' Mike said.

They started to run and jogged on past the nearest bus stop, then to the edge of the estate. They were out of breath as they came to a halt. As they waited for a bus, they heard police sirens in the distance. The sirens came nearer – they were on the estate now – then they stopped. The boys couldn't see the police cars; they must have been somewhere in the middle of the estate, by Bulwarks Road. Mike and Gregory looked at each other, horrified.

'We only just got out in time,' Gregory said.

'I know,' Mike agreed.

Five minutes later a bus arrived. It drew up and the driver opened the door.

'Someone's in trouble for sure,' he said as he checked their bus passes.

'Yep,' Mike replied, and they made their way to the back of the bus.

They sat in silence, unsure of what to say or do. If the police had gone to the Bulwarks Road address, they were done for. Their fingerprints were everywhere, and Emma would tell the police what had happened. The bus continued into town, quieter and very different from last night. Eventually the boys got off and waited for the next bus. It came a quarter of an hour later.

'We'll say we just helped,' Mike said at last. 'That Carl was responsible. That he'd planned the whole thing and saw it all through. We've got the footage from our house. It shows him pretending to kill her.'

'But that was all fake,' Gregory said. 'For the camera. Emma is good at pretending.' He paused. 'Do you think she was really ill?'

'How the hell should I know?' Mike asked. 'But one thing's for certain, she found the strength to untie herself and run away last night.'

'Or this morning. We don't know when she got free. Has Carl been in touch?' Gregory asked, peering at Mike's phone.

'No. I'll message him and tell him she's gone.'

Emma has escaped, thanks to you, he typed.

No sooner had he sent the message than Carl phoned.

'I'll call you as soon as I'm off the bus,' Mike said, and ended the call.

It was another fifteen minutes to their bus stop, where they could get off. Another passenger got off with them and they let her go on ahead before Mike called Carl.

'This is all down to you, mate,' he began, not giving Carl a chance to speak. 'Pissing around like that and letting us down. She's scarpered, gone from the house sometime last night. The police arrived while we were on the estate. So what are you going to do about it?'

Carl went quiet for a moment and then said, 'We should meet and talk about it, you know, like adults, about strategy or something.'

'I'll think about it,' Mike said.

'I think we should talk about a plan,' Carl said. 'Make sure we all get our stories straight.'

'I said I'll think about it. I need to go now. We're nearly home.' He ended the call.

'Was that wise?' Gregory asked him. 'We need to keep him on side.'

'I'll give him some time to think about it,' Mike said. 'Come on, we need to get home.'

They walked along their street and to their front door. Mike used his key to let them in. They could hear someone in the kitchen preparing food. They took off their shoes and coats and left them in the hall. Their mother was in the kitchen. Their father was nowhere to be seen.

216

'Hi, Mum,' Mike said lightly as they went in.

'Hello,' she said, and paused. 'You didn't take your football kits with you.' She was mixing a pudding for later. 'I put them out ready.'

'No, we forgot them,' Mike said easily.

'What did you use then?' she asked, turning to look at them.

'We didn't. We had to sit and watch,' Mike said, pouring himself a drink. Gregory did likewise.

'For the entire match?' she asked.

They nodded.

'Your coach called here to ask where you were,' she said. 'It wouldn't have mattered, but it was a tournament today, Coleshaw versus Maybury. You weren't there, not at all.' Her mouth was downturned – how it always got when she knew they were lying.

Fuck, Mike thought. In their haste to leave that morning and with so much on their minds, they'd forgotten all about the tournament. Gregory went to speak, but no words came out.

'We got there too late,' Mike said. 'We didn't make it on time.'

'It was an away match.' Their mother was furious. 'I heard you two leave this morning. You had plenty of time to go, with or without your football kit.'

She'd stopped what she was doing and was now staring at them. They looked at her and said nothing. The impasse continued for a few moments.

'So where have you been?' she asked at length.

217

'We had to take back a game we bought yesterday,' Mike offered.

'You could have done that after the match,' she said. 'There would have been plenty of time.'

Both boys were silent. They couldn't think of anything else to say, short of telling her the truth. She was still waiting for an explanation. 'Well?' she asked them. 'Where did you go?'

'To the gaming shop,' Mike said stubbornly, but he couldn't meet her eyes.

'And you, Gregory, where did you go?'

'The gaming shop,' he said lamely.

'You're both grounded until you tell me where you were,' she said, really angry now. 'Go to your room.'

'Where's Dad?' Mike asked.

'Outside, clearing up leaves and trying to deal with the disappointment you two are causing us.'

'Sorry, Mum,' Gregory said.

She turned and continued beating the pudding with far more force than was necessary.

The boys went upstairs to their bedroom and closed the door. Once inside, they flopped on their beds, weary and dejected.

'Perhaps we could run away,' Gregory suggested.

Mike rolled his eyes and looked to the heavens.

'It's not such a silly idea,' Gregory said. 'There's plenty of houses in the regeneration zone that have been empty for ages. We could hide in one of them like Carl did with Emma.'

'It belonged to his grandmother,' Mike said, annoyed. 'And what are we going to do all day and night? What's school going to say? And Mum and Dad would have the police out looking for us in no time.'

'They didn't find Emma,' Gregory said defiantly.

'Just shut up, will you? We'll stay here and carry on as normal, see what happens. Emma said last night that she wouldn't tell anyone what really happened if we let her go.'

'But we didn't let her go,' Gregory said. 'She escaped.'

The words hung in the air.

A while later Mike phoned Carl.

'I don't understand why the police haven't got you already,' Mike said.

'Because my real surname isn't Smith, it's Harvey – my dad's name. They're looking for the wrong person, and Gran's got dementia anyway and doesn't know what time of day it is, and she's a bit deaf, so even if they figured out we're related she probably wouldn't tell them much. She has no idea I'm wanted by the police. But if Emma starts talking then that's it. Where do you think she's gone?'

'Home, I guess, or to the hospital. She said she wasn't feeling well yesterday.'

'I'll see if I can find out,' Carl said.

TWENTY-SEVEN

The previous night, after Mike and Gregory had left 27 Bulwarks Road, Emma had cried herself to sleep. Carl had stayed most nights and brought her regular food and drink. Now he'd suddenly gone, saying only that he'd had enough for now and had to go to his gran's for a break. To hell with his gran, Emma had thought. She needed him now and she didn't like being left alone all night. There were strange noises in the house – someone could be breaking in, as they had done with many of the houses on this estate.

She listened carefully. She had no idea what time it was – around midnight, she thought. She'd slept for a while and could now see the moon through the window as it continued its slow and relentless journey across the night sky. After a while of staring into the darkness, her eyes gradually closed again and she dozed for a while, then she came to with a start and sniffed. She had a cold. Her nose kept running. She'd told Mike and Gregory yesterday and they'd given her a Lemsip, but the effects had long since worn off. She gave another sniff. It was impossible to blow her nose with her hands tied behind her back.

Time passed. The moon had nearly disappeared from view when she woke again. She flexed her hands and discovered they were tied more loosely than usual – tied to the struts in the back of the chair, which Carl never did. She wriggled and flexed them over and over again, gradually managing to work them free. Unable to believe her good luck, she quickly took off her gag and then untied her legs. She rubbed them to get the circulation back, then stood. She always felt a bit shaky after being tied to the chair. She took a few steps and the circulation returned. Suddenly she stopped again. She thought she'd heard a noise coming from outside. She stayed where she was and listened, but the noise didn't come again, so she crept across the room and downstairs.

Getting out of the house was easy. She gingerly opened the front door, then realized she didn't have her coat. Where the hell was it? She decided not to go back upstairs and look for it, and continued out, shutting the door behind her. The street was deserted and very dark. She began along Bulwarks Road, feeling clammy and unsteady. The houses she passed were all empty; no lights were on, and many had their front doors boarded up. She knew this area a little, and when they were planning all this she had agreed that Bulwarks Road was a good place for her to hide and for Carl to stay.

She kept going, feeling even weaker, and turned into

221

Crescent Road. Three doors in and she came to a house with a light on in the upstairs room. She banged loudly on the door and shouted. No one came, so she banged again, louder and more insistent this time.

A light came on in the hall downstairs, then a large man in his thirties eased the door open and looked out. He was dressed in jeans and a vest and had tattoos up both arms.

'What do you want?' he asked in a broken accent.

'My name is Emma Arnold,' she began, out of breath. 'I was kidnapped two weeks ago.' She felt faint from lack of food and water.

She took a step forward and collapsed into his arms. He pulled her into the hall.

'Who shall I call?' he asked her.

'The police,' she murmured.

'I don't want the police in my house,' he said.

'Please call them,' she begged. 'They'll know what to do.'

Still, he was hesitating. A woman called from upstairs in a language Emma didn't recognize.

'Please, help me,' Emma said.

'I'll phone them and then you can wait down the street,' he said. 'I don't want any involvement.'

'Fine.'

Emma slouched on the floor in the man's hall as he dialled 999. He said he'd found Emma Arnold in Crescent Street and gave the postcode. He cut the call and took her outside, then helped her further up the street, far enough away from his front door.

'Don't bring me into any of it,' he said again, and propped her on the ground so her back was against a house wall.

'Thank you,' she murmured. 'I won't.'

He nodded, returned to his house, closed the door, and a few minutes later all the lights were off. She was alone in the deserted street, and she prayed the police would hurry. She sat there in the still of the night, shivering, longing to hear a police siren. Ten minutes later a police car drew up and she breathed a sigh of relief. It was followed by an ambulance, and more police cars. She was saved. Two paramedics lifted her onto a portable chair and took her into the ambulance, even though she could walk. The paramedics told her their names, but she couldn't remember them. A police officer stood on guard at the entrance to the ambulance. They propped her on the bed and checked her vital signs – temperature, pulse rate, respiration and blood pressure.

'How long have you been here?' one of them asked.

'I don't know,' she lied.

When they'd finished checking her, they said they'd take her to St Mary's Hospital. They made her comfortable on the bed and, with the siren on, headed for the hospital. It was 2 a.m. when they arrived – she saw the time on the large wall clock. She was finally able to relax. She was safe at last.

TWENTY-EIGHT

At 5 a.m., Chloe McNeal was phoned by a member of the police team.

'Emma Arnold has been found, alive and well,' the officer said. 'Please tell her parents.'

'What? She's not dead? That's absolutely fantastic news, of course I will,' she said, and listened to the little information the detective had about Emma's rescue. 'That's the best news we could possibly have hoped for. I'll tell her parents now. I can't quite believe it.' It wasn't so unusual that Emma wasn't talking to the police, Chloe thought as she got ready. Whatever had happened would have badly traumatized her and it would take time for the memories to start to work their way up from her subconscious. Some of them might never be released. Also, there might be a touch of Stockholm syndrome, where someone who is kidnapped develops positive feelings towards their captors. Two weeks was a very long time.

Chloe WhatsApped her daughter, Teddy, who was

still asleep upstairs, to say she was heading out. Teddy was used to her mother leaving early. Chloe crept from the house and drove to the home of Mr and Mrs Arnold, excited that she would soon be able to give them the best news they could possibly have hoped for. She was completely delighted for them.

She arrived at the Arnolds' house and parked. A light was on, suggesting someone was up already. With her heart bursting, she got out and walked up the drive, then took a deep breath before ringing the bell. As she waited, she realized they'd never suggested she use their Christian names, which was OK by her. She liked to keep things professional. Mr Arnold answered the door, dressed and getting ready for work. Chloe was aware of their routine from all the days she'd spent there. He would normally leave at 7, but she didn't think that would happen today.

'Can I come in?' she asked, smiling. 'I have some good news.'

She went with him into the front room. 'Emma has been found, alive, safe and well. She's at St Mary's Hospital being checked over now,' she said, and gave him a hug.

Mr Arnold cried like a child. He didn't say anything, he just cried.

'Shall I fetch Mrs Arnold?' Chloe asked after some moments.

He nodded and took a handkerchief from his pocket to wipe his eyes. There was no need to fetch Mrs Arnold because just as Chloe began to make her way upstairs, Mrs

Arnold came down. Her hair was flattened from sleep, her expression scrutinizing. She was dressed in a woolly dressing gown and slippers.

'Emma has been found alive and well,' Chloe said, elated.

The poor woman looked as though she might pass out, so Chloe helped her to a chair in the living room. She gave her what details she knew and then made mugs of tea all round. She could hear the Arnolds laughing and crying for joy as she worked. This was the best part of the job – when a missing teenager turned up safe and well. It didn't matter what had led to them running away, only that they were back. By the time she'd made the tea and had carried it through to the living room they'd stopped crying and were bursting with questions. She sat next to Mrs Arnold and answered them as best she could. There wasn't a lot to tell at the moment, though.

'Emma was found in Crescent Road,' she said. 'It's on that derelict housing estate about four miles away. Apparently, a few of the properties are still lived in. The police are searching the area now.'

'Hasn't Emma told you where she was kept hidden?' Mr Arnold asked. 'She's able to talk from what you've said.'

'Yes, but she hasn't said anything about her ordeal at the moment. The main thing, though, is that she's back safely.'

'Has she been there the whole two weeks?' Mrs Arnold asked.

'We're not sure. Someone rang to say they'd found her, but that's all I know, and someone has been giving her food and drink.'

'Who?'

'I honestly don't know,' Chloe said.

'So she really hasn't told you anything?' Mr Arnold asked.

'No, not yet, I'm afraid.'

'It's bound to take a while,' Mrs Arnold sympathized. 'When can we see her?'

'As soon as you're ready. I'll take you to the hospital in my car.'

Mrs Arnold rose and quickly went upstairs to dress.

'So, you don't have any more details at all?' Mr Arnold said again, puzzled. 'Only what you've told us?'

'I'm sorry. It's not unusual. It could take some time for it all to come out.'

'Maybe she doesn't have any memories about the past two weeks,' he persisted. 'But, no, surely she must remember something?'

'We're just not sure at this stage. Perhaps there will be some news when we get to the hospital.'

He nodded thoughtfully.

Mrs Arnold reappeared and went to get her shoes and coat. Mr Arnold phoned his work and said he wouldn't be in today as his daughter had been found alive and well. He listened with a bemused expression at their words of joy and relief, and then said, 'Thank you all very much.'

'They're delighted for me,' he said as he ended the call.

'Keys?' Chloe asked them.

'Yes,' Mr Arnold said, and jangled them in his pocket.

'Will Emma be able to come home with us?' Mrs Arnold asked as they left the house.

'I don't think so, not today,' Chloe said as she shepherded them into the car. 'She'll be staying at St Mary's for a couple of days.'

The three of them fell silent as Chloe drove and remained so most of the way. It was difficult to know what to say to them with so little information, and they must be overwhelmed with emotions, Chloe thought. It was about half an hour to St Mary's Hospital. Once they'd arrived, they were shown to a side ward where a police officer was on duty outside. Chloe greeted him as they went in. Emma was in bed propped up on some pillows.

'Oh, my love!' Mrs Arnold cried, and ran to her.

Mr Arnold followed.

'We didn't think we'd ever see you again,' she said, and wrapped her arms around her daughter and wept.

Chloe drew up a second chair for Mr Arnold to sit on and the whole family cried as one. Chloe stood and watched them. When their tears had run out, Mr Arnold asked, 'What's been going on, Emma? You can tell us.'

'I don't know,' Emma said, still tearful. 'I can't remember anything. The doctor said the trauma is causing memory loss. They're going to keep me here for a bit.'

'You can't remember anything at all?' Mr Arnold pressed.

Emma shook her head.

'What about when you left the house on that Saturday morning two weeks ago? You were in a right mood with us.'

'No, I don't remember a thing after that,' she said, and shook her head. 'Sorry, nothing.'

'Leave her be,' Mrs Arnold said. 'She's been through a lot.'

At that moment, as Chloe looked at Emma, she suspected her of lying. She couldn't say why. It was just a feeling that Emma knew far more than she was prepared to say.

TWENTY-NINE

The whole of the regeneration area was crawling with police. They were searching those houses that were being lived in, and also those that weren't, looking for where Emma had been held. There were about two dozen or more police officers working on the search; two of them had brought dogs. They'd already searched Crescent Road and had now spread out. When they found someone living in a property they asked for their ID and if they'd seen anything suspicious. No one had. Sometimes they went into the person's home and searched the property. It was nearly an hour before 27 Bulwarks Road was discovered.

'Boss! In here,' one of the officers called from inside. 'This is the one, I'm sure of it.'

The other teams stood down temporarily and made their way to the property.

'This is the place for certain,' the officer said as he came out. 'You'll need lights on in there.'

'Can we have some lights, please?' DS Scrivener called.

The floodlights were brought over and set up in the various rooms. Forensics were called. It wasn't yet 8 a.m., on an overcast autumn day.

'So this is where Emma was held for two weeks,' Beth said, going in.

DS Scrivener nodded. 'Just look at it. It's not fit for a pig.'

They did a preliminary tour and then waited for forensics to arrive. They saw a teenager's coat and a number of other items that could have belonged to Emma scattered around the back bedroom. Forensics got to work and were there for a large part of the day. The other team members were told to go and return to their usual work. Forensics bagged what they needed. There was a bed in the front room with a man's jersey on it. Downstairs was a mess, with sandwich wrappers, pizza boxes and empty bottles of beer strewn everywhere. On the sink was a newish flask.

'We'll take that with us,' DS Scrivener said to forensics. 'It looks new and we might be able to identify it. Who owns this place?' he now asked Beth.

'We're not sure yet,' Beth said. 'I've left a message on the council's emergency contact number to phone me back.'

'Chase them up if they don't, please. It's freezing in here. It's a wonder Emma wasn't in a worse state when we found her,' DS Scrivener said.

He continued into the bathroom and flushed the toilet. 'At least the cold water was left on.'

Eventually, around 4 p.m., forensics had finished and cleared away. They had some good sets of fingerprints, and plenty of footprints. On the face of it, it looked as though there were three regular visitors to the house, very likely male. Hopefully, the prints would prove to be a match to someone on their computer database.

Now forensics had gone, DS Scrivener had the run of the place and he continued looking around with Beth in tow. Most of the lights had gone and the place had an unnatural feel. It was brighter outside than in. He continued to the back bedroom and looked one final time at the chair and the rope, then made sure someone would stay and oversee the boarding up of the place. He didn't want anyone getting in. He, Beth and the last few officers left. The council phoned back and she was finally told the information they needed – the property at 27 Bulwarks Road was previously owned by Mrs Edna Smith.

'Do you have a current address for her?' Beth asked.

The man on the phone gave it to her.

'Thank you,' she said, and was finally able to tell DS Scrivener.

'Let's not get overexcited,' he said. 'Smith is a very common name. Do you fancy a drive there now? It's not too far away.'

'Yes, sir,' Beth said.

Saying goodbye and thanking the last officer, they got into their police car and Beth drove the two miles to Mrs Edna Smith's house. The house was small but new, and on a modern housing estate. They had to ring the bell a number of times before the door slowly opened.

'Mrs Smith?' DS Scrivener asked her, showing ID.

'Yes. What do you want?' She was a woman in her late seventies, Beth guessed, small and wiry.

'Can we come in, please? We need to ask you some questions.'

'No. What do you want?' she said brusquely.

'I understand you used to own twenty-seven Bulwarks Road?'

'Pardon?'

'You owned number twenty-seven Bulwarks Road,' Beth repeated, raising her voice.

'That sounds familiar.'

'Does Carl Smith live here?' DS Scrivener tried.

'No. But I see my Carl sometimes.'

'Your Carl?'

'Carl Harvey, my grandson.'

'Is he here now?'

'No. I am sure he's not.'

'When's he due back?' DS Scrivener asked.

'Much later. He's a good boy and never lets me down.'

'How much later?'

'I don't know. Who did you say you were?' she asked, then before they could answer, she abruptly shut the door.

Beth thought for a moment. 'You don't think Carl Smith and Carl Harvey might be the same person, do you? Maybe we've had the wrong name all along, and that's why he never came up on any of our searches.'

'It's possible,' said DS Scrivener.

'Do you think he's in there?' Beth asked.

'He's not at twenty-seven Bulwarks Road, that's for sure.'

They returned to the car and looked up at the house.

'We'll get a search warrant and come back later,' DS Scrivener said.

'There's no need,' Beth said suddenly, for walking along the pavement behind them, coming towards the car in broad daylight, was Carl. They recognized him from the video they'd seen of him attacking Emma. They stayed where they were, charting his progress. He came steadily along the street towards them, then approached the house, and began up the path. DS Scrivener and Beth immediately jumped out of the car.

'Carl Harvey?'

'Yes,' he said, then realized who they were.

Beth pulled Carl's hands behind his back and handcuffed him. 'Carl Harvey, you do not have to say anything. But it may harm your defence if you—'

'Will you get off me!' Carl cried, struggling. 'It wasn't me.'

'You can tell us all about it at Coleshaw Police Station,' DS Scrivener said, and Beth finished the caution.

They took Carl to the car and sat him on the back seat.

'What about my gran?' Carl asked. 'I need to tell her what to do while I'm away. She's got dementia.'

Beth looked at him over the back of her seat.

'Isn't there anyone else who can help with her?' she asked.

'No one. Her husband is dead and she's estranged from her daughter – my mum. Please, I need to see her just for a second.'

'I'll go,' Beth said. 'What do you want me to say?'

'Tell her to go to bed. I'll see her when I get back, or her neighbour will call in.'

Beth got out of the car and went to the front door again. The woman answered almost immediately.

'We've got Carl in the car,' Beth said. 'He's asked me to tell you to go to bed. He's going to be with us a while, but a neighbour may call in.'

Mrs Smith peered past Beth to the car waiting outside. She smiled at Carl and waved as though she was seeing someone off at the door.

'Where's he going?' she asked.

'To Coleshaw Police Station.'

'How long will he be there?' she asked.

'We're not sure yet, but will you go to bed?'

'Tell him I'm going now.'

She gave another wave and closed the front door. Beth returned to the car, thinking this wasn't like the Carl they'd been looking for. Not at all.

'She said she'd go,' Beth reassured him.

'Thank you,' he said.

Again, Beth thought that the assumption they'd been making about 'Carl Smith' being hard-nosed, someone who just thought of himself, was wrong. So what had led him to perpetrate such a dreadful crime – to attack and try to suffocate Emma, then keep her locked up for two weeks? It didn't add up.

'I really hope Gran's all right,' Carl said worriedly as Beth drove.

'Are you sure there's no one we can call?' DS Scrivener asked, looking over his seat at Carl.

'No, there isn't. It's just me and her. When do you think I'll be able to go home?'

'It depends on what happens at the police station,' DS Scrivener said.

'I hope she's OK,' Carl said again.

'Have you had a clinical diagnosis of dementia?' Beth asked.

'Yes, but obviously there's no cure, so Gran and me muddle along as best we can. It's hard, really.'

It was clear that Carl was very worried about his gran; during the drive to the station he could talk about nothing else. Gran this and Gran that. Beth and DS Scrivener reassured him as best they could and offered again to phone someone, perhaps a neighbour, but he refused, saying she wouldn't accept anyone else's help.

They parked at the rear of the station and DS Scrivener threw Beth a look as they got out, as if to say, 'What the hell was all that about?'

It took a few minutes to process Carl at the desk and then he asked to speak to his gran again. He was allowed one phone call and he didn't want a solicitor present so they allowed it. The call was touching. He asked her how she was and if she was ready for bed. She said she was and told him that she was wearing her blue nightdress and that she'd brushed her teeth. They ended the call by blowing goodnight kisses to each other. 'I'll see you in the morning, Gran,' he said. 'Now you go to bed.'

'Yes, dear, I will.'

'I hope she does,' he said, handing back the phone.

Once he'd finished, they checked again that he didn't want a solicitor present during the interview, then showed him to the room marked Interview Room Two, where they offered him a drink.

Beth and DS Scrivener sat on one side of the table and Carl sat on the other. Beth went through the formalities of the day, time and place the interview was being held.

'How did you find me?' Carl suddenly asked.

'The council gave us your gran's address after we found Bulwarks Road,' Beth said. 'We'd been looking for Carl Smith, but you're not Smith, are you? That was clever, giving everyone a false name.'

'I didn't do anything. None of this is what you think,' he said.

'Carl,' DS Scrivener said solemnly. 'We have video footage of you trying to suffocate Emma. We all thought you'd murdered her. We've been looking for a corpse. But then you kidnapped her and hid her at twenty-seven Bulwarks Road. Why did you do it?'

Carl sighed, looked around as though collecting his thoughts, and said, 'I didn't do it.'

'Tell us in your own time what happened on that Saturday two weeks ago, when you checked into the Roomy-Space belonging to Mr and Mrs Watson.'

237

He threw them the same look and said, 'No. I won't.'

'We know you were at twenty-seven Bulwarks Road. Forensics have at least one item from you, a jersey with your name in it,' DS Scrivener said.

'That's my gran. She still insists on stitching name tags into my clothes like she did when I was at school.'

Beth and DS Scrivener looked at Carl, unsure of what to make of him.

'You want to get back to your gran, don't you? So tell us what happened,' DS Scrivener said.

Carl didn't reply.

'Do you want to spend the night here?' DS Scrivener asked.

'No,' he said.

'So tell us what's been going on.'

'I can't.'

'Who were the other lads involved?' DS Scrivener asked.

'Don't know,' Carl said, more determined than ever.

'Forensics have told us that there were three sets of male prints in the house. Who did the other two belong to?'

He shook his head and refused to answer.

And so it continued, Carl giving nothing away. After an hour of questioning, DS Scrivener wound up the interview.

'We'll be speaking more to Emma,' he said, annoyed, and stood. 'What do you think she'll tell us?'

'She won't tell you anything because there's nothing to tell,' Carl said. 'Can I go to my gran now?'

'No, you can't,' DS Scrivener said. 'You're going to a holding cell – give you a chance to think about what you want to tell us.'

'Well then, you'd just better hope my gran's all right,' Carl said as he stood.

'I am sure she will be,' Beth said.

Outside, DS Scrivener said to Beth, 'Did you notice, he didn't ask about the video footage or where it had come from?'

'Yes. I think he's trying to trick us,' Beth said.

'That's what I'm thinking. Do you fancy going to St Mary's Hospital to see Emma now?' DS Scrivener asked. 'We can go home straight from there.'

'Sure,' she said, and went to fetch her jacket and bag.

THIRTY

It was 8.30 p.m. when Beth and DS Scrivener arrived at St Mary's Hospital. They made their way to the side room where Emma was being kept. The constable on duty outside the room said good evening as they went in. Emma was awake, alone, and messaging on a phone her parents must have brought in. She looked well.

'Hi,' she said brightly.

'Hello, Emma,' Beth said. 'I'm DC Beth Mayes,' and she showed her ID.

DS Scrivener did likewise and pulled up two chairs so they could sit down. It had been a very long day and they were both more than ready to go home. They just needed to see Emma first.

'How are you?' Beth asked.

'I'm fine, thank you,' Emma replied.

'Do you feel up to making a statement yet?' she asked.

'Not really,' she said. 'I'm still very tired.' She gave a little yawn as if to prove it.

'Maybe you could just answer a few questions?' DS Scrivener suggested.

'Maybe,' she said.

'We've just detained Carl,' Beth said.

A flash of intrigue. Her eyes darted to theirs, but she said nothing.

'I believe you know him?' Beth said.

'Just a little.'

'It was our impression you knew him very well.'

They waited for a response but none came.

'You were in a relationship with him, weren't you?'

'Sort of,' Emma replied.

'We understand that two weeks ago he took you to a Roomy-Space owned by Mr and Mrs Watson. You were planning on spending the night there.'

There was no reply. Emma set down her phone and looked at them. It was very difficult to gauge what she was thinking,

'Later that night you were filmed arguing with Carl for a very long time. Then he appeared to suffocate you.' Still nothing. 'He bundled you up and kept you hostage, we assume at twenty-seven Bulwarks Road, for two weeks.'

'It wasn't like that,' Emma finally said, quietly.

'No? What was it like then?' Beth asked.

She didn't reply.

'Emma,' DS Scrivener said. 'We've spent nearly two weeks looking for you. We've used a lot of police time and money. The budget for this comes to nearly a million pounds. You'll need to tell us what happened or everyone involved will be charged.'

'Everyone?' she queried.

'Yes, there were two others visiting you at twenty-seven Bulwarks Road, weren't there?' Beth said.

Emma hesitated, then gave a small nod and looked away.

'Well? Who were they?' Beth asked.

She thought for a moment, then yawned again. 'I'm feeling very tired,' she said again, and turned her head away.

'You seemed fine when we first came in,' DS Scrivener said, a little too sharply.

Beth threw him a warning glance. This was a girl who'd been subjected to a horrendous ordeal. It would take time for the truth to come out.

'Is there nothing you can tell us then?' Beth asked, more gently.

She shook her head. 'Sorry.'

'OK, Emma,' Beth said. 'We'll let you get some rest and we'll come back first thing tomorrow.'

'Fine,' Emma said, and closed her eyes.

They left the room.

'She's young,' Beth reminded her boss.

'Yes, I know that, but this is serious, and I think she might be playing games with us.'

Beth nodded as they said goodnight to the officer outside the room and came away.

'I need to phone the station about Carl,' DS Scrivener

242

said. 'We can keep him until tomorrow, but is there any point?'

'Not really, sir. I don't think he's ready to talk yet.'

'No, I agree. We'll come back to the hospital first thing.'

DS Scrivener phoned the station and gave instructions for Carl Harvey to be released pending further investigation. They were confident he wouldn't run away, given that he needed to look after his gran.

The following morning, Beth and DS Scrivener arrived at the hospital a little after 8 a.m. to find the duty officer gone, and the room had another patient in it. DS Scrivener asked the nurse where Emma Arnold was.

'She's been discharged,' she said. 'Doctor did his rounds at 7.30 and said she was fit to go home. Her parents were pushing for it, and they were here to collect her. Your chap went too, of course.'

'Thank you,' Beth said.

'You'd have thought someone could have let us know,' DS Scrivener moaned on the way out.

'Shall we go straight to the Arnolds' house now then?' Beth asked.

'Yes. I want to talk to that young lady, and fast. Before she has a chance to hone her story.'

They drove straight to the Arnolds' house and rang the bell. Mr Arnold answered the door and looked surprised to see them.

'DS Scrivener, and this is DC Beth Mayes,' he said. 'Can we come in, please? We'd like to talk to Emma.'

He hesitated. 'It's very early.'

'Just a few questions,' Beth said.

'I suppose so. Come in.'

He showed them into their living room and asked them to wait, then disappeared upstairs. Beth scanned the room. It was as neat and well ordered as it had been when she and Matt had first come here shortly after Emma had gone missing.

Five minutes later, Emma appeared. She was wearing a dressing gown, although her mother was dressed. Beth and DS Scrivener said hello and they all sat down.

'Thank you for seeing us,' Beth said to Emma. She gave a weak smile. 'We visited you yesterday evening, but you were too tired to talk.'

'Yes, we know,' Mr Arnold put in.

'Hopefully you've recovered.' Emma gave another small smile. 'So, what can you tell us about your kidnap?' Beth asked.

'I'm not sure what you want to know,' Emma replied.

'You could start by telling us how you met Carl,' Beth prompted.

Emma considered. 'It was six months ago, I think. I met him in a coffee bar in the high street. I was there with some friends.'

'Which coffee bar?' Beth asked.

'Ozone Coffee.'

Beth nodded. 'So what happened? How did your relationship get going?'

She looked uncertain and said, 'It just did.'

'I understand that there was some hesitancy from your parents about Carl?' Beth said.

'A bit,' she agreed and glanced at them.

She was hedging, Beth thought. Not telling them everything.

'Emma, it's important you tell us the truth,' DS Scrivener put in. 'I'm sure your parents won't mind – they want to know what happened as much as we do.'

'They didn't want me seeing Carl, but I don't take any notice of what my parents say anyway,' Emma said.

'Did you know his real surname was Harvey?' Beth asked.

'No!' Emma said, looking genuinely surprised. 'I suppose I didn't know any of them very well. I just did what they wanted.'

Mr and Mrs Arnold looked at each other but held back on what they were thinking.

'So how did your relationship with Carl progress?' Beth asked. 'Was it a good one?'

'Pretty good. I mean, everyone argues sometimes, don't they? Even parents.'

'But not to the point of being suffocated,' Beth said bluntly.

Emma didn't reply.

'So what did you two like to do when you began going out together?' Beth asked.

She shrugged. 'This and that, I suppose.'

Beth looked at her carefully. 'I expect it was difficult with Carl taking care of his sick grandmother as well?'

245

'We used to go to his house quite a bit, so he could keep an eye on her.'

'So why did you book Mr and Mrs Watson's Roomy-Space on that Saturday evening?' Beth asked. 'Had you stayed in one before?'

'No. Carl suggested it, as a treat. Go for a night out. He just had to settle his gran first,' she said.

Beth nodded. 'Talk me through what happened that night, will you?'

'I don't know, really. It's all a bit hazy. I mean, I remember going there and arguing, which we did sometimes. Then I don't remember much else.'

'You don't remember Carl taking you in his car to twenty-seven Bulwarks Road?' DS Scrivener asked.

'Not really,' she said, and looked away. In fact, she was looking around quite a lot, Beth noticed.

'So, tell me what you do remember,' Beth said.

She looked thoughtful and then said, 'I really don't know what to say. I don't remember much at all.'

'You don't remember Carl trying to suffocate you and carrying you out of the room, then taking you to that old house in the derelict area?'

'No, like I said, it's all a haze. I remember everything up until the fight that night, and I can remember being tied to a chair sometimes, but that's all.'

'Who else came to the house where you were being kept?' Beth asked.

'I honestly don't know. It was dark and I didn't see their faces. Sorry, I can't be of more help.'

246

'You're doing really well, pet,' Mr Arnold put in.

DS Scrivener felt like telling him to shut up.

'So how do you feel about Carl now? Are you still together?' Beth asked.

'You'd have to ask him that.'

Beth glanced at her parents, who were sitting, expressionless. Indeed, Mrs Arnold had hardly spoken a word the whole time they'd been there.

'Do you want to see him again?' Beth said, glancing at her parents again.

Emma gave the faintest nod.

'Is that everything?' Mr Arnold said. 'Only I've got to go to work soon. I'm already late.'

Beth glanced at DS Scrivener, who said, 'For now. Thank you for your time, Emma.' He stood to leave.

'I'll give you one of my cards,' Beth said, and handed one to Emma. 'Call me when you want to talk.'

Emma said a small thank-you and her father showed them out.

They made it inside the car before DS Scrivener exploded. Beth was expecting it. He was really wound up. She'd seen him flex and unflex his knuckles during the interview.

'She's lying through her teeth,' he said furiously. 'As if we haven't wasted enough police time and money on this already!'

'I know. But why isn't she helping us? You'd have thought after everything she's been through that she would be happy to point the finger of blame at Carl.'

'And her parents have changed their tune too,' DS Scrivener said, jamming the ignition key in and starting the engine. 'They're a lot less cooperative now than they were when she was missing. I'd like to get them all for wasting police time. There's no way we can mount a prosecution with what we've been told.' He pulled away. 'I'll leave you and Matt on the case for a few more days to see if you can get anywhere, and return everyone else to their normal duties.'

'Yes,' Beth said. 'I think if we can identify the other lads in the house it would help.'

'I agree.' DS Scrivener drove to the end of the road and turned left. 'That recording doesn't make sense. Mr Watson thought he was watching a murder take place. I don't understand what happened.'

'We all thought it was real too, but maybe we didn't see what we thought we saw ...' Beth said.

He continued to drive. 'I don't suppose Carl could have given her a drug that put her in a semi-comatose state?' he said. 'Can you check with the hospital if there was anything in her system? If he did, that would explain her haziness.'

As DS Scrivener continued driving to Coleshaw Police Station, Beth phoned St Mary's Hospital and asked if anything had been found in Emma Arnold's system. The answer was only a trace of paracetamol, nothing else.

'Another dead end, sir,' she said.

THIRTY-ONE

It was nearly noon as Beth and Matt drove down the road to 27 Bulwarks Road. They let themselves in through the front door, then looked around, hoping to spot something they'd previously missed. But after half an hour of turning over rubbish they decided there was nothing else to be found and came away, locking the front door behind them.

Matt and Beth walked to the end of Bulwarks Road, then back again.

'I'm not sure what we're hoping to find here,' Beth said.

Matt sighed. 'Neither am I. We'd better get back to the police station.'

They returned to their car. As Beth drove them slowly from the estate, they passed a single-storey bus, parked up on the side.

'It's a wonder the buses still run this far out, for, what, two or three passengers a day?' Matt remarked.

'Yes, it is,' Beth replied, then she stopped the car. 'I wonder if the driver could have seen anything.'

She parked the car up and got out, leaving Matt to take a call inside, which had just come in. She went over to where the bus was parked. It was empty of passengers, its engine off, and the driver was reading a newspaper. She knocked on the doors and they opened with a pneumatic whoosh.

'We're not due to leave for another ten minutes,' the driver said, and was about to close the doors again.

'DC Beth Mayes,' she said, showing her ID. She stepped onto the deck of the bus. 'How often do you make this journey?'

'It's one bus an hour from six in the morning to ten at night,' he said. 'Not sure how much longer they'll keep this service going, though.'

'You can't get many passengers?'

'No, only about twenty people still live here, I reckon. Godforsaken place. It's time the council got them rehomed.'

'Is it you who mostly drives this route, or are there other drivers?' she asked.

'I drive this route every day apart from Sundays.'

'Over the last two weeks, has anybody used the bus who didn't before?' Beth asked.

'There was a young woman with a child last week, and two lads, as far as I can remember. Everyone else I recognized.'

'Lads ... How old were they?'

'Early to mid-teens. Brothers, I'd say. They looked similar. They got on last Saturday and a few days during the week before that. I don't work Sundays so I wouldn't

250

know about then. But they must have been bunking off school on a couple of the weekdays. I saw their school uniform under their coats. I didn't say anything, though. You can never be sure how safe you are now.'

'Do you know which school they were from?' Beth asked.

'Yes, it's that newish one on the hill. I recognized the uniform from my sister's kids.'

'Springfield?'

'Yes, that's it. Springfield.'

'Where did you drop them off?' Beth asked.

'The last stop here,' he said. The bus doesn't go any further now. They walked down that road.' He pointed in the direction of Bulwarks Road.

'Where did you take them on the way back?'

'The bus terminus in town.'

'Thank you, that's very helpful,' Beth said. 'Anything else you can remember?'

'They always sat at the back. They looked like they were up to no good, in my opinion. I guess this has something to do with the kidnapping I heard about on the news? I'm pleased the lass has been found. Fancy it being close to here!'

'Yes,' Beth said. A short press release had gone out that morning. 'Thanks again.'

'You're welcome.'

The doors swished shut as Beth returned to the car. She got in feeling pretty pleased with herself and relayed to Matt what the driver had just told her.

'Two brothers, early to mid-teens – who does that remind you of?' she asked him.

Matt looked nonplussed for a few moments and then said, 'The Watson lads?'

'Yes. That's my feeling too. They go to Springfield school, with Emma, and Teddy, although she's in a different class. I had a feeling about them when I saw them at school, but I couldn't prove anything,' Beth said.

'It's certainly an odd coincidence that they're Alfie Watson's children, and one of them is in the same class as Emma,' Matt said.

'It's more than a coincidence, I'd say.'

'We can interview them both, but I think this time we'll need to do it by the book – at the police station with an appropriate adult present.'

'Yes, I agree.'

As Beth and Matt made their way back to Coleshaw Police Station, Alfie sat at his desk at home. He had received a news update on his phone announcing that Emma had been found alive and well. He was overjoyed, although it was truly astounding. The film he'd taken had looked so real. Just goes to show, he thought.

He just needed to collect his second laptop from the police station and then they could put this whole miserable mess behind them. He hoped Jenny would forgive him in time, and his sons, well, they were just behaving like normal teenagers. True, there was still the matter of the money he'd given to Carl, and the earring reappearing. He wondered if he would ever get his money back. He phoned the police station and asked if his laptop was ready to be collected. After being passed around for a while he was told it wasn't and would still be kept for a few days.

'But why?' he asked.

'It's not my department. Try calling back in a few days,' the officer said.

Alfie put down his phone, not best pleased, and continued with his work. Then he stopped and looked at his phone, or, more precisely, at the last email Carl had sent. Yes, why not? he thought. He'd take a chance and ask for his money back, not that he stood a hope in hell of getting it.

He composed an email, brief and to the point: *I would like my money back. Alfie*, he wrote and pressed send.

It went through.

He put down his phone, but it buzzed almost immediately with an incoming message.

It's all gone – games!

Games! He stared at the message for a while and then put the phone to one side. It was such a trivial way to spend the money, but then lots of young people played games, he supposed, and continued with some work. He thought about the message periodically, then decided it wasn't worth pursuing, that he'd seen the last of that money. Just as well Carl didn't get his hands on the other ransom he'd demanded.

Meanwhile, as the afternoon progressed, at Coleshaw Police Station Beth and Matt were making preparations to bring in Mike and Gregory Watson. They had booked an appropriate adult to be with them and had worked out a strategy. They'd interview the boys separately, Gregory first. He seemed less sure of himself. They'd also have to inform Mr and Mrs Watson that their children were at the police station. Beth had already spoken to the Head of their school, Ms Clements, who'd been rather unhelpful.

'Can't it wait until the end of the school day?' she'd asked.

'I'm afraid not,' Beth had replied.

She'd finally agreed to remove both boys from their last lesson and have them wait downstairs until Beth and her colleague arrived.

'Thank you,' Beth said.

When Beth got to the school, the boys were sitting with their bags in a downstairs office that led from reception. They were looking agitated and ill at ease. The Head appeared from nowhere.

'Hello, ready?' Beth asked them.

'I think you need to contact their parents?' Ms Clements said.

'Their father's already been informed,' Beth replied. 'He's on his way to the station now. You know why you're coming with us?' she asked the lads.

Mike shook his head.

'We need to ask you some questions about Emma Arnold's abduction. We thought it best to do it at the station.'

Silently, the boys stood up, and followed Beth out of the door.

It was quiet outside – school didn't end for another fifteen minutes or so. The three of them went to the car and the boys sat in the back, dropping their bags in the footwells by their feet. Matt had been waiting in the car, and now started driving as Beth began making small talk with the boys. The conversation was one-sided and stilted. 'Yes.' 'No.' 'Don't know.' She gave up, and they sat in silence for the rest of the journey.

Having parked the car at the rear of the police station, they filed in through the back door and went to the desk for processing. Matt then took Mike to a holding cell while Gregory was taken to Interview Room One. Mr Watson had already arrived and was sitting in reception, anxiously waiting for news about his sons. The appropriate adult the police had booked to sit in on the interviews, Miss Campbell, was also in the building. She'd been called from the list and was free. Mr Watson couldn't sit in because he was involved in the case himself.

Gregory was visibly trembling as they sat down. Beth sat on one side of the table and Gregory and Miss Campbell were on the other. Beth gave the time, the date and the names of those present, then began with a smile.

'There's nothing to worry about, Gregory. Your father is just outside. I want you to tell me what you know about twenty-seven Bulwarks Road.'

Gregory fiddled with his sleeve and then said, 'It's a house that was owned by Carl's gran.'

'And what did you and Mike use it for?'

He looked at her and then began to cry. 'I'm so sorry

for all the trouble we've caused. Really, I am. It's been worrying me a lot. We should never have got involved. Dad's going to be furious when he finds out.'

Beth passed him a tissue. He wasn't a hardened criminal; he'd just got mixed up in something he wished he hadn't. Mike was older and more responsible. She waited for Gregory to quieten down and fetched him a glass of water.

'Let's go back to the beginning,' Beth said. 'Tell me what's been going on, please.'

Gregory blew his nose and began. 'Mike and me got to know Carl and he suggested we play a trick. We knew Dad had set up a spy camera in the guest bedroom and—'

'How did you know that?' Beth interrupted.

'We'd been watching Dad for months. We put cameras all round the house and Mike put a piece of spyware on his phone so we could see what he does, just for fun.'

'You could see everything?' Beth asked.

'Yes, more or less.'

'Does your father know about this?' she asked.

He shook his head.

'OK. Carry on, Gregory.'

'So that's how we knew Dad had set up the spy camera, and we thought we'd teach him a lesson. Emma had already said that she was fed up with her parents and thought doing a prank would be a laugh. So Carl pretended to suffocate Emma and then we used Carl's gran's old house to hide Emma away. We never imagined it would create the amount of attention it did. We were out of our depth, we really were.' He was on the verge of tears again.

'Did you tie Emma up?' Beth asked.

'Occasionally. She wanted to leave after a while and we needed her there. But it was with her consent – to begin with. The rest of the time she was free.'

'How often did you visit her at the house?' Beth asked.

'I think it was four or five times,' he said. 'We were supposed to be at school the first few times. And we went on Saturday too. We went back on Sunday and missed our football match. The coach phoned home so we're in trouble for that. But Emma had escaped by the time we got to the house.'

'Why did she have to escape?' Beth asked.

'I don't know. I guess she'd had enough,' he said hesitantly.

'I'm not surprised,' Beth said.

His face changed. 'I know. I'm so sorry.' He began crying again and this time couldn't stop.

'I think that's enough for now,' Miss Campbell said, looking at Beth.

Beth agreed. She'd heard more than enough. This was kids – well-brought-up kids at that – having a laugh. What a waste of police time. She'd see Mike now and listen to whatever he had to say.

'Can I go home now?' Gregory asked through his tears.

'Yes, your father is waiting for you out in reception. I'll take you to him.'

They stood and Beth took Gregory to his father,

257

who put his arms around him and gave him a hug. Miss Campbell remained where she was in the interview room.

Matt fetched Mike, who sauntered into the interview room and sat down, cockier and more self-assured than his younger brother.

'Don't believe a word he's told you,' he said once Beth had re-entered the room. 'None of it's true.' Waiting had given him time to regain his confidence and bravado, Beth thought.

'So what is the truth?' Beth asked him.

He looked at them and said, 'No comment.'

'I think you've been watching too many police dramas,' Matt said.

'How did you meet Carl Harvey?' Beth asked.

'No comment.'

'What can you tell us about twenty-seven Bulwarks Road,' she asked.

'No comment.'

'What did you do to your father's phone?'

'No comment.'

And so it continued, until after about fifteen minutes of no-comment responses, Miss Campbell turned to Beth and said, 'Excuse me, but is there any point in continuing with this interview?'

'None whatsoever,' Beth agreed, annoyed. 'You can go, Mike. We might want to see you again.'

Mike drew himself to his feet, picked up his school bag and went towards the door. Beth led the way into reception, where Mr Watson and Gregory were waiting.

They stood as they approached.

'Mr Watson, we're all done for today, but I would check your phone very carefully when you get home.'

'Why?' he asked, aghast.

'Your sons have planted some spyware on it. We're still checking your laptop – there might be something similar on it,' she said and, saying goodbye, returned to her desk.

Beth sat and wrote up her record of the boys' interviews, then turned her attention to the report on the flask they had found at 27 Bulwarks Road, which had just arrived. It showed that it had come from Tesco, and they'd sold nearly two thousand of them in the last six months in their area alone. Beth knew if she attempted to match the fingerprints on the flask they would very likely belong to one of the Watson lads or Carl Harvey, just as the shoe prints would be a match too. They didn't have the resources to follow up, and in any case, it seemed a bit pointless. She'd run it by DS Scrivener and see what he thought, but personally, she didn't think they'd secure a prosecution for any of it.

THIRTY-TWO

To say that peace in the Watson household was tenuous was an understatement. Jenny was still furious with the boys and to a slightly lesser extent with Alfie. It was her silent reprimanding looks and tuts that got to him the most. He was trying not to do anything that would upset her and make the situation worse.

DS Scrivener had more or less closed the investigation. It was decided that the whole thing, a massive waste of police time, had been kids fooling around and having what they saw as some fun. The Crown Prosecution Service had already declined to prosecute, feeling there was insufficient evidence to prosecute Alfie. He had his laptop returned to him, and he took the opportunity to apologize profusely to the police for his sons' behaviour.

'You'd better check this laptop carefully,' DC Mayes said as she handed it back to him. 'It looks like this has been tampered with too.'

He rolled his eyes as he took it.

Once home, he made himself a tea and then took the laptop upstairs to his study. Life was gradually returning to normal, he thought. The boys had confessed that they had dug up the earring, having seen him bury it through the camera in the living room, and put it back inside to confuse him. They'd also confessed to sending him an email demanding £5,000 as if it was from Carl. It was easy to set up an email account in someone's name, they said. Carl had never contacted Alfie. The money he'd paid had been spent already. He'd told them off big time, grounded them and said they had to repay the money by doing odd jobs around the house. And from now on, he would be keeping a much closer eye on them. There wasn't much more he could do. Jenny had then had a serious talk with the pair of them, telling them how very wrong it all was and that even if they were upset with their parents, this wasn't the way to deal with it. They were old enough to know better.

Alfie plugged in the laptop and got on with some work as it powered up. The battery had run right down while it had been with the police. It was only a back-up, but Beth had said to check it thoroughly, so he would. Once it had enough charge, he removed any files he didn't recognize, then downloaded a program that was supposed to protect your computer from spyware. He didn't want the boys putting anything back on there in the future. He was about to close the laptop down when he noticed a new folder on the desktop. What was this? he thought. He clicked on it and it opened. For a few seconds, he couldn't work out what he was looking at. Then his eyes adjusted and he stared at it, not understanding.

The video clip was taken in a similar room to their Roomy-Space. It was semi-dark and appeared to be empty. The camera began to move, gradually panning around the room to a chair in the middle. Alfie sat forward and stared. All was still, then suddenly a girl was dragged in and forcibly tied to it. There was no sound and she had a bag over her head. He was sure it wasn't Emma; this girl was much smaller. The film stopped as abruptly as it started. He pressed play again and looked more closely. The room could be anywhere, he decided. It wasn't necessarily theirs, but who was the girl and why was this film on his laptop? The police must have seen it. He played it through again, then phoned DC Mayes.

'It's Alfie Watson.'

'Hello.'

'You know you've just returned my laptop?' he began.

'Yes.'

'What was it you wanted me to check on it?'

'Just to look for anything abnormal, any files you don't recognize. Forensics made a note that they had found some software on it that you might not appreciate. Spyware,' DC Mayes said.

'I deleted all the temporary internet files, but I found another file dated two months ago that I didn't put there.'

'The one with the girl in the room?' DC Mayes asked.

'Yes, that's the one.'

'It was examined by forensics and they decided it was

part of the same prank your sons and Carl played,' she said.

'But the girl isn't the same one. It's not Emma Arnold.'

'I know that. But I'm certain your sons will know who she is. I would ask them when they get home.'

'Yes. Of course,' Alfie said, and he put down the phone feeling a bit of a fool.

Of course it would be his sons. They'd done this sort of thing before.

That afternoon, Alfie was ready and waiting for the boys as soon as they came in. They knew they had to come straight home from school. He had a good half an hour before Jenny came home.

'Lads,' he said in the hall. 'I need to talk to you both.'

'What about?' Mike asked.

'Come into the kitchen.'

They took off their coats and shoes and then followed him into the kitchen, where Mike began leisurely filling a glass with water. Gregory was leaning on the counter waiting for his turn.

'Stop what you're doing right now!' Alfie said, his voice much higher than usual. 'I said I need to talk to you.' They'd got away with their insolence for too long and it would stop now.

'What is it, Dad?' Mike asked, and turned from the tap.

'My laptop, this one,' he said, picking it up from the side. 'The police returned it today, but there's something I want you to see.'

He took it over to them and pressed play.

They were both expressionless as they watched the video.

'Yes?' Mike said. 'What's this got to do with us?'

'Did you put it there?'

'Never seen it before,' Mike said.

'Are you sure? DC Beth Mayes thought the most likely culprits were you two.' He looked from one to the other.

'No, nothing to do with me,' Mike said.

'Me neither,' Gregory added.

He continued to watch them as they finished getting their water. Were they telling the truth? He honestly didn't know. That was the trouble with people who consistently lied – how did you know when they were telling the truth?

'I'd let it go,' Mike said, and sauntered away.

'No, I'm not going to let it go. I've done that before. I'm going to take my laptop back to the police station now and ask them to have another look. Tell your mother I won't be long.'

'Suit yourself,' Mike said, and he headed upstairs.

His brother followed him.

Alfie closed his laptop with a bang and headed for the door. He would go to the police station now, then explain to Jenny when he got home. He texted her to say he'd be back in time for dinner, then drove to the station. The officer on duty was the one from earlier and Alfie asked to speak to DC Mayes.

'What's it in connection with?' the officer asked.

'My laptop,' Alfie said.

'I'll see if she's free. Take a seat.'

It was fifteen minutes before she arrived.

'Hello again, Mr Watson. What can I do for you?' she said with a tight smile.

'The video clip we spoke about on the phone wasn't taken by my sons,' he said. 'I've brought my laptop back so you can have another look at it.'

'Show me the clip again,' Beth said.

He sat down in reception and found the video clip, then pressed play. Beth looked at it carefully.

'It's definitely not Emma,' she said. 'That's what forensics said.' She looked at the date mark: 13 August. 'There's nothing else on here like this?'

'No. I've checked the whole laptop.'

'And you're sure it's not one of your sons fooling around?'

'As sure as I can be,' Alfie said.

'Leave it with me and I'll take another look.' He closed the laptop and passed it to her. 'Forensics may have included it in their first report. There was no need to follow it up when the case was closed. You found the spyware?'

'Yes, I did, thank you. I think I've got rid of it all. How long do you need my laptop for this time?' he asked.

'You should have it back next week.'

Alfie went home feeling positive that he had something to tell Jenny, something important that would add to his credibility. He parked the car behind hers and strolled in, only to find that the boys had already told her about the video. They were all in the kitchen talking about it.

'It's very strange,' he said, joining in the conversation. 'Beth is going to get digital forensics to take another look.'

'It's not like it's the only strange thing that's gone on around here recently,' Jenny said curtly, and began to serve dinner.

Seated at the table, they let the subject of Alfie's laptop drop and began to talk about the possibility of restarting a Roomy-Space. He and Jenny decided to wait until the new season began at Easter. It was now still October. Hopefully by then their name wouldn't be linked to the Emma Arnold case online. The boys sat quietly.

After dinner, subdued, Alfie washed up the pans as Jenny did her marking and lesson planning, then he went upstairs. The boys were in their bedroom, hopefully doing their homework. The door to the Roomy-Space was permanently closed now, but on a whim, he opened it and went in. They'd cleared up once the police had finished and it looked ready for the next guest. Just the furniture, rug and curtains remained. He spent a few moments gazing at the room, then came out and continued up to his study. He came to an abrupt halt by the door. The room, their Roomy-Space, *was* the same room as the one that had appeared in that new video clip. He was sure now he'd looked at it again.

He paused, then returned downstairs to take another look. Going in, he stood by the door and stared at the room. Take out the furniture and the room was identical – no rug, but the curtains looked similar. But then how many other Roomy-Spaces looked the same? he wondered.

Was he being silly? Paranoid? If only he had kept a copy of the video clip from his laptop. Then he remembered he'd shown it to the boys.

He went to their bedroom, knocked on the door and without waiting for them to shout 'come in', he opened it. They looked up, surprised.

'Have you two got a minute?' he said.

'Why?' Mike asked.

'It's to do with our Roomy-Space. Come with me.'

He headed across the landing to the room and went in.

'Does this room remind you of anywhere you've seen recently?' he said.

'Another Roomy-Space?' Mike suggested.

'No. The room is the same one as in the video clip I just showed you,' Alfie said. 'You saw it. It's identical, minus the furniture, of course. Look at the curtains.'

Mike looked. 'I honestly don't know,' he said. 'It could be similar, but it's like thousands of others.'

'I guess it looks a bit like it,' Gregory agreed.

Alfie looked at them and wondered if he was making a fuss unnecessarily. Had he really seen a likeness, or had he imagined it? 'It does,' he prompted.

'Yes, a bit,' Gregory agreed again.

'Is that everything?' Mike asked and Alfie nodded.

They returned to their room, leaving Alfie looking at their Roomy-Space again. The chair from the video clip that had been in the middle of the room was just like one from their dining room. He was sure of it. He went downstairs and into the dining room, where Jenny was working at the table. He pulled out one of the other chairs and studied it. It was the same as the one in the video. Identical.

'Are you OK?' Jenny asked, looking at him oddly.

He was about to tell her about his suspicions but stopped. What if he was wrong? He didn't want to make a fool of himself.

'Yes, I'm fine. Have any of these chairs ever been in the guest room?' he asked.

'No,' she said, and carried on with her schoolwork.

Alfie put the chair back under the table and went upstairs again, looking in the Roomy-Space as he went. It was the same room and chair, he was sure of it now. With a final glance around, he came out, closed the door and returned to his study, still deep in thought. He was convinced it was the same room, but how had his sons managed it? They must have been lying. There was no other explanation for it. But who was the girl on the chair? The boys must have taken the video clip some while ago and had put it on his computer. How they'd managed to clear the room without him or Jenny knowing was an absolute mystery.

It was two months ago that the video had been taken. He thought back. Beth had said the timestamp was 13 August. He flicked through his diary back to that date. It was a Sunday and they'd all gone to visit Jenny's sister for the day. All of them except Mike, who'd said he had a cold. Alfie remembered it now. He and Jenny had had a heated discussion about whether he was well enough to go or not, and had eventually decided to leave him at home. They'd been out for most of the day. Plenty of time for Mike to take out a few items of furniture and bring the chair up from the dining room. But why? Why go to all that trouble? That was the bit he couldn't get his head around. Why do it at all?

THIRTY-THREE

By 7.30 that evening, homework done in a manner of speaking, both boys were sitting on their beds, on high alert. They'd logged in to their laptops and were waiting for the meeting to begin. There were four of them in their group – Carl, Mike, Gregory and Emma – but there were plenty of other groups across the country. Worldwide there were thousands, stretching from Australia to South Africa to Alaska. They were part of an online group called the Stranger Danger Club. They operated unseen unless they were deliberately going out into the community, which they were chancing to do more often now.

The club had started several years before as a bit of fun, although their own group had only been formed nine months ago. The club was bigger now than anyone could have foreseen. There were groups all over the world containing anything from two to twenty members. It had been decided that two was the minimum and twenty the maximum for the individual groups to work.

The club set each group targets to reach, with challenges to overcome that had to be recorded online, all of which gained them points. Faking Emma's murder had been the group's most daring challenge to date, and they nearly hadn't got away with it. It had been a great challenge, because not only had they won a ton of points, but they'd also taught Emma's parents and their dad a lesson at the same time.

'Well done to us all,' Carl said when he arrived on the group chat. 'What's the next challenge?'

'It can't be about me this time,' Emma said.

'Don't be daft, of course it won't,' Mike said.

They waited in silent anticipation for the challenge to be revealed. They watched as it appeared in the top right-hand corner of their computer screens, then floated slowly down. From where it came no one knew. All they were aware of was that the challenges appeared on their computers, visible to these four club members only. They spent a moment reading what it said and then, after a few minutes, it automatically self-destructed.

Then a disembodied voice asked, 'Do you accept the challenge?'

'I don't think I can do that,' Emma said, fear in her voice.

'Me neither,' Gregory agreed.

Carl and Mike locked eyes across their screens.

They could say no, but then they'd have to start at the bottom again, nine months of hard work down the drain.

'Do you accept the challenge?' the voice repeated.

'Yes,' Mike said.

'Good luck,' the voice said, and then fell silent. That was the last they would hear from anyone in the club until the challenge was complete.

The four young people sat in silence for some moments, connected only by the video call and the thought of what they had been asked to do.

'It can't be me,' Carl said at last. 'I've been brought up by my gran.'

'Me neither,' Emma said. 'I would like to, but my parents are too old. They've had enough of me already. Any more stress and they'd have heart attacks.'

Gregory was looking down, unable to meet Mike's gaze.

'We'll do it,' Mike said.

Gregory gave the faintest of nods. Their challenge was to kidnap a parent and hide them away for a week, without letting the victim know who had taken them.

'It'll have to be Dad,' Mike said after a while. 'Mum's too clever. She'd suss us out straight away.'

Emma was still worrying. 'You'll be careful, won't you?' she said.

'Sure,' Mike agreed. 'The most difficult part will be hiding our identities. We didn't have to do that with you. If we speak, he'll realize it's us for sure. We'll blindfold him and we'll have to make sure we don't speak when he's within earshot.'

'Obviously I'll help,' Carl said.

'Thanks, mate,' Mike said. 'Where shall we take him?'

'I'd go for twenty-seven Bulwarks Road again. It's only for a week and the police have finished with it now.'

'It's a possibility. Can anyone think of anywhere else?' Mike asked.

'That house has still got police hazard tape across the front door,' Emma pointed out.

'DC Mayes told Dad the case was closed so I guess they've just left it there. Does anyone have a better suggestion?'

No one did, so they agreed on 27 Bulwarks Road.

'I don't think we should do this,' Gregory said.

'Why not?'

'Well, it's Dad. I mean, what's he ever done to us?'

'It's not so much about that. It's about completing the challenge. We can't possibly lose now. Aren't you up for it?' He looked at him questioningly.

'I guess,' Gregory said. 'But I don't think it's right. Plus, it's going to be really hard. I mean, how will you get him there for a start?'

Mike thought for a moment. 'It's Halloween on Sunday. We'll do it then. And it's just for a week. He'll be fine.'

'But how are you going to actually get him there?' Gregory asked.

Mike thought. 'Mum's still got some sleeping tablets somewhere – I heard her saying once. We'll put some of those in his drink, just to make him a bit sleepy.'

'How will we physically move him, though?' Gregory persisted.

'I can use my car like we did with Emma,' Carl offered.

'That should be all right,' Mike said. 'Does anyone have any more questions?'

The others shook their heads.

The boys ended the video call and flopped back on their beds. It was a few moments before either of them could speak again.

'I'm still not sure about this,' Gregory admitted.

Mike turned to him. 'Think of the kudos it will bring us. A member has kidnapped their father for a whole week! Others will want to copy us. You wait and see.'

'But it's not right,' Gregory lamented. 'And there will be something that goes wrong. I know there will. A week is too long. If it was for one night then maybe, but not for a week. What are you going to do – keep him tied to a chair the whole time?'

'We did with Emma – well, for a lot of the time,' Mike said.

'But that was completely different. Dad isn't supposed to know it's us. He'll guess.'

'No, he won't. Not if we keep quiet while we're in the room. Carl and Emma can do the talking. They'll have to muffle their voices.'

'I'm not convinced,' Gregory said.

'We've agreed to it now. It'll be fine,' Mike said. 'Now, let's plan it.'

The atmosphere in Mike and Gregory's room that night was a mixture of unbridled excitement and grave misgivings. Mike sat at his laptop, tapping the keys, energized and animated as he began planning the operation with military-style precision. Gregory sat silently on the other bed, only interrupting when Mike said something preposterous, when he would say 'no' and suggest an alternative. Mike would either dismiss his suggestion or take it on board with a 'good point'. By 10 p.m. they'd all but finished and the only thing that remained was to decide on a time to initiate the actual kidnap.

'It'll depend on when it gets dark on Halloween,' Mike said. 'And where Dad is in the house. I mean, which room he's in.'

'He often spends Sunday evening watching TV in the living room,' Gregory said. 'That's what he's doing whenever I come down. Mum is usually busy somewhere else.'

'So what sort of time shall we say? Eight?'

'Should be fine.' Gregory felt he was caught up in something over which he had little or no control.

'It'll be dark then, won't it?' Mike asked.

'Yes, definitely. Well before then.'

'I'll let Carl and Emma know the plan,' Mike said. He typed an email sending the details and asking if they could think of anything he'd forgotten.

Twenty minutes later Carl replied.

It should work. Let me know what time you want me outside your house.

Get here for eight, but stay out of sight until we call you, Mike replied.

Emma replied, *Sounds good.*

275

A knock sounded on their bedroom door, together with their mother's voice.

'Are you two in bed yet?' she asked.

'Nearly,' Mike called.

'See you in the morning then. Goodnight.'

'Night,' Gregory replied.

'Night,' Mike said.

The following day, both boys checked to see what time it started to get dark. They never usually took much notice of the weather or when the sun rose or fell. They were satisfied that 8 p.m. allowed them more than enough time; it was pitch dark by then.

On Saturday, they were both up early to go shopping for food and drink. They were better organized than last time. They told their parents they were just going to window shop since they were still repaying their father. They were allowed out now – they knew their grounding wouldn't last long. It never did.

They bought enough food and drink for the week and carried it to 27 Bulwarks Road. Mike unlocked the back door, as the front door still had hazard tape stuck across it. The rubbish they'd left the last time was still there. So, too, was the metal can Mike had stood on to reach in and open the fan-like window. It was dark and creepy inside, and they gingerly made their way upstairs to the back bedroom. The police had been here to, but other than items being moved around, it all seemed fine. Mike switched on the cold-water tap in the bathroom and that was still running.

'Lucky days,' he said.

'Not for Dad,' Gregory said, which Mike ignored. He had to; he was becoming nervous.

They spent about a quarter of an hour in the house making sure it was ready for tomorrow and then returned home.

'Did you see anything you wanted?' Alfie asked over dinner that night.

The boys looked at him, wondering what he was talking about. Then Gregory remembered.

'No, not this time,' he said, and continued eating.

'Are you two celebrating tomorrow?' Alfie tried. Sometimes it seemed impossible to have a proper conversation with them.

'We're going out dressed up,' Mike said. 'To a party.'

'What are you going as?' he asked.

Mike didn't reply.

'I'm going as Black Panther,' Gregory said. 'And Mike is going as Godzilla. They're—'

He didn't get any further. Mike had kicked him under the table and was now glaring at him.

'Have a good time,' Alfie said, ignoring his elder son's lack of conversation.

'I hope we don't get too many trick-or-treaters,' Jenny said.

'We'll do what we did last year – put off the lights and go to bed early,' Alfie replied, and winked at his wife.

THIRTY-FOUR

The most difficult part of the whole challenge was going to be how to remove their father from the house and get him into the waiting car, the boys had decided in their bedroom, as they ran through the details one last time on the Sunday. They'd also decided it would be best if Gregory side-tracked their mother upstairs, to distract her. Mike, taller and broader than his father, would then be able to bundle Alfie into the car.

At 7.15, Gregory went downstairs for a drink. He glanced into the living room, expecting to see his father lightly dozing in his chair. His mother was there watching TV, but his father was nowhere to be seen.

'Where's Dad?' he asked casually. He knew that Mike had already crushed the sleeping tablets and added them to his father's evening meal.

'I'm not sure, love. Upstairs somewhere, I think.'

Taking his glass of water, he immediately went up the two flights of stairs to his father's study. His father often went there in the evening to be alone. He knocked on the door. There was no reply, so Gregory gingerly opened it. The room was empty. He closed the door again and went down a flight of stairs to his parents' bedroom. There was nowhere else his dad could be. He gave a small knock on the door. Again, there was no reply.

'Are you in there, Dad?' he asked, giving the door another small knock.

Still no reply. He gingerly opened the door and there was his father, flat on his back, fast asleep on the bed. His jaw was hanging open and he was snoring lightly. He wasn't supposed to be asleep yet! It was too early. Gregory silently closed the door and went to his bedroom.

'Dad's fast asleep,' he said to Mike, going in. 'He's in his bedroom. How many tablets did you give him?'

'Four,' Mike said.

'That's a lot! He's out cold.'

Mike thought for a second. 'We'll get into our costumes now then. We can leave before eight. I'll message Carl and tell him.'

He sent a quick WhatsApp to Carl saying to be there by 7.45 at the latest, then, putting down his phone, he struggled into his Godzilla costume. Gregory put on his Black Panther outfit. They checked the results in the mirror. They certainly looked the part. The dark costumes covered them from head to toe, and they included rubber face masks, which they then put on. You couldn't see who it was beneath the costume at all.

They stood for a moment looking at their reflections

in the mirror. Mike had to admit to himself that he was nervous at the thought of actually removing his father from the house and taking him to the car, but he said nothing. Gregory had been freaking out ever since they'd been given the challenge. He took a deep breath and adjusted his costume.

At 7.40 they were ready, and Mike slightly opened their bedroom door. The sounds of the TV drifted up. Their mother was still in the living room and clearly engrossed.

'Do we show her our costumes?' Gregory whispered to Mike.

'No, she can use her imagination,' Mike replied. He pulled a disparaging face beneath the mask.

A message arrived from Carl, saying he was parked outside. Mike messaged back that they were on their way and closed their bedroom door.

They quietly crossed the landing and slipped into their parents' bedroom. Their father was still out cold, flat on his back, snoring more loudly than before. They tiptoed quietly over the carpet to the bed. They placed their hands under his armpits and lifted him into a sitting position. He was a dead weight. His head flopped to one side and his whole body collapsed onto the bed.

'Four tablets was too many,' Gregory hissed. 'Mum only takes one.'

'It's too late now,' Mike said. 'You get on the other side and we'll try again.'

Gregory manoeuvred into position and together, with

a big heave, they sat Alfie up. He groaned but didn't open his eyes. They waited until he'd settled and then moved him round so his legs were hanging over the edge of the bed.

'On the count of three,' Mike whispered. 'One, two, three.'

They pulled him into a semi-standing position, but his legs buckled and collapsed. Mike had to grab him to stop him from falling back on the bed. They sat him on the edge of the bed again. He was a lot heavier than they'd thought he would be.

'Let's try again,' Mike said, his breath coming fast and low.

Taking a side each, they managed to pull Alfie upwards and got him onto his feet. He stayed there swaying.

'A step at a time,' Mike cautioned.

They began slowly towards the door, half carrying and half dragging him. His feet had a way of disappearing backwards, underneath him. Finally, they were at the door, they opened it and listened. It was still quiet downstairs.

'Now or never,' Mike said, and with Gregory helping, they pulled their father to the top of the stairs.

They made their way carefully down the stairs one step at a time. There were eight steps before they were level with their mother. Gregory counted each one. He hadn't ever wanted to do this and now he felt justified – this was scary as hell. He could see his mother's back in the living room. The television was turned up and their mother was engrossed. They waited a moment. There was still no movement from her, so they continued downstairs. As they neared the last step, Gregory wondered what his mother would see if she were to turn. Black Panther and Godzilla heaving their father downstairs. They quickly went past her line of vision and to the door. She heard them.

'Have a nice time!' she called from the living room, but she didn't come to the door.

'We will!' Mike called back.

They headed down the path. Straight ahead was Carl's car. The rear door was already open. Thank goodness. They breathed a sigh of relief as together they bundled their father in. Emma was on the back seat and helped pull him towards her. She was dressed for Halloween, glammed up in a wicked-witch costume, but without a mask. Carl was sitting in the driver's seat and turned to look at them. He gave a small laugh. He was wearing a dark hooded robe. 'Grim Reaper,' he said with another laugh.

Alfie was in the car now and Gregory got into the back next to him and slammed shut the door. Their father's head fell to one side, lolling onto Emma's shoulder. She pushed it back, but it immediately fell down again. Mike was in the front passenger seat.

'Let's go,' Mike said. 'Halloween challenge, here we come.'

They pulled away into the depths of the night.

They kept their masks on in the car, but they didn't

stand out because the streets were full of trick-or-treaters having fun. Many of them had clearly had a drink.

They made their way into town and out the other side, then Mike and Gregory took off their masks for some fresh air.

The atmosphere in the car was quiet and sombre as they continued to drive towards the regeneration area. Occasionally one of them made a comment and it was met with a nod. Alfie slept on in the back with no sign of waking. His head kept lolling onto Emma's shoulder. Eventually she gave up trying to push it back and accepted the extra baggage.

The roads were clear now and they were gathering speed towards 27 Bulwarks Road. It was very dark as they entered the regeneration site; only a few street lamps had been left on in the roads where there were inhabitants. Emma gave a shiver as they drove down Bulwarks Road, past the house where she'd been held, and then they turned right. There was an alleyway that ran behind the row of houses, but it wasn't wide enough for a car.

'Let's stop here,' Carl said, and he brought the car to a halt.

They looked out at the deserted streets.

'Can I keep my mask off?' Gregory asked.

'No. We don't know when he's going to wake up,' Mike said.

They got out of the car and looked around. There was a nearly full moon, it was now 8.30 p.m. They stood where they were, looking and listening. It was all quiet.

Alfie was still in the car, the top half of him had fallen across the back seat as Emma had got out.

'It's spooky,' she said, and shivered again.

Mike and Carl reached into the car and began to pull Alfie out.

'Jesus, he's a weight,' Carl said. 'What did you give him?'

'Mum's sleeping tablets,' Mike said.

'They don't have this effect on my gran,' Carl said.

'Try four,' Gregory replied.

Alfie was out of the car now and lying on his back on the ground, still sleeping.

'If we take an arm and a leg each?' Mike suggested.

Carl shut the car doors and they bent down. Mike and Carl put their hands under Alfie's arms and Gregory and Emma took a leg each.

'On the count of three we lift,' Mike said.

They lifted him with a series of grunts and, holding him aloft, began manoeuvring him along the alley.

'Which one is twenty-seven?' Carl asked, peering into what he could see of the rear gardens. They were all unlit and he'd never had to use the back entrance before.

'It's over there,' Mike said, and tripped over a tin can. 'Shit!'

'Keep the noise down,' Carl hissed. 'How do we get in?'

'Through the back gate,' Mike said, and led the way into the back garden of Number 27.

They struggled with Alfie to the rear of the house and put him down. Emma looked up at the room she'd been kept in. 'I don't know how I survived for so long here,' she said.

Mike took the key from his jacket pocket and unlocked the back door. He'd taken the key with them on their last visit when Emma had been here. He pushed the door wide open. They picked up Alfie and struggled in with him. It was pitch dark inside.

'Just look at what I had to put up with,' Emma said in a sulky tone.

Suddenly a noise could be heard, a strange scuttling sound, and a rat ran across the kitchen floor. Emma screamed and dropped the leg she was holding.

'Sshh,' Carl hissed. 'Get a grip.'

They waited until she'd composed herself.

'Pick up his leg,' Mike told her, and Emma, still bleating about the rat, did as she was told.

They steered Alfie down the hall, turned left and began hauling him up the stairs. Mike and Carl took most of the weight at the back, but even so it was a struggle. At the top of the stairs they went straight into the back bedroom.

They continued across the floor and sat Alfie on the chair in the middle of the room. He was still fast asleep and kept toppling off, his top half flopping forwards. Mike got Carl to hold him in place while he took the rope from the items they'd bought yesterday. He began wrapping it around his dad's upper half, a dozen or more times. It didn't take long and then Alfie was secure. They four of them stood back to admire their work – the Grim Reaper, Godzilla, Black Panther and a witch.

'Shall we wait until he wakes up?' Carl asked, looking at the others.

'We don't know when that will be,' Mike said.

'I think we should,' Emma said. 'It's horrible waking up here alone.'

'But supposing he doesn't stir until the morning?' Mike said. 'I don't know how long four tablets last.'

They continued to look at Alfie, who sat on the chair, out for the count.

'When did you give him the tablets?' Carl asked Mike.

'Just after six o'clock, with his dinner,' Mike replied.

'I don't think he's going to wake until morning,' Carl said.

They sat on the floor with their costumes on and watched Alfie for another half an hour, during which time he snored, occasionally trying to right his head, but it flopped back down again. He remained fast asleep. Carl decided it was time to leave.

'I'll be back here by nine tomorrow morning,' he said. 'Then, Mike and Gregory, you two can come after school.'

'How many days do we have to do the challenge for?' Gregory asked.

'It ends at the weekend,' Mike said.

'Are you sure he won't wake until tomorrow?' Emma asked, worried.

'Yes, positive,' Mike said. 'Look, he's completely out of it.' And to prove it he slapped his father's cheek.

'OK, then I'll give you all a lift back,' Carl said.

Before he left the room, he picked up a cloth and tied

it around Alfie's eyes as a blindfold.

'Is that necessary?' Gregory asked, glancing at Mike.

Mike nodded.

With a final glance back, they went downstairs where Mike told them to leave their costumes. 'That way we can put them on each time before we come up here.'

They struggled out of their Halloween suits and dumped them in the hall.

'Anyone fancy going for a drink?' Carl asked. 'It's only just gone nine.'

'Yes, sure, why not?' Mike agreed.

They went out the back door, which Mike locked. He left the key under a large stone. The four of them went down the back garden to the car they'd left in the alleyway.

'How about the Green Dragon?' Mike suggested. 'They serve underage kids out the back.'

They clambered into the car and set off for a night out. It was Halloween, after all.

THIRTY-FIVE

At 4 a.m. the following day, Alfie began to surface from a bad dream. He couldn't move his hands, legs or the upper part of his body, and it was very dark. It felt as though he was blindfolded and sitting on a chair. Indeed, he felt as if something was holding him to it.

He swallowed hard; his mouth was so dry. What had he had to eat? He tried to stand, hoping to get a drink, but he couldn't. He was tied to a chair and couldn't see. He *did* have a blindfold on. What the hell! Where was he?

'Hello, is anyone there?' he asked, his voice croaky from being so parched.

No one replied, so he tried again. 'Hello, anyone?'

Nothing. The atmosphere in the room suggested he was alone; it was cold and there didn't appear to be any heating on. There was an empty feel to wherever he was. It had an echo, as if it was devoid of furniture. It was like being in a Kafkaesque nightmare. He sat for a moment and then tried shouting again. 'Is there anyone there?'

No one replied and there was no suggestion that anyone had heard him.

He tried to flex his hands, to wriggle his fingers, but they wouldn't budge – the top half of his body was held tightly to the chair by what felt like rope. This was a strange nightmare.

'Help! Is anyone there?' he tried once again, and waited, sitting very still and quiet.

What had happened to him? He thought. He remembered eating his dinner on Sunday evening, then he'd told Jenny he was going for a lie down. He'd suddenly come over very tired. He remembered lying on his bed with his clothes on, and after that there was nothing. He tried to think back to how he might have come to be wherever he was, but it was a blank. Was he in hospital? Had he had a stroke? He didn't think so. He didn't feel as though he'd had a stroke. His arms and legs felt normal. Perhaps it was a massive seizure? Was he on life support? He'd read somewhere that you could suffer from strange dreams when on life support, but again it didn't feel like he was in a hospital ward. There were no tubes or monitors, and why hadn't a nurse come in when he'd shouted? They certainly wouldn't have blindfolded him.

So where the hell was he?

He tried shouting again. 'Hello? Is there anyone there?'

Nothing. No one appeared.

He began to feel afraid and strained against his bindings, but other than making his hands and legs sore, nothing happened.

He then tried to calm himself, breathing deeply in and out. Where were Jenny and the boys? He called out.

'Jenny! Mike! Gregory!'

No one came.

He suddenly came over very sleepy again, and at some point he must have dropped off. His last thought was that when he woke, the nightmare would have ended. He prayed it would.

An hour or so later, Alfie's eyes opened again. It was still pitch black. His hands, legs and upper body were still tied to the chair. Everything was the same. Darkness was all around him and he was still bound to a chair. He came fully to and realized it wasn't a nightmare at all. This was for real.

Alfie began to struggle and call out, but no one came. He was captive. Presumably whoever had brought him here would return? He needed to calm down. He wasn't dead, no one had murdered him, so for that he had to be grateful. What time was it? What day was it? He thought maybe Monday, and if it was, he had an appointment that morning with a new client at 9 a.m. That clearly wasn't going to happen now. He kept thinking about what the hell could have happened, but before long, he fell into another deep sleep for about another hour or so.

At 6.45 a.m. in the Watson household, Jenny was first up. It was always difficult on a Monday morning, after the weekend. The bed beside her was empty and she assumed that Alfie was in his study getting ready for his 9 a.m. appointment. He'd been in there last night too when she'd come up to bed. It must be an important meeting, she thought. She woke up both her sons and then went downstairs where she made them all breakfast. She called goodbye from the hall.

'I'll be a bit late tonight,' she added. 'It's the monthly staff meeting.'

'OK. Bye, Mum,' Gregory shouted, and looked at Mike to do the same.

'Bye, Mum,' he called.

They heard the front door slam shut.

'She hasn't missed him!' Gregory exclaimed.

'No, and she won't either. Straight after his meeting this morning, he'll send a message telling her he's had an emergency call from his sister, Julie, and has gone to visit her. She's ill again like last year. Do you remember?'

'You've got his phone?' Gregory asked.

'Yes, so there's nothing for you to worry about.'

The boys got dressed and ready for school. Gregory was very nervous and kept dropping things. Once they were ready, they had breakfast, put their father's bowl in the dishwasher with their own, and left the house.

'What do you think Dad is doing?' Gregory asked his brother as they walked to the bus stop.

'Sleeping or just coming round, I guess,' he said. 'Carl will be there in under an hour so stop worrying.'

Another boy joined them at the bus stop so further conversation on the matter was impossible. Then on the bus there was a group of lads from school, though at school they went their separate ways. Mike went to his classroom, where Emma stood in a small circle with a group of girls. She knew not to say anything and carried on as normal. When she chanced to glance over, Mike gave her a thumbs-up sign and she smiled.

The teacher arrived and took the register. Before they switched off their phones, Mike texted Gregory.

You OK?

Back came Gregory's reply: *Yes.*

See you after school. Don't be late.

Mike worried that Gregory didn't have the stomach for this, like he and Carl did. He would be all right during the day, but this evening, when they were home with their mother, it would be difficult for him. Mike had already decided to watch him like a hawk to make sure he didn't give them away.

They were allowed to turn on their phones at morning break and Mike texted Gregory again.

Still OK? He asked.

Yes.

It was now just before 9 a.m. at 27 Bulwarks Road. Alfie was wide awake, the effects of the tablets having finally worn off. He was panic-stricken, trying to work out what to say when his captors arrived. They'd got the wrong person, Alfie was convinced of it. He'd been kidnapped and he would be killed if no one paid whatever ransom they'd asked for. And of course no one *would* pay because they'd got him instead of whoever they were supposed to

292

kidnap. He'd worked it all out in the hours he'd sat there. It was the only explanation for him being held captive. Somehow, whoever was responsible had kidnapped the wrong person and had brought him here while the person they were supposed to have targeted was walking around freely. He vaguely wondered who the intended target was and if this whole thing was somehow connected to Emma. But if that was the case, he had no idea how. Certainly his sons couldn't be responsible. They wouldn't do something like this to their own father.

He stayed very still. Then suddenly he heard a noise. He listened in petrified silence. If he wasn't mistaken it sounded as though a door somewhere was being opened. He sat still and listened intently, and as he did so, he heard a door close. Had someone come in? It sounded like a back door. He listened hard and then heard footsteps in the distance. Should he cry out? He decided not to. He needed to be seen to be cooperating. He sat still, sweat pouring off him and running down his back.

It was very quiet for a minute or so, then he heard what sounded like footsteps coming up the stairs. Alfie sat in absolute terror, waiting and listening. The footsteps came slowly closer, then into the room he was in, and then they stopped. Alfie waited.

'Hello?' he said at last, his voice trembling.

Another step towards him, then a voice penetrated the silence.

'Hello, Alfie.'

'Who are you?' he asked.

'Never you mind.'

Alfie sat in the dark. All his previous thoughts about him being the wrong person had now gone. This man knew his name.

Alfie heard him take a couple of steps to his chair and then touch his face.

'Don't hurt me, please,' he begged, and drew back.

'I'm not going to harm you,' the man laughed.

'What do you want with me then? Money?'

'No, although that wouldn't go amiss,' he said. 'We have other plans for you.'

'Like what?'

'We're going to keep you here for the rest of the week, then we'll let you go.'

'I don't believe you,' Alfie said, getting in a state. 'You're lying. You're going to kill me. I know it.'

Another laugh.

'Believe that if you wish, but I promise you it's not true.'

'But why would you let me go?' he asked, still not believing him.

'Because we can,' the man said. 'What do you need now?'

'The toilet,' Alfie said. In fact, he was bursting and couldn't hold it for much longer. 'Then to call my wife.'

'I can take you to the toilet, but I can't let you speak to your wife.'

'Why not?' Alfie asked, the full horror of his situation returning.

'You ask too many questions,' the man said, and, stepping around him, he began to untie his hands and legs.

He felt big and Alfie decided he was too well built for him to try to overpower him. He allowed his hands to be untied and then the man helped him to his feet. He was very stiff and wobbly from sitting for so long.

'This way,' his kidnapper said, and began to guide him out of the room. His blindfold was still in place.

They turned left on the landing and into what Alfie assumed was the bathroom.

'I'll wait here while you go,' the man said.

Alfie found his flies and went to the toilet, then, once he'd finished, he zipped himself up again.

'Can I wash my hands?' he asked.

'Sure. The sink's over here to your right.'

The man ran the cold water and Alfie washed his hands.

'Is there anything to dry them on?' he asked.

'Just your clothes.'

Alfie wiped his hands down the front of his clothes, then the man slowly steered him back to his chair and sat him down. He didn't retie his hands. Alfie heard a squeak of paper being torn, then a supermarket sandwich was put in his hands.

'It's a BLT,' the kidnapper said. 'Your favourite.'

'Thanks,' he managed to say, and began eating, wondering how this person knew what his favourite sandwich was. Surely his sons couldn't be involved, could they?

'Where am I? Really?' he asked after a moment.

'I've told you all you need to know. All you have to do is behave yourself and you'll be released at the end of the week.'

Alfie didn't believe him and was unsure of what to say next. He didn't want to antagonize him. He ate his sandwich and then gave him the empty packet.

'Do you want a drink?' the man asked. 'Coffee?'

'Yes, please.'

Alfie heard him unscrewing what sounded like the top of a flask and pour out some coffee. He was sure it was coffee. He could smell it.

'Here you go,' the man said, and placed the cup firmly in his hands.

Alfie took a sip. It *was* coffee, just as he liked it. He took another sip and another.

'How did you know this is how I like it?' he asked.

'Never you mind,' came the reply.

Alfie drank the coffee as he thought about his kidnapper: a man who'd brought him here, tied him to a chair and left him blindfolded, but brought him a sandwich, and coffee just as he liked it in a Thermos flask. It didn't make any sense.

Once he'd finished the coffee, Alfie handed the cup back and he heard the man screw it back on to the top of the flask.

'What happens now?' Alfie asked with some trepidation.

'If there's nothing else you need, I'll tie you up again

and be off.'

Alfie gave a humourless laugh. 'You mean, other than for you to let me go?'

'Put your hands behind your back,' the man said.

As Alfie moved his hands, he quickly pulled up his blindfold. He couldn't believe his eyes. It was the Grim Reaper. Before he could take in what he was seeing, he felt a blow to his cheek. He winced as the man yanked down the blindfold.

'Don't ever do that again,' he said in a threatening tone.

'But I don't understand what's going on here,' Alfie said. 'Why would you be dressed like that and keep me here for a week?'

The man didn't reply, but continued to tie Alfie's hands behind his back, more tightly than before. Then he tied his legs together and to the chair.

'That's too tight,' Alfie said. 'I can feel the chair digging into my legs.'

'You should have thought of that before you peeked,' the man replied.

He checked the bindings, then stood behind Alfie and retied the blindfold, again tighter than before. He left the room in silence and went onto the landing. Then his footsteps sounded on the stairs. Alfie struggled with his ties, but to no avail. His kidnapper paused at the foot of the stairs for a minute or so.

'Are you still there?' Alfie shouted.

No reply.

Then Alfie heard him reach the back door, which he

opened and closed. The key turned in the lock, and Alfie was completely alone again. He should never have pulled up his blindfold – he'd just made things worse. From now on, he'd do as he was told.

THIRTY-SIX

At lunchtime on Monday, Mike switched on his phone. A message from Carl came up first.

Make sure you wear your face masks. He tried to remove his blindfold.

Did you give him a sandwich? Mike replied.

Yes.

Mike answered a few more messages from friends and checked Gregory was still holding up. Then he took out his father's phone and sent a message to his mother.

Sorry I disappeared. I'm going straight to Julie's after the meeting. She's very poorly again. Will be in touch. Love Alfie x

To which his mother replied: *Give her my love x*

Alfie's single sister Julie had been ill for years and no one seemed to know what was wrong with her. Every so often she worsened and Alfie went to visit her. This suited Mike's plan just fine.

It was soon the afternoon lessons, and the day couldn't

pass quickly enough. Mike willed away the time. Emma wouldn't be coming this afternoon to the house, but she had promised to come tomorrow.

Mike and Gregory met outside school and then waited for the bus that would take them straight into the regeneration area. It arrived after about ten minutes. The driver seemed to keep looking at them in his interior mirror, or was it their imagination? They got off at the stop nearest to the house. It was now 4.40 p.m. Their mother wouldn't be home yet as she had a meeting after school.

Mike and Gregory continued towards 27 Bulwarks Road and went round the back. Mike took the key from under the stone and opened the door. There'd still be enough sandwiches for today, then tomorrow they'd get him something else to eat.

The place smelt stale and shut up, but all was quiet. They went to the foot of the stairs in silence and changed into their Halloween costumes, leaving their school uniforms and bags in the hall. They began up the stairs, Godzilla and Black Panther, and into the back bedroom. Alfie was sitting on the chair, bound and blindfolded.

'Is it the Grim Reaper?' he asked, thinking it must be the same man who'd come before.

'No,' Mike said, using a voice-changing app on his phone

'Who are you then?' he said, alarmed.

Mike motioned to Gregory not to reply but went to the chair and began untying his father's arms. The less they spoke, the less chance there was of him recognizing one of them.

'Who are you?' Alfie asked again, fear in his voice.

Mike kept untying the rope. Carl had certainly done a good job. It was tighter than when they'd left him.

'Talk to me,' Alfie said. 'Have you got my phone?'

Mike untied the rope until his father's hands were free. He immediately drew them forwards and began massaging them.

'That was too tight,' he said.

Neither of the boys replied.

'Can I go to the toilet?' Alfie asked.

Mike untied his legs and took him into the bathroom.

'The other man let me wash my hands,' he said when he'd finished.

Mike steered him to the sink, turned on the cold water and waited while he washed his hands, then turned the tap off again. His father rubbed his hands down his clothes. Mike put a hand under his armpit and steered him back into the room where Gregory was waiting, then into the chair.

'Can you please tell me who you are,' Alfie asked.

They gave no reply. Mike began retying Alfie's legs. Gregory was rummaging in the supermarket carrier bag for a sandwich. He tore the packet open and handed it to his father.

'Thank you,' Alfie said gratefully.

He ate ravenously and then drank the packet of juice he was given and a Bakewell tart from a packet.

301

'No coffee?' Alfie asked hopefully.

The boys looked at each other and Mike said, 'No,' using his voice-changing app.

Once he'd finished eating, Mike began tying Alfie's hands behind the chair again.

'Are you going?' Alfie asked.

There was no reply.

'Won't you stay and talk to me?'

Mike continued to tie his hands.

'We can't,' Gregory said, lowering his voice behind his mask. Mike threw him a warning glance.

'Why not?' Alfie asked hesitantly.

Mike shook his head at Gregory, signalling for him not to reply.

Once Alfie was bound, the boys left the room in silence and went downstairs. They paused at the foot of the stairs to take off their costumes, then picked up their school bags and went outside, locking the door behind them.

'Come on, cheer up,' Mike said as they waited at the bus stop. 'Only another five days to go.'

'It's not right,' Gregory blurted out. 'Whichever way you look at it, it isn't. If we get caught, we'll be in serious trouble, and if we don't, we'll have to live with what we've done forever. This could scar Dad for life.'

'Dad's fine,' Mike said. 'You saw him. He'll be OK until the weekend so stop worrying about him, please.'

Back at 27 Bulwarks Road, Alfie's head was clearing fast. The last effects of whatever drugs he'd been given had completely worn off now and he'd been doing a lot of thinking. He thought about the two visitors he'd had just now. He thought of the man who had come this morning and said far more than the other two. His thoughts eventually went to his phone. Where was it? He tried to think. He'd had it with him when he'd gone up for a lie down, but he didn't have it now. What had happened to it? Had it been left on the bedside cabinet? Had it been lost outside somewhere when they kidnapped him? Or had the kidnappers stolen it? And how did they get him from the house to here? He couldn't remember anything from when he went upstairs for a lie down. Whatever had happened next?

It was nearly six o'clock when Mike and Gregory arrived home, five minutes before their mother was due back. They had just enough time to get upstairs to their room and change out of their school uniforms before the front door opened and she came in.

'Have you put the casserole in the oven?' she called up, already knowing they hadn't. There was no smell coming from the oven.

Gregory went downstairs and took the casserole his mother had already prepared from the fridge and put it in the oven to heat up.

'*Thank you*,' she said tightly.

Gregory returned upstairs, aware that his father usually saw to dinner when his mother was going to be late. Gregory wasn't a mind-reader though; he needed to be told what to do. He went back to his bedroom, where he and Mike waited for the call to dinner. By the time they came down, their mother had recovered somewhat and was in a better mood. It often took her time to recover after a bad day at school. They sat at the table and ate.

'Your father has gone to see his sister,' she said, raising her eyebrows. 'I don't know what's the matter with her. She's always ill. I'll give him a ring later and see how she is.'

'Do you think that's a good idea?' Mike asked. 'I mean, if she's very ill he might not be able to answer his phone.'

'Then I'll leave a message,' she said.

Just to be certain she didn't phone Alfie, after dinner Mike used his father's phone and texted her.

Best not call, love. Julie is very poorly. I'll phone you when there's any news.

Their mother clearly thought nothing of it and replied, *I'll wait until I hear from you x*

On Tuesday morning on the way to school, Mike texted Carl to make sure he was going to see their father. He replied that he was. Mike thanked him and said they'd be there this afternoon after school and wished him luck. He and Gregory went to their respective classrooms. Emma was with the same group of girls as she had been yesterday, and messaged him across the classroom to say she wasn't able to meet them tonight. Mike replied that that was OK, but quietly he doubted that she wanted to be involved at all. Oh well. There were still three of them and sometimes people dropped out.

*

At 9 a.m., Beth was at her desk at Coleshaw Police Station. She'd finally found the time to take another look at Alfie Watson's file on his laptop. She was watching the video clip that showed a girl being dragged into a bare room and forcibly tied to a chair. There was no sound. The girl had a bag over her head. It definitely wasn't Emma; this girl was much smaller. The film stopped as abruptly as it started, and Beth replayed it.

It was unsettling to watch, but if, as Beth thought, it was a prank, presumably by Alfie's sons, then did she have the time to follow it up? No one was missing who matched the girl's description. She checked the rest of the laptop and found that, as Alfie had said, it just contained surveyors' back-up files. She looked again at the video clip. It was certainly disturbing. It was dated 13 August, over two months ago. Alfie had said he'd approached both his sons and they'd denied all knowledge. Could they be believed? Beth wasn't so sure based on their past behaviour.

She picked up her phone and dialled Alfie's number. It went through to voicemail and she left a message asking him to phone her. Then she got on with some other work. At lunchtime she tried his phone again with the same result. She might call in to his house on her way home.

THIRTY-SEVEN

Alfie sat alone in the room and thought some more. He was still worrying about his phone, but the only explanation was that his captors had it.

The question he kept asking himself was: why? Why had they brought him here in the first place? Jenny had been downstairs with the boys when he'd gone to his room. It was unlike him to suddenly come over all tired so early in the evening. Very unlike him, and then very unlike him, too, to be unable to remember a single thing about that night or about coming here. He assumed he must have been drugged, especially given how much he had slept when he'd first got here. It was only now that some memories were starting to come back. Could he remember what he ate for dinner on Sunday night? Yes, it was a full roast. He remembered enjoying it. Then what had happened? After he'd gone upstairs, could he then have got up, gone outside and been attacked? But why?

He didn't have any money, and this morning, when he'd asked the man again why he'd been brought here, he hadn't given him a reason. He'd taken him to the toilet, then given him a sandwich and some coffee and said the others would be in tonight. Who were the other two? He pondered. They'd hardly spoken at all.

Alfie sat there with no idea of the time, listening to the faint noises that drifted in from outside. He was sure there were rats downstairs. He could hear them scuttling around. At one point he'd banged his feet on the floor and they'd scuttled away. He couldn't stand rats.

With nothing else to do, Alfie continued to think. Some of the thoughts he had were quite bizarre. For example, it crossed his mind that the two people who came in yesterday afternoon could be his sons. He didn't have any solid reason to believe this. It was just a feeling in the way one of them had spoken. And they had just been caught out in a kidnapping prank. But he didn't want to believe it. He dismissed the idea. Why would they bring him here? It was a ridiculous thought.

But if his sons *were* involved, he persisted, why do this? He thought and thought, and couldn't work it out. Of course it wouldn't be his sons. What would they be doing keeping him tied up in this god-damn awful place? The idea was ludicrous.

But it would explain – to some degree – how he was taken from home without his knowledge or his phone. Where did Jenny think he was? Had she reported him missing? Were the police out looking for him? He assumed so. You couldn't just disappear and not be reported missing, could you?

Alfie was suddenly jolted from his thoughts as the back door opened. He listened carefully and heard it close again. Then he heard two sets of footsteps making their way to the bottom of the stairs. It was them; they'd returned. They stopped briefly before continuing up the stairs, the same way they'd done yesterday. The footsteps continued across the landing, then came into his room, stopping just inside the door.

'Hello,' Alfie tentatively said.

There was no reply.

'Can I use the toilet?' he asked. 'I'm desperate.'

One of them moved towards him, then around his back. He felt his hands being untied, then his legs. His blindfold was still on. He massaged his arms and legs and got to his feet. He stood still for a moment, trying to get his balance, and then began gingerly across the room. One of the lads had a hand under his arm, steering him in the direction of the bathroom. Once there, he waited to his right while Alfie used the toilet.

When finished, he found the handle and flushed it. He heard a small laugh come from his captor. It sounded familiar. He took the step to the washbasin and in a split second he pulled up his mask and looked into the face of Godzilla. But in that moment, he knew those were the eyes of his son.

'Mike!' he cried, in disgust and horror. 'What the hell are you doing?'

308

'It's not Mike,' the person said, and made a lunge to pull down Alfie's blindfold again.

'Yes, it bloody well is,' Alfie said and tore off his blindfold entirely.

They stood there staring at each other, unsure of what to do or say next. Then the other lad came in dressed as Black Panther.

'Gregory!' Alfie exclaimed. 'What the hell do you two think you're doing to me? I'm your bloody father!'

His heart was racing, and he felt hot and cold, as the two boys stayed where they were, frozen between denying and admitting it.

'Well? What have you got to say for yourselves?' he asked. 'What do you two idiots want with me?'

There was a moment's hesitation when they continued to stand there and stare, then Gregory took off his mask.

'Sorry, Dad,' he said.

'Sorry!' Alfie exclaimed in anger, shaking. 'What do you mean, you're sorry? Mike, you'd better take off your mask too. You look absurd standing there with that on.'

Gradually Mike put his hand to his head and pulled off the mask.

'Well? What is this? What do you think you're playing at?' Alfie demanded. He was panting and struggling to get his breath.

There was a long silence before Gregory spoke. 'It was a test, a challenge,' he said.

'What do you mean – a challenge?' Alfie asked.

Gregory glanced at Mike and when Mike said nothing

he began to explain.

'We're members of the Stranger Danger Club and—'

'You're members of what?' Alfie asked in a derisory tone.

'It's an online club,' Gregory continued. 'It's world-wide,' he added as if that would make it all right. 'After the success of fake-murdering Emma, our next challenge was to kidnap a parent, and we chose you. We had to keep you here until the weekend, then let you go.'

Alfie opened and closed his mouth as if to speak, but nothing came out. He hadn't a clue what to say to his sons. They were both deranged.

'An online club?' he asked after a moment. 'And who is in this club?'

'It was supposed to be us two, Carl and Emma for this challenge. There are hundreds of other challenges going on right now all over the world.'

Alfie looked at Mike, who was still saying very little.

'I suppose you put Gregory up to all of this?' he asked him.

'It was both of us,' Mike replied.

'Does your mother know about it?' he asked, looking again at Gregory.

'No. She thinks you're visiting Julie.'

'She what?'

'Your sister – you texted her and said your sister was very ill again.'

'But I haven't got my bleeding phone,' Alfie snapped, without thinking.

'No, I've got it.'

He took the phone from his trouser pocket and handed it to his father.

'I should have guessed,' he said. 'I nearly did. I need to sit down.'

He went into the back bedroom where he had been held captive and sat on the chair where he'd been held. He put his head in his hands.

'I don't believe it,' he said after a moment. 'I thought I was a goner.' He shook his head and felt like he might cry. 'I really did. I am so angry with you two.'

'You'd have been fine, Dad,' Gregory said, stepping forward and touching him.

Alfie pulled his arm away.

'You said there were four of you – I take it the Grim Reaper was Carl, but where's Emma? She hasn't been here at all.'

'She's been busy. We think she might not want to play any more,' Gregory said.

Alfie sat there shaking his head.

'How did you two get here?' he asked at length.

'On the bus,' Gregory replied. 'Straight after school. We brought you here on Sunday in Carl's car.'

'What did you give me to make me sleep?'

Gregory looked at Mike. 'Mum's sleeping tablets,' Mike said. 'We'll go back home in Carl's car. I'll phone him now.'

Mike went outside the door to phone Carl. He told him the game was over because Alfie had found out who they were.

'Oh shit,' Carl said, then, 'Don't worry. There'll be another challenge.'

'Not for us. Dad's not going to let us out of his sight,' Mike said despondently. 'Can you come and pick us up?'

'Sure. Is he very angry?'

'More disappointed than anything, I think.'

Alfie had a cold-water wash, then took a look around the house while he waited for Carl to arrive with the car. He desperately needed a shower and a change of clothes, but that would have to wait until he was home. He was still struggling to believe what had happened. The boys had given him his phone back, so he texted Jenny to say he was on his way home. She replied, *Great. How's Julie?*

I'll tell you later. He would tell her the full story as soon as he was home.

While they waited for Carl to arrive, Alfie also phoned the client he was supposed to have visited on Monday morning, apologized for missing his appointment and rescheduled it for the following week. He began to feel a bit better now. He was back in the real world.

After twenty minutes, Carl finally arrived. He messaged Mike to say he was there.

The three of them went downstairs and out of the back door, which Mike locked. He put the key under the stone, and they walked through what had once been the back garden and was now more of a rubbish tip. Carl's car was waiting at the end of the alleyway.

'Hello, Carl,' Alfie said, getting into the back of the

car. 'We meet again.'

Carl gave a snort of laughter. 'Too right, Mr Watson. How are you? Wasn't much of a challenge in the end, was it?'

'It was a challenge for me all right,' Alfie said, and fastened his seatbelt.

Mike got into the front and Gregory the back.

'I've told the group what has happened and that we failed our challenge,' Carl said to Mike. 'They said they'd email.'

Mike nodded. Carl started the car and headed for the Watsons' home. For the rest of the journey they were all silent, Alfie, Mike and Gregory gazing out of their side windows. The light was fading but Alfie looked out and savoured life afresh. He was pleased to be alive and well. He looked at his sons and truly wondered about them. What had made them do this? It was beyond teenage rebelliousness.

As they drew up outside their house, Mike turned in his seat and asked Alfie, 'Are you going to tell Mum?'

'I might,' Alfie said. 'I'm thinking about it.' He knew he held this as a trump card and would make them sweat for a while before he made a decision.

Jenny's car was parked on the drive, so she was home. The three of them got out, Mike and Gregory said goodbye to Carl, and they went indoors.

'I'm home,' Alfie called from the hall.

'Great. I was going to give you a ring tonight,' Jenny called back.

'Well, I'm here now, love.'

Alfie took off his shoes and went straight upstairs without seeing Jenny, who was cooking dinner. He showered, then went to his bedroom and spent a while looking around it. For a moment there, he'd thought he'd never see it again. Everything seemed so fresh and vibrant. He was grateful to be home. He threw his dirty clothes into the laundry basket, then he chose a fresh outfit from his wardrobe. Once dressed, he checked his appearance in the mirror and went downstairs, happy to be alive.

Jenny was putting the finishing touches to dinner as he entered the kitchen. He went over and kissed her on the cheek.

'That was nice,' she said with a smile and kissed him back.

'Can I do anything?' he asked.

'No, we're nearly ready.'

The front doorbell suddenly gave a long peal. Jenny parted the blinds and looked out. 'It's the police,' she said. 'Whatever do they want with us tonight? Alfie, can you answer it, please? I'm busy here.'

'Sure,' he said, and immediately felt his heart go into his mouth. Whatever did they want?

THIRTY-EIGHT

'Good evening, Alfie,' DC Beth Mayes said. 'Can I come in? I'd like to talk to you.'

'I suppose so,' he replied, and led the way into their sitting room.

Jenny came in too.

'Good evening,' DC Mayes said to her. 'How are you both?'

'Fine, thank you,' Jenny said.

'Are your sons available? I'd like to speak to them.'

'They're upstairs in their room. Can I ask why you want to speak to them?'

'It's about the video on your husband's laptop.'

Video on his laptop? Alfie had to think – there'd been so much going on in the last few days. Then he remembered.

'You can have this back for now,' DC Mayes said, taking the laptop from her bag and laying it on the table.

'I'll go and fetch the boys,' Jenny said.

Jenny left Alfie in the sitting room while she went upstairs, wondering all manner of things. She gave a perfunctory knock on the boys' door and went in.

'The police are here to speak to you two. You'd better come down now. I hope you haven't got into more trouble,' she added, stressed.

Both boys were silent as they made their way downstairs. They looked alarmed and nervous as they went into the living room. Both were on high alert.

'Hi, Mike, Gregory,' DC Mayes said. 'Take a seat, please.'

Gingerly they sat on the sofa. The smell of dinner floated into the room.

'We've had your father's laptop at the station for a while now,' DC Mayes began. 'I share his concerns about a video of a young girl on it.' She paused and waited for their reaction.

Neither of the boys said anything. Gregory was concentrating on the floor.

'I've seen it, and it looks like the room we use for Roomy-Space, only without the furniture,' Alfie put in.

Both boys were looking down now, clearly unsettled. Beth concentrated on Mike.

'Do you know anything about it?' she asked him.

He gave a small nod. 'Yes,' he said. 'I took the video. The girl is in Gregory's class at school.'

Alfie and Jenny both looked shocked as Beth calmly took out a pen and notepad and said, 'Her name and address, please?'

There was a short silence before Mike said, 'She lives at number twenty-three. Her family moved in a few months back. Her name is Beverly Peters.'

'I remember them,' Alfie exclaimed. 'I went to their home.'

'I'll visit them when I've finished here,' Beth said. 'Tell me about the video clip. Where were your parents while you were shooting it?'

'Out for the day,' Mike said with reluctance. 'I didn't want to go so I said I wasn't feeling well and got left behind.'

'Yes?' Beth prompted when Mike stopped.

'I took out most of the furniture from the Roomy-Space and called Beverly. She came straight away and we shot it. That's all there was to it. She was in on the whole thing.'

Beth wrote. Alfie took a deep sigh. This was nothing compared to his time imprisoned in that house. Jenny, though, was hopping mad.

'What the hell!' she exclaimed. 'You betrayed our trust, yet again. You'll never stay at home alone again. Ever.'

'What were you going to do with the video clip?' Beth asked Mike.

'Similar to what we did with Emma,' he replied. 'Get some money. There was no challenge involved, though.'

'You were going to kidnap Beverly and blackmail her family?'

Mike shrugged.

'And did you ever use the video?'

'No. We didn't get the chance.'

'When you say "we" are you referring to Gregory?'

He gave a nod.

Jenny was still furious but seemed now to be keeping it under control, at least.

'Are there any other videos like this on any devices?' Beth asked.

'No,' Mike said emphatically. 'No.'

'Why was it on your father's laptop and not yours?' Beth asked.

'It was when we had the place wired up. You know, when we put a camera in every room. We used Dad's spare laptop to transfer the files and one must have got left behind.'

'You've got no business using my laptop,' Alfie said angrily. 'I'll have to start locking my study door in future.'

There was a pause as everything started to sink in, then Beth said to the boys, 'Is there anything else you want to tell me?'

Mike and Gregory glanced at their father, who looked away, disappointed and disgusted with his sons.

'No,' Mike said quietly.

'I need you two to think carefully about what you've done,' Beth said. She stood and made her way to the sitting-room door. 'I hope I don't see you again,' she said to the lads, and walked from the sitting room.

Alfie and Jenny went with her to see her out.

Beth left her car parked in the road outside the Watson household and walked to Number 23, wondering how kids entertained themselves before the advent of the internet. She'd look into the Stranger Danger Club; it was clearly a sinister operation. She knocked on the door and it was opened by Mr Peters, who still had his coat on, having just got home from work.

'I'm sorry to trouble you. I'm Detective Constable Beth Mayes,' she said, showing her ID. 'This won't take long. There are some safeguarding issues I need to discuss with you.'

'Safeguarding issues?' he repeated, frowning, puzzled.

'It's in connection with your daughter, Beverly.'

He looked uncertain. 'You'd better come in,' he said, taking off his coat.

Beverly was in the living room with the TV on. She was on her phone. Mr Peters called his wife to come as he and Beth went in.

'It's the police,' he said.

Beth turned and smiled at Mrs Peters. 'It's about Beverly. I understand she's thirteen?'

'Yes, that's right,' Mr Peters said.

'I've just come from speaking to Mr and Mrs Watson,' Beth continued, glancing at Beverly. 'They live a few doors up from you.'

'I'm sorry, we don't know them,' Mr Peters said.

Turning her attention to Beverly, she asked, 'Do you know Mike and Gregory Watson?'

'Put down your phone,' Mr Peters said crossly to his daughter and, picking up the remote, he switched off the television. 'Do you know them?' he demanded of her.

'You haven't done anything wrong,' Beth added.

'A bit,' Beverly replied, looking very self-conscious.

'I want to make sure you're all right?' Beth said.

'All right? Why shouldn't she be?' Mr Peters said. 'Beverly, what have you been doing?'

She immediately burst into tears and blurted out the full story. 'I know the Watson boys from school. Two or three months ago Mike phoned me. We chatted for a while, then he said the rest of his family had gone out for the day and why didn't I go to his, so I went.'

'You did what?' Mr Peters yelled at his daughter. 'What have I told you about teenage boys?'

'I don't think you two even noticed I'd gone,' Beverly said angrily through her tears. 'While I was there we chatted for a while and then Mike suggested he take a short video clip of me being fake-kidnapped. That was it, really. I did it.' She sniffed and looked at her father.

'Show me the video clip,' he demanded.

Reluctantly she found it on her phone and passed it to him.

'Is that it?' he asked.

She nodded.

'But I can't even see who it is. There's a bag over your head.'

'That's it,' Beverly repeated. 'I was going to do an Emma Arnold and get some money out of it.'

'That's my understanding too,' Beth said. 'You're sure there are no more videos?'

She looked gloomy as she shook her head. 'Honestly, I'm sure.'

'I think that's the end of the matter then, unless you want to take it further?' Beth said.

'No, I think Beverly's learnt her lesson,' Mr Peters replied. 'But I'd like to give that Mike a telling-off.'

'I've spoken to him. Can I just have a quick look around your house? I'll be off then,' Beth said.

'It's not very tidy,' Mrs Peters said, and began plumping cushions.

Beth left the Peters family in the living room and wandered into the kitchen-diner, which had a similar layout to the Watsons'. Their houses were built at the same time and in a similar style. She peeped through the curtains into the garden but couldn't see much as it was dark outside now. She went upstairs and looked in the three bedrooms. There was no attic conversion, so she came down again and returned to the living room. Mr and Mrs Peters came towards her.

'Thank you,' Beth said to them. Then, 'Goodbye, Beverly. Look after yourself.'

She went to the front door. Mr and Mrs Peters came with her.

'Is that everything?' Mr Peters asked.

'Yes, thank you.'

The front door closed behind her as Beth walked down the path. She sat for a moment in her car thinking about all that had happened. She was pleased this investigation was now finally over. Tomorrow she'd file her last report.

THIRTY-NINE

Six months later, at Easter, Alfie and Jenny Watson began their Roomy-Space again. The story of Emma Arnold on the internet had died down and you had to search quite hard to find anything significant about the incident online. She'd moved away with her parents and Carl hadn't been in touch again. Alfie's sons had promised there would be no more Stranger Danger Club and Alfie took them at their word.

Christmas had come and gone. Jenny had given the Roomy-Space a coat of paint in the interim and bought new bed linen. The police had the old sheets and Jenny said that forensics could dispose of them. Now, as the Easter holidays approached, they had their first paying guest, who left three days later with a five-star review. They were back in business!

After a few months, life had gone back to normal, Alfie thought. Jenny still taught at a secondary school and the boys were typical growing teenagers. Alfie was reasonably busy with his surveying work. Then one afternoon, with the house empty, he left his study and went down to the Roomy-Space. He didn't usually come in here; it held bad memories for him, but this time he went in and looked around. On the spur of the moment, he decided to buy another miniature spy camera, not to replace the one in the bedside clock, which the police still had, but for the larger wall clock they'd bought recently. It sat proudly in the middle of the wall.

He returned to his study with a growing sense of excitement – he was doing something very naughty, prohibited – and ordered another one. He might not use it, he thought, but it would be there just in case. He might keep it in his desk drawer forever, but even just knowing it was there spiced up his day. It was a get-out clause for real life, which could become tedious at times.

The miniature spy camera arrived the following day, with next-day delivery. The post came just before 11 a.m. Alfie was waiting for it. Straight away he knew what it was. He carefully carried the box to his study, unwrapped it, and sat there admiring it for some time, examining it and turning it over in his hands. Then he connected it through his computer, using the app. It was like old times, he thought. He moved the camera around his study to get a better picture. Delighted with what he saw, he went downstairs and took his screwdrivers from the drawer in the garage, then went up to the Roomy-Space. He went in and closed the door. The room didn't hold the demons any more, he thought, as he worked.

He had to lift the clock from the wall to fix the spy camera in place. It was only a five-minute job, then he replaced the clock, stood back and truly admired his work. You couldn't see the camera at all, even if you looked really hard. He'd bought a better-quality one this time. He went up to his study to test it on his laptop. It was perfect. It had a better lens than the old one, which made the picture even sharper.

His heart fluttered with anticipation as he closed the app and did some work on his computer. Every so often he'd stop and take a peep at the room, all throughout the afternoon.

When his sons arrived home he went down to greet them.

'Good day?' he asked them.

'Yes, thanks,' Gregory replied. Mike gave a small nod. They were the same old lads, only bigger each day.

Later, after dinner, Alfie took a mug of coffee up to his study, settled at his desk and opened his laptop. It was all quiet in the room, like a film set. Then he watched Jenny go in and check it over. She smoothed the sheets and, satisfied, left it for the following day when they had guests.

It was a Saturday, and the Roomy-Space booking was for one night only. The whole Watson family was out for the evening. They'd pre-booked cinema tickets. They left the key in the safe spot. The guests weren't there when they arrived home, so they left the front door unlocked. Again, nothing unusual in that, Alfie thought. Jenny and the boys went to bed and Alfie followed.

'I hope they're not too late,' Jenny said as she climbed into bed.

'So do I,' he said.

Alfie slept through until Sunday. There was no noise coming from the Roomy-Space when Alfie got up. He made Jenny a cup of tea and took it to her, then he bumped into Gregory on the landing, who was going to the bathroom. At 11 a.m., when there still wasn't any noise coming from the Roomy-Space, and it was half an hour after check-out, Alfie knocked on the door. There was no reply, so he knocked again, then gently opened it. The room was empty, there were no personal belongings and the key to the room was on the table. The bed was made and looked as though it hadn't been slept in. Strange, he thought.

'Guests are generally pretty tidy,' Jenny said when he told her he thought it was a bit odd. He thought no more about it.

Alfie went to his study and opened his laptop. He was intrigued to know what time the guests had left. He logged into the app and at 11.30 p.m. a young couple could be seen arriving. They sat on the bed with their backs to the camera and began to argue. Alfie straightened and peered more closely as the argument continued. There was something familiar about the couple. He stared at the screen and tried to work out what it was. Their argument began to escalate. Suddenly they both turned to face the camera and Alfie nearly fell backwards. He knew who they were. It was Carl and Emma, looking straight at the wall clock, at him.

SUGGESTED TOPICS FOR READING-GROUP DISCUSSION

1. How is Alfie and Jenny's relationship at the start of the book?

2. Does their relationship change much during the course of the book?

3. How would you describe Alfie?

4. What sort of father is Alfie to his sons?

5. Would you describe Mike and Gregory as typical teenagers?

6. Could both Alfie and Jenny have taken more of an interest in their sons? Would this have produced a better outcome?

7. Police always search the home of a missing person. Why do they do this?

8. Describe the regeneration area? Most of us know somewhere like this.

9. What do you make of the ending?

A friendly reunion...

After ten years, Sarah and her husband Roshan are looking forward to catching up with their closest school friends. So when one of them invites the group to spend a week in a beautiful converted church, they eagerly accept.

A vision of fear...

Very quickly though, Sarah becomes unsettled. She is frightened by the church's creepy surroundings, and she thinks she might be seeing ghosts. Even more disturbing, a masked woman is committing armed robberies in the area – and the police can't catch her.

A terrifying secret...

As Sarah and the others begin to have more frightening visions, the armed woman strikes again. The group of friends begin to wonder just what they've got themselves into...

An isolated cottage…

After losing her job and boyfriend, Jan Hamlin is
in desperate need of a fresh start. So she jumps at
the chance to rent a secluded cottage on the edge of
Coleshaw Woods.

A tap at the window…

Very quickly though, things take a dark turn. At night,
Jan hears strange noises, and faint taps at the window.
Something, or someone, is out there.

A forest that hides many secrets…

Jan refuses to be scared off. But whoever is outside
isn't going away, and it soon becomes clear that the
nightmare is only just beginning…

Have you seen Leila?

8-year-old Leila Smith has seen and heard things that
no child should ever have to. On the Hawthorn Estate,
where she lives, she often stays out after dark
to avoid going home.

But what Leila doesn't know is that someone has
been watching her in the playground. One day, she
disappears without a trace...

The police start a nationwide search but it's as if Leila
has vanished into thin air. Who kidnapped her?
What do they want? Will she return home safely or
is she lost forever?